# THE MERCHANT PRINCE

## TALES OF THE MISPLACED - BOOK 2

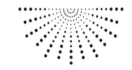

## ADAM K. WATTS

# CHARACTERS

**Akshira:** *Rorujhen* spouse to Farukan and mother of Barashan.

**Alénia:** A human woman living in the Shifara area. She is an expert with the long-sword and seeks out any who re proficient to challenge them.

**Ancaera:** *Ashae* widow to Vaelir, whom she had married out of convenience to maintain control of her family estate of Shianri.

**Arané-Li:** *Ulané Jhinura* Chamberlain in Su Lariano.

**Arnelas:** *Ulané Jhinura* Minister of Trade in Su Lariano.

**Arugak:** Founding king of Pokorah-Vo.

**Astrina:** Astrina Ulané Poloso. *Ulané Jhinura* queen of Su Lariano.

**Azadi:** *Ga-Né-Mo Ri* healer in Aganaté.

**Barashan:** *Rorujhen* son of Farukan and Akshira.

**Bardian:** *Ga-Né-Mo Ri* king in Aganaté.

**Bavrana:** An *Urgaban* merchant and the Merchant Guildmaster in Pokorah-Vo. Part owner with Mira of the Raven's Nest Restaurant in Su Lariano.

**Bijoux:** *Jahgreet* cub. Rispan's companion.

**Chevis:** *Ogaré* father to Gaetan.

**Darkstar:** *Rorujhen* slave owned by Dimétrian.

**Darusa:** *Urgaban* merchant in Pokorah-Vo. Aligned with the slavers.

**Démka:** *Loiala Fé* Guard in Shifara.

**Deneven:** *Ulané Jhinura* Chief Forester in Su Lariano.

**Dimas:** *Ashae* City Guard in Shifara.

**Dimétrian:** *Ashae* Master of the White Riders.

**Dobarek:** *Urgaban* Slaver Guildmaster in Pokorah-Vo.

**Duskovek:** *Urgaban* Captain of the Guard from Laraksha-Vo. Sent with the delegation to Su Lariano.

**Dzurala:** *Ulané Jhinura* General of the Investigations and Intelligence Branch (IIB) in Su Lariano.

**Farlen:** *Ulané Jhinura* who assisted in kidnapping Mira.

**Farukan:** The *Rorujhen* formerly enslaved by Vaelir. He serves Mira as mount and partner. Spouse to Akshira and father of Barashan.

**Felgar:** See Mouse.

**Felora:** *Ulané Jhinura* tailor and shopkeeper in the Su Lariano outer town. Wife to Gylan and mother to Tesia.

**Gaetan:** Young *Ogaré* whose actions resulted in him being sentenced by his people to follow and assist Genevané until such time as she can forgive him.

**Genevané:** *Darakanos* befriended by Rispan.

**Giang:** *Pilané Jhin* working for the Royal Court in Shifara Castle.

**Gilglys:** *Ulané Jhinura* who assisted in kidnapping Mira.

**Gradela:** *Urgaban* mercenary working for Dobarek.

**Gralbast:** An *Urgaban* merchant. Formerly the Merchant's Guildmaster. Mira's business partner in Pokorah-Vo.

**Grangor:** *Urgaban* diplomat sent to Su Lariano from Laraksha-Vo.

**Gylan:** *Ulané Jhinura* leatherworker and armorer in Su Lariano. Husband to Felora and father to Tesia.

**Icolan:** *Ulané Jhinura* bodyguard assigned to protect Mira. Rank of Bar, equivalent to private, with the Su Lariano Palace Guard.

**Jakeda:** *Urgaban* hired by Bavrana to be the head chef at the Raven's Nest restaurant.

**Jaleya:** *Ga-Né-Mo Ri* queen of Aganaté.

**Javen:** *Urgaban* mercenary adopted by Mira to be Farukan's groom.

**Jill Ramirez:** Mira's foster-mother on Earth.

**Kaerélios:** Childhood *Ashae* friend to Ancaera, also a White Rider. Pledged to Mira and assigned to protect Ancaera and Shianri.

**Karis Ulané Panalira:** Missing younger cousin of Neelu.

**Karugan:** *Urgaban* king in Laraksha-Vo.

**Kalisan:** Long-deceased husband to Neelu's missing sister, Reelu.

**Kergak:** Deceased *Urgaban* king of Pokorah-Vo. Father to King Vegak and son of King Arugak.

**Kholinaer:** The *Ashae* king in Shifara Castle.

**Khuyen:** *Pilané Jhin* queen and only survivor of the massacre of her people led by Arugak long ago. Leader of *Chados*, the resistance of Pokorah-Vo.

**Kiarash:** *Ga-Né-Mo Ri* scout and resistance member. Befriended by Rispan.

**Kirsat:** *Ulané Jhinura* friend to Mira from her military training in Su Lariano. Part of the original mission to Pokorah-Vo and who did not survive the journey.

**Kooras:** *Ulané Jhinura* friend to Mira from her military training in Su Lariano. Part of the original mission to Pokorah-Vo and who did not survive the journey.

**Lacela:** *Ulané Jhinura* student healer in Su Lariano.

**Laruna:** *Ulané Jhinura* mage and magic instructor in Su Lariano. Became a fugitive when it became known she orchestrated Mira's kidnapping.

**Lengel:** *Ulané Jhinura* aide to General Dzurala in Su Lariano.

**Meshin:** *Ulané Jhinura* general of the army and City Guard of Su Lariano.

**Mikolosk:** *Urgaban* who serves as Gralbast's right hand and personal assistant.

**Mira:** Mirabela Cervantes Ramirez. Child of Earth who finds herself stranded on Daoine.

**Mooren:** *Ulané Jhinura* assigned to accompany Mira and advise and protect her on her missions to Pokorah-Vo and Shifara. Holds the rank of Lance with the Su Lariano Palace Guard, which is equivalent to corporal.

**Mouse:** Also known as Felgar. Close *Ulané Jhinura* friend to Mira and Rispan since her early days in Su Lariano. Becomes manager for the Raven's Nest Restaurant.

**Nadezhda:** Healer in a *Loiala Fé* village.

**Naga:** Name of the *reshan* eagle that serves as Kiarash's mount.

**Nazreela:** *Urgaban* queen in Laraksha-Vo.

**Néci:** *Loiala Fé* house servant in Shianri.

**Neelu:** Neelu Ulané Pulakasado. *Ulané Jhinura* daughter of Queen Astrina. Mira's first friend in Daoine.

**Niden:** *Loiala Fé* groom in Shianri.

**Niklos:** Vaelir's *Ashae* nephew.

**Nirellen:** *Ulané Jhinura* commander in charge of Mira's platoon in military training in Su Lariano. Holds the rank of Tree, which is equivalent to Staff Sergeant.

**Nora:** Leanora Leland. Mira's foster-sister on Earth.

**Reelu:** Reelu Ulané Pulakaloso. Missing older sister to Neelu.

**Réni:** *Ulané Jhinura* Assistant Minister of Trade in Su Lariano. Assigned to accompany Mira on her mission to Pokorah-Vo.

**Rhesaeda:** *Ashae* Minister of Internal Relations in Shifara Castle.

**Rispan:** Close friend to Mira and Mouse since her early days in Su Lariano. Is assigned to join her mission to Pokorah-Vo.

**Rizina:** *Ulané Jhinura* bodyguard assigned to protect Mira. Holds the rank of Bar, equivalent to private, with the Su Lariano Palace Guard.

**Sabela:** *Ulané Jhinura* friend to Mira from her military training in Su Lariano. Part of the original mission to Pokorah-Vo and a highly skilled tracker.

**Shaluza:** Part of the *Urgaban* delegation to Su Lariano from

Laraksha-Vo. Assigned to accompany Mira on her mission to Pokorah-Vo.

**Shéna:** Korashéna Ulané Sharavi. Last surviving member of the royal family of the *Ulané Jhinura* city of Su Astonil. Enslaved in Pokorah-Vo all her life until she was freed by Rispan.

**Shigara:** *Ulané Jhinura* Chief Healer for Queen Astrina in Su Lariano.

**Tabalin:** *Ulané Jhinura* Forrester scout assigned to accompany Mira on her mission to Shifara.

**Tarana:** *Ulané Jhinura* friend to Mira from her military training in Su Lariano. Part of the original mission to Pokorah-Vo and who did not survive the journey.

**Tesia:** *Ulané Jhinura* master mage in Su Lariano. Friend to Neelu and daughter of Felora and Gylan. Trains Mira in magic and accompanies her on her mission to Shifara.

**Tony Ramirez:** Mira's foster-father on Earth.

**Vaelir:** *Ashae* White Rider who is killed by Mira when he attacks her and her team on their way to Pokorah-Vo.

**Veeluthun:** Veeluthun Ulané Gabolé. Younger brother to Neelu in Su Lariano.

**Vegak:** *Urgaban* king in Pokorah-Vo.

**Veron:** *Ulané Jhinura* weapon's master in Su Lariano. Oversaw training for Mira in martial arts.

**Veselek:** *Urgaban* working as Bavrana's right-hand.

**Yarmilla:** *Urgaban* sent from Laraksha-Vo as a junior diplomat to assist Grangor.

**Ysiola:** *Ashae* queen in Shifara Castle.

MAP OF DAOINE

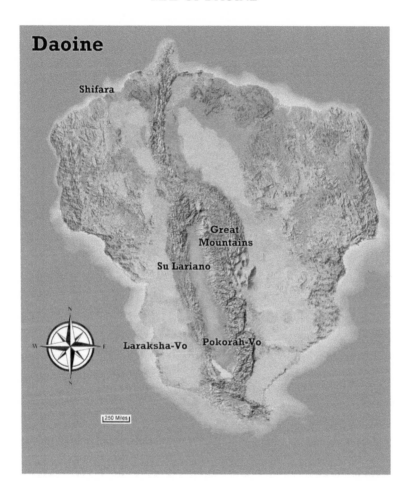

*This book is dedicated to artists and dreamers everywhere. You are the soul of the world; don't ever forget it.*

# CHAPTER ONE

## MIRA

*G*ralbast says there are two types of people, the takers and the took. I know he's not really that cynical, but I also see a level of practicality to that approach. The truth is, life's not that simple, and there are more colors to the universe than black and white.

The more I saw of Pokorah-Vo, the more colors I saw in that spectrum. Not in the *Urgaban* themselves. Physically, they were all pretty much the same shade; kind of a pale yellow, not quite green. And they mainly seemed to be just under four and a half feet tall, so at five foot two, I was hard to disguise.

That's the thing though; I was in disguise.

A couple of assassination attempts convinced me it might be wise to make people think the last one succeeded. So instead of being seventeen-year-old Mira, I was Raven. A man and a trader of goods. A merchant. Partner to Gralbast, an *Urgaban* of Pokorah-Vo, a city founded by exiles and criminals.

*Urgaban* was the real name for what humans called goblins. It seemed like humans made up a lot of names for races that already had names for themselves. Goblins, *Urgaban*, had a bad reputation.

"Look," Gralbast was saying to me, "We both know there's

more to you being in Pokorah-Vo than a little trading. All I'm saying is that the more you tell me, the more I can help you."

We were seated at a table in his home, and he had his familiar pipe in his hand. My team and I had only arrived at Pokorah-Vo a few days earlier. I'd given him the story of our trip from Su Lariano, but otherwise, Gralbast and I hadn't discussed anything beyond trade.

"Help me?" I cocked an eyebrow at him in amusement. "All out of the goodness of your greedy little heart?"

His eyebrows shot up, "You wound me, *Raven*." He put extra emphasis on my assumed name to remind me he was already keeping secrets for me. "Sure, there's profit in stability. But we're in this world for more than profit. You know me better than that I would think."

I nodded as I thought about what he'd said. He wasn't lying. I knew how he felt about slavers and that he'd taken an occasional loss by acquiring and discreetly freeing a slave or two. But what if it came to deciding between his people and other races?

"I'll tell you what," I said, "let's speak hypothetically."

I noticed the flash of victory that showed in his eyes before he had a chance to hide it.

"Alright." He nodded. "Hypothetically."

"Let's say that until recently, no one knew that this city existed. As far as anyone knew, there were just random bands of *Urgaban* running around causing problems. Attacking and enslaving travelers... Occasionally eating them..." His face flushed a bit at that last part, but he couldn't deny it. "You could see how *some* might think it would be a good idea to get together and just eradicate these bands. Yes?"

"Eradicate?" He gaped at me. "You can't be serious!"

"But," I went on, "when it was discovered there was an actual city and how big that city was, those same people might have decided they needed to figure out a different approach."

His eyes narrowed as he put his first reaction behind him and started to examine the problem objectively, drawing from his pipe as he thought.

"And there are really only so many different approaches they could take," he mused.

"Right." I nodded. "But in all cases, the approach would have to result in ending the attacks and the slavery."

"Slavers." He looked like he had a bad taste in his mouth. "That's going to be tough." He met my eyes. "A lot of powerful people, and not just in Pokorah-Vo, make a great deal of money in the slave trade. They aren't going to want to let that go."

"So, if you were trying to solve this little problem, what would be your solution?"

"Well," he said, "the first problem these hypothetical people would have, is that they don't know anything about the power structure in this city. Without that, there's no way they could formulate any kind of effective strategy. They'd send someone to gather intelligence. I'd already figured out you were here for that. But they must need whatever you can get for them before they can even start to put together a plan."

I just looked at him without comment.

"Alright." He nodded. "I'll help you to get your information. But let me tell you why. This is my city, the good and the bad."

"And the ugly," I supplied.

"Even so," he agreed, not knowing the reference, "but I'm no traitor. And there are good people here. People that deserve a better life for themselves and their families. If we can bring Pokorah-Vo into the open, to trade and deal equally with the other races, it will help my people. But my people can't get there without help. I'm going to help you because in the end it will make a better life for them."

"Well," I grinned at him, "if I *were* on such a mission, I'm sure I would include that in my report!"

He shook his head, "No more nonsense about hypothetical. You need a plan. That's what this is really about. You need a way to make Pokorah-Vo a peaceful, contributing ally. And without going through a bloody war and subjugation to do it. Yes?"

I hesitated a moment, then nodded.

"I have the connections and the knowledge," he said, "and if truth be told, I've been looking for a way to change things around here for a while. But I didn't have the resources to do it on my own. A little external... motivation. That can do wonders. We're not just going to send information to let someone else try to figure it out. We'll send the information *and* the plan."

"You're very ambitious."

"A fellow never made a copper without a little ambition." He grinned.

"Then I'd make a bet you aren't running low on coppers."

He just grinned at me in response.

"Gralbast, there are also some other things that people are curious about. Like why they haven't heard from the *Ulané Jhinura* from the local forest. From Su Astonil."

All levity left his face, and he no longer met my eyes.

"That was mostly before my time," was all he said.

"You might as well tell me," I prompted him. "I'm going to find out eventually."

The eyes he raised to mine were hardened steel. "I'll not sugarcoat this. You asked about ugly. This is about as ugly as it gets."

"Tell me."

"I understand it started when some *Urgaban* wandered into a forest garden. All but one were slaughtered by the little creatures that lived there."

"The *Pilané Jhin* and the *Sula Jhinara*," I supplied. "The pixies and the sylphs."

"Aye." He nodded. "This survivor. His name was Arugak. He got mad and gathered a bunch of others and they started burning all the gardens they could find."

"What?" I was horrified. "Then the *Ulané Jhinura* must have tried to stop them!"

"Yes," he agreed. "The *Ulané Jhinura* attacked them and drove them back out of the forest."

"Naturally," I said, trying to control my revulsion at what the *Urgaban* had done to the *Pilané Jhin* and *Sula Jhinara*. "Their entire purpose is to protect the forest."

"Well, Arugak gathered more men. By then, he'd proclaimed himself the first king of the outcast *Urgaban*. He had tracked the *Ulané Jhinura* to their city. I've heard of your Su Lariano. This Su Astonil wasn't nearly so large. With a combination of fires and cave-ins, they were overwhelmed. Most were killed in the attacks. Or shortly thereafter, in the feasts." ·

"In the feasts?" I felt myself wanting to lock down, to block him out. I didn't want to hear it. But I needed him to confirm.

"They were eaten," he spoke those three words through clenched teeth. "Those who survived were made into slaves."

My mind reeled from the brutality and pure evil of Arugak's atrocities. I wanted to run from it, but I couldn't. I needed to know.

"How many... lost?" I forced myself to ask.

"Tens of thousands."

"How many slaves?"

"Hundreds. A few thousand at most."

Grief pierced my chest like a hot blade. Then it turned into fury. I needed to get out. I needed to strike. I stood abruptly, and my chair fell over behind me. I grabbed my staff and strode into the courtyard.

"Mooren!" I called out. "I need to spar! Now!"

Mooren looked up from where he was talking with Rispan. One look at my face sent him scrambling for his weapons.

I didn't wait for him to get set before I launched my attack. I just kept driving forward, letting my grief at the atrocity flow out through my strikes, the rage that tightly clenched every muscle and joint of my body.

*Monsters!*

Mooren was still on the defensive as I drove him back and

back. His *shyngur* swinging smoothly to block my wild strikes. The handles shifting easily in his grip, extending at ninety degrees from the shafts.

*They must pay!*

I couldn't contain it any longer and I screamed, sinking to my knees.

*All those lives!*

I could see them in my mind. Running. Afraid. Fighting. Dying. Burning. My grief combined with images of Tarana. Of Kirsat and Kooras. All dead.

My body was racked with sobs as Mooren silently put his arms around me, not understanding, but there.

# CHAPTER TWO

## RISPAN

"*M*ooren!" I heard Mira shout as she slammed out of the door from the house. "I need to spar! Now!"

I watched as Mooren grabbed those *shyngur* he was so fond of and barely got them up in time to avoid strikes from Mira's staff. She was scary good with that thing. But then, Mooren was pretty good, too.

Something was wrong. I'd never seen the intensity of emotion I now saw on Mira's face. She occasionally got a little melancholy, but she would pull herself out of it within a few minutes. She'd never talked about it, so I'd never asked. I was there for her. Always. No question. But I would respect her privacy, too.

This was different.

Something had upset her. Badly. I turned my eyes to the door of the house.

Mira's scream brought my gaze back to her. She was crying and Mooren had his arms around her.

Mira was crying.

I stormed across the yard and through the door to where Gralbast was sitting at his table.

"Rispan." He nodded to me.

"What happened?" I demanded.

Gralbast sighed. He put his pipe down and reached over to a side table. He picked up a glass and set it down next to the partially full one that already sat in front of him. He gestured to the other side of the table as he poured from the bottle. The chair across from him was knocked over, so I picked it up and sat down. He slid the glass toward me.

"What happened?" I asked again.

"She asked, and I answered."

"What did you say?"

I listened as he repeated the story he had told Mira. By the time he was finished, I was angry enough to want to kill Arugak and anyone who stood with him. But I could see how this would hit Mira. Mira was too good. She cared too much. Not that I would ever say she was weak. She was one of the strongest people I knew. But she always saw the good in people. Always believed that the best things would happen in the end. I knew better. I knew life was a shit-show and you just make the best of it while you can.

My time in the kid's home hadn't been horrible. But it hadn't been wonderful, either. I'd been a little small for my age for as long as I could remember. There were always those who would take advantage.

That's why I didn't hate the *Urgaban*. I knew that *Ulané Jhinura* could be just as cruel. Maybe not to the point of eating other races, but you know what I mean. Wherever you went, there were good and bad people. *Ulané Jhinura. Urgaban. Ashae.* Whatever.

I took a swallow of the goblin grog he'd put in front of me.

"It might have been better to let her find out about it over time," I said to him.

He shrugged. "Perhaps. But then she wouldn't trust me if I'd kept it from her."

Gralbast was a trader. He made his living by making deals.

By getting people to buy whatever he was selling. I knew he was good at it.

"I think it's time you and I came to an understanding," I said to him. "I don't know what your goals are or what plans you have. And I really don't care. But if you ever betray her or hurt her, I will be feeding you your own guts."

I don't know what I expected. Anger. Denial. Some sort of confrontation. But his eyes softened as he looked at me.

"Ah lad, I know that." He nodded. "You forget. I was there the day she came for you and your friend. When she charged through the whole forest on a pony she didn't know how to ride. How she put herself in danger for your freedom. And I saw your face."

I nodded once, remembering.

"No lad." He shook his head. "Enemies, she'll have aplenty, but I won't be one of them. If she survives, she will bring a lot of change to Daoine. She can't help it. But it will be a good change. For *Ulané Jhinura*. For *Urgaban*. For other races. So, I will do what I can to help her."

"If she survives."

"Yes." Gralbast leaned forward on the table, refilling our glasses. "Why don't we see what we can do to make sure that happens."

That's when I started secretly working with Gralbast. He knew the people who needed to be watched or listened to. After my years in the kid's home, I had become very good at getting around quietly without being noticed. Mira knew — I should say Raven. Raven knew I was sneaking out to gather information, and as long as I was getting results, she was happy and didn't bother me with other assignments very often. But she didn't know that I was getting my targets from Gralbast.

We weren't trying to work around her. We were working to support her. She had Sabela, Shaluza, and Ergak gathering general information while Mooren and Réni were in place to keep her cover as a trader working. Gralbast had already provided the general information, but she had to confirm it with her own team before reporting it. I was working with Gralbast to get answers to the questions she didn't know she needed to ask yet.

Another thing I got from Gralbast: an enchanted ring. Most *Urgaban* spoke *Urgan* instead of the common tongue. The ring's enchantment made it so that I could understand what the rest were saying in their language. I could even respond in kind if needed. He said it wasn't uncommon where mixed languages were spoken, so it wouldn't be suspicious if it was discovered. I was pretty sure Raven's amulet did something similar.

I mainly spent the first several days walking the streets of the city to get familiar with the layout. Gralbast had given us maps, but there's nothing like seeing it firsthand. It was the only way to really know important things about a city. Like foot traffic patterns. Where people were walking or where they tended to gather. Knowing where to find different kinds of shops or businesses, and what kinds of people frequented them.

There were also subterranean levels to the city, but they weren't very extensive. It seemed that a lot of the city was built before there was any real plan. And even when the area seemed to have a plan, it wasn't consistent. This was nothing like Su Lariano, where everything was meticulously planned.

It was surprising that not much of Pokorah-Vo was underground. I'd gathered that Laraksha-Vo was similar to Su Lariano in that much of it was built into underground caverns, but the builders of Pokorah-Vo evidently hadn't wanted to work that hard. I'd hated City Maintenance duty, so I could relate. Though I had to say, this mess did give me a better appreciation for all the work that went into Su Lariano. After I'd gotten familiar with the city layout, he started sending me to watch and listen to people. Specific targets. What they were saying and who they were saying it to.

Tonight, Gralbast had given me a name. Darusa. She would be paying a visit to someone named Valdeg at his business after hours. I had no idea how Gralbast had come across this information. The *Urgaban* clearly had resources he didn't talk about.

The sun had long since set and I waited in the shadows by an alley across the street where I could watch the building and its approach. My clothes were dark to match the shadows.

Darusa wasn't hard to miss. She walked with two guards ahead and two behind. They looked very alert and competent. I was still getting used to the hairlessness of the *Urgaban*. Especially on the women. Raven's newly shaved head kept catching me by surprise, too. Though I couldn't deny her disguise was pretty effective for anyone who didn't know her well.

Two of the guards followed Darusa in and the other two took a position outside the door. The guards presented a problem, and I was going to have to get a lot closer to find out what was going on in the meeting.

I ducked back down the alley to circle around a couple of buildings so I could cross the street where the guards wouldn't see me in the dark. I crossed the street and went down an alley on the other side to come up behind Valdeg's building. There was a door in the back, but my gentle nudging got me nowhere. It was likely barred from the inside.

I could hear voices inside, but not well enough to make out the words. If only Gralbast's ring could make voices louder, too.

I could see light coming out of a window on the side of the building. I crept up to it, hoping I could hear better. As I reached the edge of the window, I nearly stepped into a hole that angled from the alley toward the building. Some kind of animal warren. I could easily have twisted or broken my ankle if I hadn't seen it at the last moment.

I'd started to reach for my dagger to pry up the window, but I was in luck, and it was already cracked open. Darusa and Valdeg were in the room beyond.

"We just need to be patient," the male voice must have been Valdeg. "That's worked for us so far."

11

"The situation has changed," a woman's voice. Darusa. "We must change with it."

"That idiot Vegak is still following our lead," Valdeg returned. "The merchants aren't going to get any traction so long as he opposes them."

I'd already learned that Vegak was the current king of Poko-rah-Vo. Grandson to the monster Arugak, their first king.

"But they *are* getting traction," Darusa insisted. "The Merchant Guild Council is split down the middle, and some of the conservatives are starting to waver. This new partner of the merchant Gralbast isn't helping, bringing in these new goods and promising more volume. They're going to want a piece of that business."

"What if we give them a small piece of the slave trade?" he suggested. "Say a merger between the Slaver and the Merchant Guilds?"

"Nonsense! The Slaver Guild would never give them an inch."

"Then what would you suggest." Valdeg sighed.

"Maybe we should look at removing some pieces from the board."

"If we are too blatant," he objected, "they will align against us. It's too risky."

"I don't need you to teach me how to grow mushrooms!" She napped. "Of course, we can't be blatant."

"Apologies," his voice was heavy with sarcasm. "What did you have in mind?"

"What if this new partner of Gralbast had brought in some-thing volatile, and it caused a fire? It would be a shame if he and his partner were to perish in the blaze."

"We would still be suspected."

"Yes," she agreed. "But if we get the rumor of a secret substance going first, we can easily manage the optics. Give me a few days and I'll have everything ready."

There was a pause before Valdeg answered. "Agreed."

"Now, on to other business."

A guttural hissing sound from near my feet snapped my attention back to the alley. I looked toward the sound to find a relak on its hind legs, staring at me with angry, beady eyes, its claws extended from its raised, front legs. Relaks were large rodents, their bodies about two feet long. They could be vicious, but rarely attacked people. I was guessing that didn't hold true if you were standing on its doorstep.

It hissed at me again, threateningly, and I slowly moved away from it towards the back of the building. The thing watched me the whole time, hissing. I'd almost reached the corner when one of the guards stuck his head into the alley from the front of the building. I instantly froze.

The guard said something over his shoulder and started down the alley. Slowly, I pressed myself against the building.

"It's a relak!" he called out as the thing spun to face him, hissing at a new target.

"Well kill the *zergish* thing," came the answer.

The guard backed away from the relak.

"Not me," he said. "I hate those things. You want it dead? You kill it."

The other guard was laughing loudly.

"Don't mock me!" The first guard angrily stomped back toward the street. "You're not the one with the thing hissing in his face."

Quietly I turned the corner of the building and moved away. Their voices fading with the distance. I didn't find out as much as I hoped, but I was glad I'd found out what I did.

# CHAPTER THREE

## MIRA

*I* set down the pen and leaned back from the table in Gralbast's study, massaging my hand. I'd like to find one of those writers that made it look like being a spy was exciting and give them a few good whacks with my staff. So far, it had just been either boring, tedious or monotonous.

Mikolosk brought me a cup of hot tea. Mikolosk worked for Gralbast and looked as old as dirt. He was butler, assistant, foreman, legal advisor, and anything else Gralbast needed him to be. I wouldn't exactly call him kindly, but he was definitely attentive and dutiful.

"Thank you, Mikolosk," I said, picking up the mug.

"Rasha tea has certain restorative properties," he told me. "You looked like you could use some. From what I have seen of your preferences, I took liberty to sweeten it."

Before I could say anything else, he turned and walked out of the room. I turned my attention back to the work in front of me.

We'd been in Pokorah-Vo for nearly two weeks now and a lot of my time was spent reviewing and consolidating the information my team was bringing in. We'd done a few deals with the trade goods we brought, a little here and there to spread it around, but we were stalling so we could prolong our stay in the city and gather more information.

Rispan came in and I saw right away from his face that something was up.

"Hang on," I told him. "Let's get Mooren and Gralbast."

Once the four of us were assembled, Rispan filled us in on what he'd overheard.

"*Zerg!*" Gralbast pounded the side of his fist on the table. "I knew those two were up to something!"

I'd suspected Gralbast was supplying Rispan with information on who to look into, and this confirmed it. But as long as they were getting results, I'd let them run with it.

"We can't sit around waiting for them to burn us out." Mooren scowled.

Their conversation faded to the background as I pondered the problem. The strategy against us was pretty solid. But that was because we were sitting as an easy target. Something had to change quickly, and we couldn't reveal we were on to them.

"How fast can we offload what's left of our goods?" My question cut across some rant from Gralbast.

His eyes narrowed speculatively, "That depends on how cheaply you let it go. Why?"

"And what about a return caravan? How soon can goods be made ready to ship out to Su Lariano?"

"On my own," he answered, "a decent shipment would take a couple of weeks to put together. I take it you want to move faster than that?"

"I do."

"How much faster?"

"I want to be on the road in three days."

Gralbast let out a long breath.

"And," I added, "I don't want them to know we're leaving until after we're gone."

Gralbast stared at me, his face blank. Then he chuckled.

"Alright. I think it can be done. But we'll need more ready resources than what I have."

He tapped his fingers on the table, thinking. Coming to some conclusion, he stood.

"Well, we've no time to lose," he said. "We'll need to talk to someone tonight. She's the only one that can make this happen."

On the way out the door I grabbed my cloak and settled it over my shoulder with the raven clasp that Rispan had found for me someplace. He'd asked and, using my amulet, I gave him an image of what a raven looked like. A few days later, he'd shown up with the clasp.

We walked with Mooren ranging ahead and Rispan coming up behind. After about ten minutes of brisk walking, we approached a large shop, and the lights were still on. The door was barred from the inside however, and Gralbast pounded on the wood between the glass panes until someone came.

It was a bulky *Urgaban*, his face was scarred and battered from old injuries. One look at him told me I probably didn't want to see the other guy. He pulled the bar from the door and cracked the door enough to speak with us.

"Shop's closed," he growled. "Whad'ya want?"

"Please tell Bavrana that Gralbast and his partner Raven are here to see her," Gralbast told him.

The man looked over his shoulder and I could see a woman give him a nod. He opened the door and motioned for us to pass. He closed and barred the door behind us while we faced the woman.

"Gralbast," she nodded to him. "And you must be Raven." She looked at me.

"You are well informed as always," Gralbast told her. "Forgive the late hour, but we needed to speak with you on a matter of some urgency."

A slim smile formed at the corner of her mouth. "I love it when someone comes to me on a matter of some urgency. It means they are desperate, and I'll get a better deal."

"That's one way it could turn out." I smiled. "Or they could just decide the deal isn't good enough and they'll hold off until they have time for a proper negotiation."

"Oh, I like this one Gralbast," she said, eyeing me. "I wondered why you would be willing to take on a partner. He definitely—" she paused for a moment, studying me. Then her eyes widened in surprise. "*She* definitely has potential."

I glanced anxiously around, but of course, there was no one else in the shop.

She smiled, "Don't worry. Your disguise will fool almost anyone in Pokorah-Vo. It would have fooled me as well if I hadn't spent some time trading at the human settlement." She turned and headed toward the back of the shop. "Let's speak in my office."

Her office held a large desk in the center. Shelves along one wall seemed to contain ledgers and records. Behind her was a cabinet and she pulled a bottle and three glasses from the shelf and put it on the desk as we took a seat. Rispan and Mooren stood by the door, looking like hired muscle.

She filled her own glass and set the bottle down, motioning for us to help ourselves.

Gralbast poured and we each tipped our glasses to our hostess and took a sip. It was very smooth with a hint of smoky cherry.

"As I am sure you've surmised," Gralbast started, "I'm in the process of establishing trade relations with the *Ulané Jhinura*. Specifically, this is with the city of Su Lariano."

"It had come to my attention," she said dryly.

"As head of the Merchant's Guild, you—"

She held up her hand to stop him.

"When you were head of the Guild, you could lecture on what the position meant," she cautioned him. "When you gave up the position, you also gave up that right."

"Of course." The new expression I was seeing on his face could only be called contrite. "Poor phraseology on my part.

17

What I mean to say is that from what I understand of your policy, I believe you would be in favor of such relations."

"Perhaps."

"Particularly, if you were brought in on the ground floor as a key player?"

"I'm listening," was all she said.

She was probably a really good poker player, because I wasn't getting anything from her, even with my amulet.

"I'm sure you've seen some of the goods we brought," I cut in. I couldn't let Gralbast run this. I needed to establish my position.

Bavrana seemed to sense the shift and she turned her attention to me. "Yes." She nodded. "I have acquired some to see for myself."

"You probably haven't seen much silk in a long time," I said. "Su Lariano has an exclusive deal with Laraksha-Vo for silk. You can only get it through us."

"Us as in you and Gralbast?" she asked. "Or as in Su Lariano?"

"I represent certain people in Su Lariano." I leaned forward. "People who would like to establish friendly relations with Pokorah-Vo. Relations that included open trade. Relations that also brought an end to slavery and raids."

"An end to slavery?" Her eyes widened. "That alone will earn you some enemies. Opening trade will also make you a target for those who profit from the black market. Either way, you're a threat."

I leaned back in my chair.

"It's unlikely anyone would know about your aims for slavery," she mused. Then her eyes flicked back and forth between me and Gralbast. "But the others. That's why you're here." She looked hard at Gralbast, "This one still has his connections. He found something out." She turned back to me. "What is the situation and what are you proposing? No hedging. You aren't here for a deal; you need another partner."

She was right. This wouldn't work if we weren't really on the same side.

"Rumors will be going around in the next few days about our shipment including some secret, volatile substance," I told her. "When Gralbast and I die in the subsequent fire, few questions would be asked." She had raised her glass to take a drink, but it froze halfway to her lips. "I don't plan to be in Pokorah-Vo that long. We need to sell the rest of our cargo and load up a caravan back to Su Lariano. I want to be on the road in three days and I don't want them to know what we are doing."

"Bold." She nodded. "This is doable. I'll take your remaining goods. I'll pay your going rate minus ten percent." She smiled at my raised eyebrows. "Bulk discount. We'll worry about the tallies later." She winked. "Veselek!"

Immediately the scarred doorman stepped into the room.

"Get a dozen of your most discreet teamsters. We have goods to move tonight. Put it in the warehouse by the east wall." She looked back at me. "They'll need someone to go along and show them."

"Mooren?" I asked him.

He nodded and followed Veselek out the door.

"Now then." She tapped a finger against her lips. "What do we send on the caravan?"

"I'm sure we can take as much *Kerelahin* as you have."

"What?"

"Sorry, it's what we are calling your singing sculptures," I explained.

"Gralbast *has* been busy." She glanced at him. "That can be arranged. What else?"

"We need Réni," I told her. I turned. "Rispan, can you get Réni please?"

"Don't worry about the front door," Bavrana called after his already retreating form. "Veselek has guards watching outside."

She turned back to me thoughtfully, "What else are you trading with Laraksha-Vo besides silk?"

19

"I really don't know."

Her expression told me she didn't believe me.

"Seriously," I told her. "They came to us about some political alliance. It wasn't until we were looking at coming here as traders that the subject of trade with them even came up."

She gaped at me, "How can you expect to bring people together if you don't start trading goods?"

"That's the same thing Réni said."

"At least someone in Su Lariano has a good head on their shoulders." She rolled her eyes. "This is the one you sent for just now?"

I nodded. "She knows about trade a lot more than me."

"About trade, perhaps," she said. "But I imagine you can hold your own quite nicely when it comes to trading." She put emphasis on the last syllable. "What was this political alliance supposed to be for anyway?"

"I don't know all the details, but something about an equal voice for all the races, and open interaction."

"I see," she mused. "And how is this equality project working out?"

I thought about that and scowled, remembering how some of the *Ulané Jhinura* had felt about me.

"Not so well?" she guessed. "Yet they made you a citizen, yes?"

I thought about that. "I suppose so. An honorary one, anyway."

"And if you can come here as a trader *for* Su Lariano, it would only be logical that you would be able to do business *in* Su Lariano, yes?" Her eyes were bright as she looked at me.

"I know that look," Gralbast said. "What are you getting at?"

"We are going to have a side venture, you and I," she said to me.

"We are?"

"I've traded with practically every race on this world, and do you know what I have found that *Urgaban* can do better than anyone else?"

I shrugged.

"Cook! You are going to open a restaurant in Su Lariano, with me as a partner."

"I am?"

"Yes." She grinned. "You are!"

Gralbast chuckled, "I must be getting old. I should have thought of that."

"I don't get it," I told them.

"This is not only about trade and profit," Bavrana said, "though there is going to be a lot of profit. If we open a high-end *Urgaban* restaurant in Su Lariano, everybody who is anybody is going to want to be there. This will create a demand and lead to lower end *Urgaban* restaurants opening. This is going to require ongoing trade in order to keep the right spices and ingredients on-hand. It also means you will need, at least initially, *Urgaban* chefs to cook it. *Urgaban*, living among the *Ulané Jhinura*."

She went on with all the ways this could be leveraged to assist in an alliance, but also how the proposed alliance could be used to bolster launching the restaurant. Finally, Rispan returned with Réni.

"Réni," I said, "thank you for coming. This is Bavrana. She's in charge of the Pokorah-Vo Merchant's Guild. She's also a new partner. Please work with her to figure out what we will send on a caravan back to Su Lariano."

"Of course." She smiled at Bavrana. "Pleased to meet you."

"One more thing," I said to her. "We will be on the road in three days."

Réni's smile faltered, but she nodded.

"What do you have there?" Bavrana asked. She was looking past me to where Rispan stood, trying to suppress a grin.

From behind his back, he produced a black felt hat. It had a wide brim, and one side was pinned up and sported an iridescent, multicolored feather.

"I saw this on one of the shelves as I went by," he said, holding it out to me. "It's perfect for you."

Curious, I put the hat on my head.

"He's right," Bavrana observed, "and it will enhance your disguise."

There was no mirror handy, so I had to take their word for it. I doffed the hat in a mock bow and put it back on my head.

"That will be one silver," Bavrana said to Rispan.

"A whole silver?"

She shrugged. "An experimental hat from some unknown hat maker… on your head… Maybe three coppers. But — A gift for the great trader Raven, which will come to be known as his hallmark? That's worth at *least* a silver."

Rispan just laughed and tossed her a silver coin he pulled out of his purse.

# CHAPTER FOUR

## RISPAN

*T*he rumors started circulating the next day. I'd gone into a local tavern to catch a late breakfast when I heard it. I wore a cloak with the hood up, and I'd applied cream to my skin to hide my eyebrows and make my coloring match the *Urgaban*. I also had a wrap the color of *Urgaban* skin over my scalp to hide my hair. This disguise had proved handy for blending in.

"I don't know what it is," one man was saying, "but I heard it's not safe. Best to stay far away from that place."

"I heard it was a dragon," I said, speaking across the room. I had an idea for turning the rumors into something that would make it a more challenging cover story.

"Dragon?" One of the others turned to me. "Where'd you hear that?"

"I can't say too much," I answered, looking around as if I was afraid of being overheard, "but I heard they cut the wings off a dragon and were trying to get it to lay eggs."

There were general exclamations from around the room.

"How do you know about it?" the first one asked. "You see it?"

I shook my head vigorously, "Not me! I wouldn't go near it.

But my old friend Yasek. He was working for them. He told me of it. Said they were keeping it in one of their warehouses — no way they could hide it at the shop. He said," I looked around again, "he said they were having a hard time getting it to eat regular meat." I sighed. "Poor Yasek."

"What happened?"

"I don't know." I shrugged. "Don't let on I told you, but Yasek went to work three nights ago and never came back." I paused dramatically. "I hear they're hiring again."

The conversation after that went into speculation about the dragon, its eggs, and how many workers they'd been feeding it. I slipped out and paid a similar visit to several other taverns, telling the same story about the unfortunate Yasek. Sometimes, I even mentioned his poor widow and six kids. The last place I went, they were already talking about it. Here, I was informed that Yasek had two cousins who had also disappeared.

The day was busy. We'd gotten our wagons loaded with goods from Gralbast's warehouse. Even the shelves in his store were looking bare. The bulk of the caravan would be in the six additional wagons from Bavrana that she would be loading the following day. One of the wagons was to be entirely dedicated to supplies for opening a restaurant.

Tonight, I had two others to check in on. Dobarek and Vesna. They were both prominent members of the Slavers Guild. I hadn't spent much time in the slave quarter. Just the feel of the place made me itch. It wasn't the best smelling section of the city, and the stench of waste and unwashed bodies was everywhere. You would think they would take better care of the slaves if they valued them, but it seemed that part of the desire to own another person was the need to humiliate and degrade them.

It wasn't quite dark yet as I approached the building where they held their auctions, just adjacent to the warehouse where they kept their "stock." I passed by the front and didn't hear any sounds from inside. As I reached the corner, I turned quickly and went down the alley between the buildings. If they weren't in, maybe I could get inside and find some useful information.

The back door was locked from the outside with iron bindings and a heavy padlock. I did find a window near the back that I was able to lever open with my dagger. I quietly raised the pane and climbed through.

The room was only dimly lit and didn't have much in the way of furniture. From the size, I'd guess it took up the back half of the building. There was a heavy door on one wall that evidently led to the front room. I quietly approached the door and tried it, but it wouldn't budge.

Frustrated with my luck, I headed back to the window. Maybe there'd be another way into the front. I reached for the windowsill, but my hand was blocked only inches away from it by some invisible barrier. I put both hands up in front of me, testing the air and found the barrier to be solid. I pulled out my dagger and tried stabbing it, but the blade just bounced back.

"You can't get out that way," I heard from behind me.

I spun and looked for the source of the voice. A small movement brought my attention to the corner of the room.

"The window is enchanted to prevent escape." The voice was female. "Not even sound can escape this room."

*Of course! They brought the slaves in here when they were about to sell them! That's why the back door was locked from the outside!*

She stood and walked toward me. "Why did you come here?" I could see her features more clearly as she approached. She was *Ulané Jhinura*. Her clothing was not much more than rags.

"You're a slave?" I asked her.

She shrugged.

"There must be another way out of this room."

"If there is," she said. "I don't know it."

"What's your name?"

"I am Korashéna," she said. "Just Korashéna."

25

"Korashéna, my name is Rispan," I told her. "What is your clan? Your city?"

"I have none."

"But your people," I persisted. "Where are they from?"

"Su Astonil."

"Su Astonil? But it was destroyed!"

"In the time of my grandparents," she said. "Yes."

That means she'd been a slave all her life. I felt the anger rising in my chest and pushed it back down.

She looked at me. "You are *Ulané Jhinura*. I don't know you. What is your clan?"

"Su Lariano," I told her.

She spat. "I have heard of your Su Lariano. They abandoned us." For the first time, her voice held something more than boredom. More than apathy.

"What?"

"With help, we could have defeated Arugak and his men. The story is passed down so none will forget the treachery of Su Lariano!"

"I swear to you, this is not true. We received no word."

"Easy lies," she said, her voice returning to the tones of boredom from earlier. She squatted where she stood and sat cross-legged on the floor. "Save your words. They mean nothing to me."

I tried to tell her that Su Lariano hadn't received any messages, that we were here to find out what happened, but she wouldn't respond. Finally, I gave up and turned my attention to the room and how I could get out.

I tried sliding across the wall toward the window, but the magical barrier still stopped me.

"Told you," she said, not even looking at me.

I went to the door leading to the front of the building. It was a heavy monstrosity, and the hinges were on the other side. Striking it with my shoulder got me nothing more than a bored chuckle from my companion.

26

"Just because you've given up hope, doesn't mean I have," I growled at her.

Her head snapped up. She stood and strode across the room to me and slapped me across the face.

"Do not *dare* to speak to me of *hope!*" she snarled. "You know *nothing!*"

"You're right," I said. "I'm sorry. I was out of line."

She turned and went back to her spot and sat back down.

"How long before someone will come?" I asked her.

"They probably won't come tonight," she said. "They like to make me wait in the dark. I let them think it scares me." The corner of her mouth curled in a slim smile.

An examination of the walls, ceiling and floor left me with no hope of creating an exit. It was getting darker outside and before long the room was sheathed in blackness. I passed the time telling her about Su Lariano. I told her about how Poko-rah-Vo came from the criminals of Laraksha-Vo. I told her about my friends. About Mira. Of course, I called her Raven, not Mira.

Eventually, my stories ran down and we had silence for a while.

"I *am* going to get away from them," I said. "You should come with me."

"And do what?"

I didn't know what to say to that question. "I'm talking about your freedom."

"I've been a slave all my life. What would I know of freedom?"

"But—"

"Keep your stories to yourself, Lariano," she said. "I'll not bed you this night."

"I'm not trying to buy your favor, Korashéna. Will you come?"

"Ask me when the time comes," she answered. "We'll see."

I don't know how long it was before I dozed off, but the next thing I knew, light was coming in through the window and there were noises coming from the front room.

I moved to the front wall, about three feet to the side of the door. I slid my double-sticks from the case on my back and waited. I could hear occasional voices, but I couldn't make out the words.

I heard a soft chuckle from Korashéna.

I heard a door open and close, and it went quiet in the front room. I settled down to wait. I could be patient.

I must have dozed off again because a sound from the front room snapped my eyes open. Judging from the light and shadows from the window, several hours had passed. Though it was hard to know for sure since the light was reflected off of the building next door. Voices again, and the front door opened and closed. Steps approached and I quietly got to my feet as I heard the bar being worked on the heavy door. The door opened out.

"Okay, princess," a voice called into the room. "Stand where I can see you."

Korashéna got to her feet and stood towards the back of the room.

"Did you miss me, little one." The man chuckled. He strode into the room toward her. He went right past me. He started to say something but stopped when he noticed the window was open. "How—"

I was on him before he knew I was there and he collapsed to the floor, unconscious. I was tempted to hit him again, but I didn't want to waste the time.

"It's time, Korashéna," I said to her. "Will you come?"

Her eyes went from the fallen *Urgaban* to me, and then through the door to the front room. Finally, she nodded.

We went through the door, and I pushed it closed behind us, setting the bar.

"That should buy us some time," I told her.

There was more light in the front room, and I could get a better look at her. Those rags were going to stand out. There was also some kind of heavy metal bracelet on her wrist, and even I could sense the power coming off of it.

"What's that?"

"They can track me with it."

That was going to be a problem. "One thing at a time." I looked around and found a cloak that must have belonged to that guard or whoever he was. I grabbed it. "Put this on."

I returned my double-sticks to their case, and we went to the front door of the building. She had the cloak wrapped around her and I pulled the hood up over her head.

"Alright," I said. "Stay close, but don't rush. If you run, you'll only draw attention."

We slipped out the door and headed down the street. It took us several minutes before we were out of the slave district.

"What have I done." She looked back, wide-eyed. "They're going to find me. I'll be punished for running away."

"They won't find you," I assured her. "I'll make sure of it."

She shook her head. "You're a fool, Lariano. And I'm a fool for listening."

It took us forty minutes to get back to Gralbast's house where we were staying. Raven was the first one to see me as we stepped into the courtyard. She was talking with Gralbast. Good.

"Rispan! You're back! We were worried." Raven looked over my shoulder. "Who's your friend?"

"Raven," I said. "This is Korashéna. Of Su Astonil."

"What?"

"Hang on," I told her. "Questions later. Gralbast, we need to get this removed quickly."

I held up Korashéna's arm, showing the tracker.

Gralbast paled, "You brought her here with that?" He shook his head. "Never mind. Inside."

He ushered us through the house and into the shop that faced the street on the other side of the block. He pulled open a cabinet and brought out some tools.

"These things are designed to be easily tracked," he said, "but they aren't that hard to break if you know how."

There was a raised section on his back counter, with a solid block of metal mounted on top. He placed her arm and the tracker on it so that the metal was against the block. He laid a chisel against it and struck with a heavy mallet. On the third strike, it snapped. He grabbed the two sides and bent them outwards, freeing her arm.

"This is still enchanted," he said. "We need to get this thing as far from here as we can."

"I'll take care of it," I told him.

"Rispan," Raven started.

"Sorry boss." I grinned. "No time. Just keep her safe. She's coming with us. I'll be back."

Korashéna's eyes fell on Gralbast, and I could see the suspicion there.

"Don't worry." I put my hand on her shoulder. "You're in good hands. Meanwhile," I held up the broken iron bracelet, "I need to do something with these."

She started to say something else, but I was already walking and was out the door. Some people want to talk when they should be moving. It had been nearly an hour since we broke out. They'd be finding that guard inside the room at any time. Maybe we'd get lucky, and no one would check until tomorrow, but I wasn't going to count on it.

Now, what was I going to do with this thing? An idea came to mind, and I turned the next corner and headed towards Valdeg's shop. I grinned as I thought about the slavers giving Valdeg a hard time about their missing slave, with the evidence right in his shop.

I hadn't been walking more than five minutes when I noticed an unpleasant looking bunch of *Urgaban* coming up the other side of the street. I was curious, but only because they stood out against the more relaxed pace of others on the street.

I continued on toward the next corner when loud voices behind me drew my attention.

"You said it was in front of us!"

"It was! I told you it seemed like it was moving. Now it's behind us!"

I turned to see what they were doing as one of them was looking around, up and down the street. His eyes fell on me, and I made eye contact. I saw his expression change and I spun and ran around the corner.

*Rookie move!*

I heard the yelling behind me, and I could tell they were splitting up, cutting down alleys and streets to head me off. I tossed the tracker and kept moving. I wasn't going to be able to ruin Valdeg's day after all.

I turned right at the next street and doubled back at the second alley I came to. Then left and kept going. I felt a burning in my side and looked down to see three inches of arrow sticking out from under my ribs. That wasn't good. I had to push on before my body realized what had happened. Left at the next alley. They were getting closer. The next street was Merchant Square. It was full of market carts, people selling goods on the street. I was hoping to lose myself in the crowd, but I'd be too easily spotted with this arrow sticking out of me.

I stumbled once and got up. There! On the side of the Square! Pokorah-Vo's Merchant Square had one of the few storm drains in the city. I ducked down and slid through the opening, the arrow catching painfully as I fell through.

# CHAPTER FIVE

## MIRA

*R*ispan had rushed out the door before I could say anything else. He was right though; he needed to get that tracker out of here right away. Korashéna's cloak had been set aside while Gralbast was removing the bracelet. I could see she hadn't been treated well. She was filthy. Her hair was matted and the bits of clothing she was wearing were dirty and barely covered her. There were also bruises showing; some of them looked recent and others were at various stages of healing. I reached out my hand and stopped when I saw her tense up.

"Probably the first thing we should do is get you cleaned up and into some proper clothes." I smiled, trying to put her at ease.

Then I realized that, appearing as a man, I probably wasn't the best person for this.

"Come with me, please," I said to her and headed back toward the courtyard. She followed behind me, giving Gralbast a wary look from the corner of her eye.

"Sabela!" I called out once we were out the back door.

"Here!" She appeared from the stable area.

"Sabela, this is Korashéna," I told her. "Could you help her please? She's going to be traveling with us. She needs a bath and some clothes. I figured she'd do better with a female touch."

Sabela frowned for a moment before realizing, "Right! No problem, Raven." She winked. Turning to Korashéna, she smiled. "Come on. I'm sure you'll be happy to get rid of those things."

Satisfied she was in good hands, I went back inside to resume going over the details of our caravan with Gralbast. We'd filled the three wagons that we'd brought with us, plus two more of Gralbast's. Bavrana had expanded her portion to eight wagons. This part of the work was wearying. Réni was better suited to it, but she had gone to see Bavrana to check on a few details. And technically, I was in charge of this caravan, so I did need to know everything about it. Maybe I was taking the role-playing too seriously, but I didn't like to do anything in half-measures.

Things were coming together nicely. We were still worried about Valdeg and Darusa burning Gralbast's shop after we left, though the shift in rumor from some vague volatile substance to a captive dragon had thrown a monkey wrench in their cover story. I suspected Rispan had a hand in that, but he'd just smiled and looked away when the subject came up.

I'd sent Ergek and Sharuza out to appear to be bored and looking for work. They would complain loudly about having been let go by the trader Raven as soon as all his goods were sold. There was no way that a fire could be easily passed off as Darusa had planned. We still needed to be sharp, though. She would probably come up with something else if we gave her half a chance.

It seemed like no time had passed before Sabela brought a dramatically altered Korashéna to me. Her hair was clean and brushed, with a sheen I could only envy. The bruises were mostly covered by her clothes. She was also young, maybe my age or younger.

"I borrowed some from Réni's things," Sabela told me. "It was the best fit. But we'll need to get her some things of her own."

I pulled my purse from where it was tied at my belt and

tossed it to her. "You know her size well enough now," I said. "Would you please go out and see if you can find several changes of clothes for her? If need be, just get her *Urgaban* clothes and she can roll the sleeves up." I turned to Korashéna, "Once we get to Su Lariano, you can go to a shop and choose for yourself. But for now, I think it would be better to keep you hidden."

Sabala was already out the door when Gralbast spoke.

"I've been thinking about that bracelet," he said. "They are expensive to make. *Urgaban* can learn to use them, but we don't have the ability to make them. That's why they aren't used very often. Only very valuable or special slaves have them."

I looked at Korashéna questioningly. Her eyes darted back and forth between us.

Her eyes dropped for a moment, then she pulled her shoulders back.

"My full name is Korashéna Ulané Sharavi, nya Su Astonil."

"Ulané?" I was not expecting that. "You're from the royal family?"

She nodded.

"I hadn't heard there were any survivors."

She opened her mouth to speak, but then clenched her teeth together as her gaze back fell to the floor.

"There aren't," she said after a moment. She still hadn't raised her head. "Not anymore. I am the last."

"All the more reason to get her out of Pokorah-Vo," Gralbast said, "and they'll be looking for her that much harder."

"You should be safe once we're out of the city," I said to her.

"You plan to take me to Su Lariano?" Her eyes had narrowed with the question.

"Yes," I told her. "By tomorrow we—"

"I would not go to the city of traitors." She glared. "I will go my own way."

I was at a loss for words while I tried to digest that. "I... I don't understand. City of traitors?"

"You are of Su Lariano? You are not *Ulané Jhinura.*"

"No. I mean, yes. I'm human. I've only been on this world a short time. Su Lariano has taken me in."

"Do not trust them. They will betray you. As they did the people of Su Astonil."

I looked at Gralbast, but he just shrugged.

"From what I've seen," I said, "they seem to be honorable. At least for the most part."

"Honorable?" She scoffed at my words. "Is it honorable to abandon your allies? They left us to perish at the hands of these monsters!" She flung her hand in Gralbast's direction. "Three times!" Her anger was rising. "I know the tales well! Three times we sent messengers, asking for help. Each message, more desperate than the last. All were ignored!"

"My understanding is that they've had no communication from Su Astonil," I told her. "One of my goals in coming here was to find out why Su Astonil had cut communications."

"Lies!" she snarled. "We even sent the seal of our city with the first messenger, so there could be no question. We waited, but there was nothing. We sent a second messenger. We had no seal, so as proof of our message we sent the royal scepter."

"A platinum scepter," Gralbast said. "With gold trim. And sapphires and diamonds."

"Yes!" Her eyes flashed at him. "Still, no help came. When we sent the third messenger, my people had nearly given up hope. The messenger was sent with—"

"A crown," Gralbast cut in. "Also, platinum with gold trim. With sapphires and a great ruby in front."

"Yes!" She glared at him. "How can you know this?"

"They are on display in the palace," he said. Eyes downcast. "Arugak's palace. Now Vegak's. You weren't betrayed, Korashéna'u. The messengers never made it through."

Korashéna gaped at him.

"Arugak had scouts posted for miles to watch the edge of the forest," he said. "They never had a chance."

I could see her walls crumbling, the focus of her hate, of her blame, was taken from her. My amulet was giving me an understanding that would have been beyond me otherwise. Her one anchor was suddenly cut loose, leaving her to flounder. She needed something new.

"Korashéna Ulané Sharavi." I got her attention. "We will end slavery in this city. Your people will need you. They will need your strength."

I could see her taking hold of that concept, grasping it, taking it as her own. Making it her new foundation. She wasn't stable with it yet, but it was a start.

We had taken to having dinner inside Gralbast's house. Sharuza and Ergek would cook, and we would all gather around the large dining table to eat. I introduced Korashéna to everyone, not using her title or full name.

"Please," she told us, "just call me Shéna."

I'd fill Mooren in on her identity later. It's not that I didn't trust everyone on our team, I just wanted to avoid open discussion. What if we weren't the only ones sending out spies? I'd bring Sabela, Sharuza and Ergek in on it, too, and Rispan as well, at an appropriate time.

I watched her eating from the corner of my eye, and I could tell she was trying to hide how much the food was overwhelming her. Judging by how she looked when she got to us, I doubted she'd tasted anything decent her whole life. Réni had rejoined us, reporting that Bavrana was ready to go.

I looked up at the sound of the door, expected to see Rispan come in, but it was Sabela with a bundle under her arms.

"Plenty of clothes." She smiled, putting the bundle next to Shéna. "Mission successful!"

Rispan still hadn't returned by the time we'd finished eating and the dishes were cleared away.

"We should all turn in early," I said. "We have an early day tomorrow." I turned to Gralbast. "If you could have one of your guards wake me at four-thirty?"

He nodded and I turned to face Shéna. Where was I going to put her? We needed to keep her out of sight.

"Come with me," I told her.

I led her to my wagon and ushered her inside.

"We're going to have to share," I said, closing the door behind us.

"I see." Her head was bowed. "And this is where I am to show my appreciation to the great Raven for keeping me safe from the *Urgaban*."

"What?" I looked at her, then shook my head. "Um. No."

I started undressing and I could see this was upsetting her.

"There are a couple of things you should know about me," I said as I continued undressing. "One of them is, my name isn't really Raven. It's Mira."

My shirt came off and her eyes widened when she saw the bindings on my chest.

"You're a woman!"

"Yeah." I smirked. "That's the other thing."

I could see she was trying to reconcile a few things in her head.

"So… you are a woman," she said. "And… you prefer…"

I saw where she was going and stopped her cold. "You are only in this wagon because we need to keep you hidden. I am Raven. This is my caravan, and this is my wagon. I would never give it up to anyone. So. We share. And it will be a bit crowded because I am already sharing with Réni. Once we're out of the city, we can look at other options if you like."

Réni came in not long after and soon we were all trying to sleep. It was going to be interesting though, since Réni tended to flail about in her sleep a bit and latch onto anything warm. When the light tap sounded on my door at four-thirty, my sleep had been fitful at best.

The center of the courtyard was lit up with light stones. I could see figures moving in the shadows around the edges, bringing up teams to hook to the wagons. The night still had a chill; my breath showed only briefly in the air. I pulled my cloak tighter, wishing for a pair of gloves. I'd have to talk to Felora about that when we got back to Su Lariano.

At least this ridiculous hat Rispan had picked for me would help to keep my head warm. I never realized how much hair helped for that until I'd cut mine off.

I went to check on Farukan and found out that Rispan still hadn't returned. His bedding, which was laid out near Farukan's stall, hadn't been slept in.

"Mira," Farukan's voice rumbled in my head. "*I don't see my groom.*"

"*Good morning.*" I spoke to him with my mind. "*He didn't come back last night. We're going to have to enlist someone else.*"

I knew he preferred to have a consistent groom working with him, but we'd have to make allowances.

"*I'll send Sabela,*" I told him. "*She'll be good. Be nice to her.*"

His chuckle seemed to echo in my head, and I couldn't tell if that meant he was going to be nice or was planning to give her a hard time.

"*Another thing, Farukan,*" I said to him. "*I've been thinking about this secret of ours.*"

"*That we can speak mind to mind?*"

"*Yes. I think it would be helpful for a few others to know. At least your groom.*"

"*The White Riders strictly forbade anyone else knowing.*"

"*Yeah, I know. It seems like they had a lot of bad habits. I wanted to tell Rispan first,*" I said. "*I'm worried that he's not back.*"

"Sabela!" I saw her walking across the yard. She changed direction and came toward me at my call. "Rispan didn't make it back yet. I need you to take over for him with Farukan."

"Do you think he's alright? What if he's not back before we leave?"

"I doubt he's going to be showing up in the next few minutes. We can't wait." I shook my head. "We can only hope he's okay and that he'll catch up with us."

She nodded. "He's a bit of a rascal," she said, "but he always comes through in the end."

"Pack his things up for him, will you?" I asked her. "He probably won't have time."

I sounded more positive than I felt. There was no way Rispan wouldn't have been back by now unless something was very wrong. I was very afraid that this mission of mine had gotten another of my friends killed. I couldn't afford to think like that, though. As Mouse would say, that's not getting any onions chopped.

I could see Gralbast having a last-minute conversation with Mikolosk. Mikolosk maintained Gralbast's business and managed his affairs whenever he was gone.

Mooren was getting the team hooked up to my wagon when Sabela brought Farukan to me, fully saddled and ready to go. As always, he knelt so I could mount his giant frame. I surveyed the scene from my new height.

"Are we ready to go?" I called out. "I'd like to beat Bavrana to the main gate."

"Where's Rispan," Mooren asked.

"He'll have to catch up," I told him.

"We are ready, Captain," Gralbast called from his seat on one of his wagons. He didn't have a sleeper wagon like I did, just the two freight wagons. He'd also supplemented our team so that all of the wagon benches were loaded three across.

"Captain?" I asked him.

He laughed. "You are our captain, are you not? Captain of this caravan? Or would you prefer the title of Master?"

"No." I didn't like that at all. "I suppose Captain is fine. But I'd prefer Raven."

He just shrugged with a grin.

"Alright," I said. "Let's move out."

Mooren drove my wagon and the others fell into line behind him. The gates would open at sunrise, and we were to meet Bavrana and her wagons there. It didn't take us much more than ten minutes to reach the gate from Gralbast's place. We still had a few minutes before they would open. Quite a few more guards were at the gate than I would have expected. Especially for the early hour.

An *Urgaban* gave one of the guards a shove towards us.

The guard strode forward, "We'll be searching your wagons before you can pass." He motioned his men who started for the wagons.

"Here now," Gralbast called out. "What's the meaning of this?"

"Gralbast," the one who had shoved the guard spoke. His voice sounded like a greasy knife. "I thought you'd be smarter than this."

"Dobarek?" Gralbast peered at him. "What do you want? You've no call to stop us."

"I do if you've stolen one of my slaves!"

"We don't trade in slaves," I cut in. "There's enough filth around that deals in that."

Dobarek snapped his gaze to me. "Who are you?"

"I am Raven," I said to him. "This is *my* caravan you are accosting."

"I don't know you."

"That's right," I said. "I don't travel in your circles. I can't take the stench." I found that I *really* hated slavers.

He opened his mouth, but before he could say anything, I heard a scream and someone was pulling a struggling, hooded figure out of the back of my wagon.

"What do we have here?" the woman was saying.

Farukan was already moving, and I threw my leg over his back and launched myself off just as the woman pulled back the hood of the cloak to reveal Réni.

I already had my knife against the woman's throat.

"What you have there is my bookkeeper," I growled at her, "and I'll have your blood if you don't let her go this instant."

The woman froze, but she didn't release Réni. Her eyes went to Dobarek.

"Let her go, Gradela," he said. "That's not her."

Gradela stepped back from Réni, and I turned to face Dobarek.

"I have no business with you or your kind." I glared at him. "Step aside or when that gate opens, we will ride through over your corpse."

It was a bluff because the numbers were pretty even.

"Gradela?"

"She's not here, sir," she answered. "We'd have found her."

"Very well," he said. "Let them pass."

Just then there was some noise from the rear, and I saw that Bavrana had arrived with her wagons. Bavrana was on a brown horse and was moving past the wagons toward us. The first rays of the sun highlighted the look of concern on her face.

"That," I said, "is the rest of my caravan. You will *not* interfere."

With all of Bavrana's people, the numbers were now in our favor, and he hesitated. Aside from two teamsters per wagon, she had an additional eight on horseback for security. Farukan knelt by my side, and I mounted. Dobarek glared at me and then gave a dismissive gesture to his men.

I turned to the chief of the guards, "I believe you are late in opening the gates."

He nodded and signaled to his men, and they worked the crank to pull back the bars. Once they were drawn, they pushed the gates open.

"Move out!" I called. I held my position to the side, my eye on Dobarek, until the last wagon was through. He started to say something, but I'd turned Farukan, and we were out the gate.

# CHAPTER SIX

## MIRA

*I* could feel Dobarek's eyes on my back as Farukan carried me to the front of the caravan. Réni had taken her spot on the bench next to Mooren.

"That was close," I said as we came up alongside. "Where's Shéna? How did they not find her?"

"As soon as I heard the guard at the gate talking about searching the wagons," Réni told me, "I put her in the hidden compartment."

"What hidden compartment?"

"The one under the floor," she said. "That was the easiest."

"There's more than one?" *Why didn't anyone tell me about this?*

She nodded. "Rispan showed them to me."

"He did, did he?" I was going to have a talk with Rispan and find out what else he might have forgotten to share with me. That is, as soon as he caught up with us. I didn't want to think about that right now. "Where is she now?

"She's still in the compartment."

I glanced back at Pokorah-Vo. "Alright. She's going to have to stay there until we are out of sight of the city. I imagine it can't be very comfortable, but it's best not to risk it."

By midmorning we had passed the hill that overlooked Pokorah-Vo. Hidden from view, I called a halt long enough to let Shéna out of the compartment. Réni showed me how the molding along the wall flipped up to allow you to slip a hand under the edge of the floorboards to one side and pull up a two-foot-wide section that ran about three feet long.

The compartment was both wider and longer than the cover. Laying down, Shéna had plenty of room. As she climbed out, I noted she wasn't the only thing in the compartment. The sword and all of the gear of the White Rider was stashed in there.

*Rispan!*

I'd told him I didn't want anything of the White Rider's. That's something else I'd have to talk with him about when he got back. If he got back.

*Damn it!*

It was hard to be mad at him and worry about him at the same time. That just added annoyance to the list. We got moving again and Shéna joined Réni and Mooren on the bench. Coaching from Farukan was making me a better rider, but by the noon break I was more than ready to join the others on the wagon bench, too. In fact, I may even have called it a bit early.

It hadn't rained since we'd come through the other way, so the ground wasn't as soft, and we made good time. The hills around us were still lush and green.

Bavrana had brought Jakeda, who she had evidently poached from a restaurant in Pokorah-Vo. Bavrana planned for Jakeda to be the head chef at our restaurant once we opened it in Su Lariano. Shaluza and Ergak had been collaborating with her for our meals on the trail. Despite the occasional arguments over correct ingredients and proper technique, they actually got along quite well.

Four days in, Rispan still hadn't caught up and we suspected we were being followed.

"It must be Darusa or Valdeg," Gralbast was saying over dinner. "Everyone does a little unofficial trading, but almost all of the smuggling in and out of Laraksha-Vo goes through their hands. They stand to lose the most by an agreement between Pokorah-Vo and Su Lariano and Laraksha-Vo."

"Not to mention they must be frustrated with how things went for their plans when we left the city." Mooren grinned. "You *know* they aren't happy about that."

"Don't forget," Bavrana put in around a mouthful of rabbit and a spicy pepper sauce, "they had planned for Raven and Gralbast to die in a fire. Disappearing on the trail would work just as well."

"Alright, you two know the trail best," I said to Gralbast and Bavrana. "If it was you, where would be the best place to come at us?"

"After we turn north," Bavrana answered.

Gralbast nodded. "I'd cut across country to get ahead. Set up a nice little ambush."

"And they know our numbers," Bavrana went on. "They'll have enough to feel comfortable with the advantage. There's no shortage of thugs for hire in Pokorah-Vo."

I brought out my map and studied the route. I could see what they were saying. The road went west from Pokorah-Vo along the river, and then turned sharply north when we hit the mountains. If they cut across, they could be waiting anywhere along the trail north.

"What if we don't turn north?" I asked. "What if we take the pass through the mountains instead and then turn north?"

"It takes a little longer," Gralbast said. "The road though the pass gets steep, and once we are through, we have a few streams to ford. They'd figure it out pretty quickly and come up behind us. But we'd bypass the ambush."

"Maybe we can have a surprise waiting for them," Mooren suggested. "Trim the odds a bit."

Of all the studying we'd done, one of the things that had fascinated me the most was tactics and strategy. Rispan had been good at it too, and sometimes we'd pose situations for each other to come up with a plan. It was more fun than playing chess.

Even Tree Nirellen said we had a natural talent for it. I already had a plan formulating in my head.

Sabela was probably the best scout we had, but for now, I needed to keep her close for Farukan. I had Bavrana send her two best scouts ahead to confirm whether we had any surprises waiting for us. They returned the next evening, reporting that there was a group of about sixty well-armed *Urgaban* in the woods about a half day north of the turn. That was about half again as many as our group, and not all of us were fighters.

By midafternoon the next day, we were approaching the turning point. I rode Farukan up alongside Gralbast.

"These wagons make an awful lot of noise when they're moving," I said to him. "Is there any way to make them quieter?"

"We'd have to tie everything down to minimize motion," he said. "Wrap anything that jingles with cloth. Even the horses' hooves and the wheels would need to be wrapped. And we'd need to travel a bit more slowly."

"Do we have enough cloth to do it?"

He thought about that. "We can probably have the men use their spare clothing and blankets to wrap things in the wagons and the trace chains and gear. That would just leave the wheels and the horses' hooves. We could cut up some tarps for that."

We reached the turn and I headed us north, but I called an early halt an hour and a half later. We had come up to a small, wooded area off to the side of the road and we brought the wagons into the trees.

"Set up camp," I said, "and collect extra firewood."

"What are you planning?" Mooren asked.

Ignoring his question, I turned to Gralbast. "Let's do what we discussed. Cut up the tents if we have to. Worst case scenario, we have cloth in our trade goods."

"Well, let's hope we don't have to dig that deeply," he answered.

ADAM K. WATTS

"It's a last resort," I nodded, "but let's get everyone started on getting that ready."

"Are you going to tell me what you have planned?" Mooren smiled. "Or do you want to see if I can guess?"

"Come on." I grinned. "They drilled those basic principles into us over and over again."

"It's been a while since I did Basic," he chuckled, "and I haven't looked at strategy since. It's not my area."

"The most basic principle of warfare?" I prompted him.

He thought for a moment. "Deception. I wondered why you turned north when I was pretty sure you'd decided to take the pass. We're going to double-back?"

I nodded. "Most of us are."

"Most of us?

"What's the first rule when facing an opponent who has superior numbers?" I asked.

Mooren shrugged. "Don't engage directly."

"Exactly. Guerilla tactics. Engage his flanks and fade away before he can organize."

"What did you have in mind?" Bavrana had heard the last comment as she approached.

"We'll send the wagons back and into the pass tonight," I told her. "Meanwhile, we'll try to make them think we're staying in these trees for as long as we can. If you can leave those of your people on horseback?" She nodded. "Good. I figure me, Sabela, and your eight can do some damage and stay mobile." We'd kept the best three of the horses we'd inherited from our attackers on the way into Pokorah-Vo. Sabela could use one of those.

"And me," Mooren said.

I shook my head. "No, I need you to stick with the caravan in case something happens." I wasn't going into this blind; I knew there were risks.

"In case something happens is why I'm here," he objected. "I'm supposed to keep anything from happening to you."

46

"Not this time," I told him. "Someone has to give a report to Dzurala. Me, you, or Sabela. And Sabela's our best scout. I need her."

I could tell he didn't like it.

"Fine," he said after a moment. "I'd suggest I stay with Sabela, and you go with the wagons, but I'm not going to waste my breath with that argument."

"It's my plan." I smiled. "I can't just leave it for others to do."

As the sun was setting, the caravan had been muffled. All except for the stove and cooking gear that Sharuza and Ergek were using to prepare dinner.

"Once you've eaten," I told everyone, "get some rest. Be ready to move out at midnight."

I took a seat near the fire. Mooren brought his bowl and joined me, and we sat in a sort of companionable silence as we ate.

"I don't have to tell you how dangerous this will be," he said after he'd scraped the last of the stew from his bowl.

"I know. We might not all come back."

"Make sure *you* come back."

Something about the way he'd said that made my stomach jump.

"I'm worried about Rispan." I changed the subject. "I hope he's alright."

"He's a resourceful guy," he told me. "He's sly like a fox."

"Yeah," I agreed. "But even a fox can be caught. I understand fox hunts used to be quite the thing."

"Just don't let your worry for him distract you."

"I won't," I told him. "I want you to get the wagons through the pass as soon as you can. Stop often enough to keep the horses from wearing out but keep going. The maps didn't have great details of the pass. If you come across a really good defensible spot in the pass, a bottleneck, someplace they couldn't get around behind us, stop there and fortify. Otherwise, push through."

I went to my wagon to try taking a nap. Shéna was sitting on the back steps.

"Still no word of Rispan?" she asked.

I shook my head.

"It's my fault." She hung her head.

That startled me. "Come again?"

"He was getting rid of my tracker," she said. "If anything happens to him, it's my fault."

I never realized how common self-blame could be. I'd done it with Tarana. So had Kirsat. I would really have to stay on top of that kind of thing.

"First of all," I told her, "Rispan makes his own decisions, and good or bad, Rispan does what Rispan wants to do. If he got himself into trouble, it was from his choices, not yours. Second, Rispan is only on this mission because of me. He does what he does based on my mission, my needs, and my orders. So that makes it my responsibility. But I'm only here because of the situation and it had to be somebody. We can trace things further and further back looking for who to blame. Slavers. Arugak for starting the war against your people."

"You're saying bad things happen and no one is to blame?"

"No." I shook my head. "Bad things don't *happen* by themselves. People *do* bad things. And they should definitely be held accountable. And make no mistake," I met her gaze, "if someone has done something bad to Rispan, they *will* pay."

At midnight, the wagons set off into the night, back down the trail we'd just come up. Sabela stood next to me as we watched them go.

"What's next?" she asked.

"Nothing for now. I figure we can stall for maybe a day, making them think we're all still camped here. We just keep the fire going and smoky. If they see the smoke, they'll be relaxed at first about where we are."

"And then?"

"Then they'll start to get anxious and want to take a closer look. We'll need to be watching for scouts. We keep an eye on them and we'll know when we're out of time. That's when the fun starts."

As soon as it was light, I had them erect false walls around the edge of the trees. Just loose branches, woven together to stay upright and make it so you couldn't easily see what was behind them. That would make it harder to see that the wagons were gone.

In the center of the little woods was an odd-looking tree. It was long since dead and nothing remained but a husk of what had once been really magnificent.

"What kind of tree was that?" I asked Sabela.

"That was the tree of a *Jhiné Boré*," she said.

*Jhiné Boré*. That was what humans call a dryad, a kind of a nymph.

"What happened?"

"A *Jhiné Boré* and their tree are bonded," she told me. "Neither can survive without the other. When this tree lost its *Jhiné Boré*, it simply withered and died."

Lost its *Jhiné Boré*. She meant when it had been killed. Here along the road out of Pokorah-Vo, I could imagine what had happened.

I had two of the *Urgaban* posted on hilltops with a good range of vision to watch for scouts. A pair of scouts had been spotted about a half-mile up the road, but so far, they were just watching from a distance. I had three of our *Urgaban* scouts circle around behind them. Meanwhile, I had two others just riding their horses back and forth on the road just past the trees. This would make the two scouts curious and keep them focused, trying to figure out what we were doing. By noon, our guys signaled that they'd taken out the scouts. Their orders were to erase all signs of the enemy scouts and see who came looking.

By dinner time, two more had shown up. I mounted Farukan and we started up the road at a walk. I'd gone maybe halfway when our scouts came down the road towards me. Distraction had worked again, and the new spies were out of the picture. The four of us rode back to the others in the trees.

"Okay," I said. "When they don't hear back from those last two, they will know something's up. So now it's time for phase two of my plan."

We split into two groups. Me, Sabela and three of the *Urgaban* scouts in one group, and Bavrana's chief guard, Veselek, and the other three scouts in the other. Leaving the fire set up to keep burning, we headed north. Veselek's group would circle around on the east side, while my team would circle around to the west.

I assumed that when they didn't hear back from their scouts, they'd send a larger party in the morning, maybe even the whole lot of them. Our first objective would be their horses.

I was wrong.

They had packed up and were already on the move south. We waited in the hills as they passed, riding down the road, my clever plan in shambles. A movement back down the road caught my eye and I looked toward the wooded area where they'd been camped. Not everyone had left. I signaled to the others, and we made our way through the hills to get a closer look.

Two *Urgaban* were just finishing loading up four packhorses and were evidently preparing to follow the others. This must be their supplies. It took resources to keep sixty men fed on the trail for several days. We might be able to salvage some part of my plan after all. I didn't want to take any risks, so we got closer and took them out with a couple of well-placed arrows.

I really didn't like all the killing, but I didn't have any illusions about what they were here to do. The whole caravan was depending on me. I couldn't afford to be soft. When it came to choosing between the lives of my people and the lives of those would who attack them, there wasn't even a question. Would I have been able to look at things so coldly a year ago? I didn't know. Despite all the changes, I didn't feel like a different person. I'd heard growing older was like that, though; you didn't feel any older, but suddenly you realized you were.

We gathered up the horses and packhorses and headed out. Tomorrow morning, there were going to be a lot of unhappy people asking about breakfast.

We slowly gained ground on the main group and watched when they pulled up at the last rise that looked down on the little woods where our fire was still going. They'd been smarter than I'd hoped so far, and I needed to give them more credit.

So far, they knew we'd eliminated their scouts. They knew they had the advantage of numbers. What would I do? One option was to try riding over my enemy and overpower them before they could get set. That was dangerous though, because they couldn't know our defenses. We didn't have any, but they didn't know that.

Another option was to try a sneak attack during the night. They'd have to be quiet, but they could take their time on the approach. But would they do that on foot or on horseback? I knew Veselek was out there, not knowing what I was planning to do. At this point, I was waiting to see how things would shape up.

Then I noticed a couple of horsemen closely circling the small group of trees where our wagons were supposedly camped. *Veselek!* He was preserving the illusion of our camp by putting out visible sentries. That would also make it hard for Valdeg or whoever was running this group to get a clear picture of what was inside the trees. They'd have to wait until dark to try sneaking in a scout. Every hour of delay was another hour of travel that Mooren and the others were gaining through the pass.

I stood next to Sabela, just below the crown of a small hill. We could see over the top, but its bulk prevented our bodies from being seen.

"Sabela," I said to her, "I need you to get down there and talk to Veselek. That sentry idea was brilliant. Have him put up torches once it gets dark."

"Too bad we didn't hang onto any of the light stones."

"That would have made it easier, for sure," I nodded, "but if we set up a ring of torches it will make it very hard to sneak in a scout. Tell him we'll watch from out here."

"No problem. Anything else you want me to tell him?"

"If I get the chance, I'll still try to go for their horses. So just tell him to be ready to support as we discussed in our original plans. Take the packhorses with you," I added. "Stash them south in a good hiding place. We can pick them up later on our way and I don't want to worry about them falling back into enemy hands."

"You got it, boss!" She grinned.

The afternoon turned into dusk and then into twilight. Veselek put up the torches as directed so that the perimeter of the woods was fairly well lit. There was a flaw though that I could see from here; there was one section on the west side where the light from the torch was blocked by some foliage and cast a shadow that a good scout could use to sneak in. And there was no way I could let Veselek know.

Sabela was back, but I didn't want to risk sending her back out. I could only hope the scout, and I knew they'd send one, wouldn't see that the wagons weren't really there. As soon as that was known, Valdeg or Darusa or whoever this was would head straight for the pass. It was the only other route. I wanted to do some damage to them before they found that out.

The waiting was frustrating. By midnight, Veselek had replenished the torches, but unfortunately, he hadn't fixed the gap. Sure enough, from our angle we could see a scout moving across the open meadow that ran up to the edge of the trees. He stayed in the shadows, moving from bush to clump of grass to hollow. He angled his path toward the gap and disappeared into the shadows of the woods.

Meanwhile, Veselek still had two sentries riding the perimeter. It was only a matter of time now. Soon, the scout would come back and report what he saw. An hour passed and the scout still hadn't returned. Another half hour, and he still hadn't come back out.

*Veselek, you genius!*

The gap hadn't been an accident, it had been a trap. That scout had come in right where Veselek wanted him to, and they'd been waiting. Today had definitely shown me that I'm not the only smart one around. And maybe not the smartest, either.

Evidently the bad guys had figured out their scout wasn't coming back. Or maybe they were just tired of waiting. But they were moving forward now, and the good news was it looked like they were going on foot. Veselek's sentries had made a circuit and were now on the other side of the woods. Actually, they were overdue. They were probably getting ready for the attack.

Now it was our turn, we needed to find their horses.

# CHAPTER SEVEN

## MIRA

We knew where they'd been gathered, but we didn't know how many guards they'd left behind, if any. We took a wide loop around to come from behind. Hopefully, coming up from behind where we estimated their horses to be would help to hide any noise we might make in our approach.

Their horses were held in a makeshift rope corral. We approached as quietly as we could, slowly making our way.

I heard voices ahead and motioned the others to stop.

"I tell you I heard something," one voice said.

"It's just the horses being restless," another voice said.

"I don't think so. It sounded like it was coming from farther away."

They were speaking Urgan, but my pendant let me understand what they were saying. I was tempted to have Bavrana's scouts handle the guards, but it wasn't fair to have them do all the dirty work. I motioned to Sabela, and she dismounted while Farukan knelt for me to get to my feet.

We crept forward, listening and watching for the guards. I had my daggers in my hands.

"See?" the second voice spoke again. "There's nothing out there."

I could see them now in the darkness. Moonlight reflected off of their faces and the metal heads of their spears. They stood several feet from the horses, looking out in our direction. Sabela was already nearing one as they started to turn back to the horses. I stepped forward and my boot caught on a root, causing me to stumble slightly. Both guards spun instantly in my direction.

Sabela took advantage of their focus and attacked one from behind, her knife sinking in at the base of his skull. His companion turned to her, ready to thrust with his spear, but I was already moving, and he was shortly on the ground next to his friend. I didn't even stop to think about how easy it had been for me to kill. I knew it was coming, and when the time came, I had just acted. I had to. People were depending on me.

It had been fast and quiet, but the horses nearby were suddenly restless. Maybe it was the smell of blood. They were all saddled, so it wasn't the plan to leave them for long. Our enemies probably expected to overwhelm our camp quickly and return. Trying not to upset the horses further, we cut down the ropes holding them in and went back to our own mounts.

"*Farukan,*" I asked him, "*what's the best way to get these horses to stampede out of here?*"

"*What direction do you want them to go?*" His voice rumbled in my head.

I considered that for a moment.

"*Could we get them to run through that meadow below us, where those* Urgaban *are trying to sneak up on the woods?*"

"*Charge your people forward,*" he answered. "*Make noise and be loud. I'll do the rest. They can hear and understand me to a degree.*"

I turned to my team. "Ready?" They nodded, shifting in their saddles, and adjusting the grips on their reins. "Then let's go!"

Farukan shot forward, and I screamed, "Yaaaaaaaaahhhh!"

The others were on my heels, doing the same.

*"Run cousins!"* I could hear Farukan. *"Run through the night and don't stop! Run!"*

The entire herd launched in an instant, running hard over the hill and down across the open plain. We followed on their heels, urging them on.

Heads turned toward us in the field, panic on their faces.

"Stampede!"

I saw several of them being run down and then we were past them. We kept the horses going past the trees and Veselek and his team joined us. Our pace slowed after the first mile or so, but we kept riding until we reached the fork in the road. Along the way, Sabela had split off and then caught back up, leading the packhorses she'd stashed earlier.

We'd done it! We'd gotten their horses and supplies, and none of our team had been hurt. I grinned at Sabela.

"Nicely done!" Veselek said to me.

"Back atcha, Ves. That little trap you laid was brilliant!"

I glanced down and saw a splash of blood on my sleeve from the guard I'd killed. That brought my mood down a bit. Our team might have come through unscathed, but there had been death today. It was a waste. How many of them had families waiting for them?

I knew there would be more death before we were through. This would delay them, but eventually they'd round up some of their horses and come after us again. It would give us more time to prepare, and put us in a stronger position, but this was far from over.

We made a cold camp and I had them get a few hours rest. I was too restless to sleep though, so I kept watch. By first light, we were moving, following the trail that led through the pass. The trail entered a canyon that cut into the mountain. The sides climbed quickly to tower high above us. Some of the loose horses had come this way. As we came upon them, we either tied them in line to bring along or pushed them ahead of us.

By the morning of the fourth day, we had rounded up a dozen of them.

From my knowledge of the trail, we should be reaching the summit of the pass soon. The elevation had been steadily rising since the first day. We were coming through a section with a rock wall on one side that leaned over the canyon, and a steep slope of loose shale on the other. Ahead, I could see the way narrowed considerably. It had probably been just wide enough for the wagons to get through.

"Took you long enough!" a voice called from ahead.

I looked up to see Mooren's grinning face from where he stood on top of a huge boulder.

"Did you miss me?" I teased.

"Every moment." His grin only seemed bigger. Why did my face feel so hot?

Ignoring his grin, I looked at the bottleneck and the area leading up to it.

"You decided to dig in here?" I asked. "This looks like a good spot."

"Yes," he answered. "It has the higher ground, a good field of vision, and a narrow choke point so they can't come at us very many at a time."

"What if they come at us from above?"

He shook his head. "They'd have to go back two days to find a place they could get to the top. The overhang above actually protects us on this side, and on the other side, the range from beyond the shale is too far for bows. There's an easy way to the top not much further along, and I have scouts stationed to keep an eye in case they try circling around us."

"Wow! Talk about a perfect spot!" I was impressed. "Let's get ready. I'm sure they'll show up tonight or tomorrow. A lot of them will be on foot, and they're going to be hungry."

Mooren looked at me, waiting for me to explain.

"We scattered all of their horses, and," I pointed to the pack-horses, "we took all of their supplies."

"Cruel," he said, shaking his head. "You should have just killed them quickly and put them out of their misery."

"We did kill some of them," the smile had left my face, "but there are still too many of them."

"Don't worry," he said. "There's no way they can take the pass."

"Any sign of Rispan?" I asked him.

He shook his head.

On the other side of the bottleneck, the canyon quickly widened again into a large, grassy meadow. It was at least a mile long and maybe a half mile at its widest point. The meadow sloped gently upwards and at the far end turned more to granite and bare ground at the summit of the pass. Around the bottleneck, they had built up additional defenses. The wagons were circled, and the horses were all moved to a safe distance. It smelled like our chefs had another wonderful surprise they were cooking up for us. Sabela led the dozen extra horses we'd picked up to graze with the others.

Scattering their horses had just been a delaying tactic. I wanted Mooren to have time to get settled into a defensive position. I knew it would have taken them at least several hours to round up horses to come after us. Maybe a full day. Then they would have followed us into the pass, riding hard to make up for lost time. Mooren had found a good place to stand them off.

We saw the dust before we saw them. Almost all of our people had bows, and we were going to take full advantage of that. As the riders rushed up the canyon, they couldn't see that we were lying in wait.

"That's definitely Valdeg," Gralbast said from beside me. I didn't know which one he was talking about. "The rest are just hired thugs."

When they were halfway across the open ground between the cliff and the shale slope, I signaled for everyone to draw. At fifty yards, I signaled them to release.

Both men and horses fell, and the riders turned quickly to

head back down the canyon. Our archers got off a few more rounds before they got out of range. On the ground, I could see at least eight of them, and two horses. I felt sad for the horses, but not so much for the *Urgaban* who'd been charging up here to kill my people.

On the far side of the open ground, I could see a few of them standing and looking over the approach to the bottleneck. I could only imagine what they were saying, but I knew they didn't like what they saw.

I glanced at Mooren where he stood atop the same large boulder he'd greeted me from earlier.

"What do you think they'll do?" I asked him.

"They know we have the approach covered," he answered. "They'll probably wait until dark and try to get close when we can't see them. Coming across that open ground in broad daylight is suicide."

I nodded, "Sounds likely."

"We should keep an eye on that shale slope though," he added. "They may have someone try to come around it to get a look at our defenses."

They weren't going to come charging at us anytime soon. We did have several people watching though, just to be sure. Now that I knew where they were, I felt like I could relax more. Earlier, I'd been too tense. I sat down with my back to a boulder and took a look around the camp to get a feel for things beyond basic defenses.

Shéna and Réni were sitting on the steps at the back of our wagon, talking about something. Sabela was giving Farukan a good brushing. Gralbast and Bavrana were sitting near the cook fire with some sort of board game set up between them. Our three chefs were caught up in some collaboration that they were adding things to and tasting, sometimes with a nod and sometimes shaking their heads. The rest of our company was either on duty and keeping an eye out or relaxing around camp.

If I didn't know there were close to fifty *Urgaban* just down the canyon wanting to kill us all, I would have thought everything was just peachy. But I did know. And I noticed that when one of the teamsters jumped down from a wagon where he'd been dozing, Gralbast's head snapped around at the sound before returning to his game with Bavrana. And I noticed that while Réni and Shéna were very involved in their conversation, their eyes still turned to occasionally scan the area with a wary glance.

They weren't really relaxed. They were ready to jump to their feet at the slightest hint of the trouble they knew was coming.

I felt a slow anger rising inside me.

I had seen so many wonderful things since coming to this world. But I'd also seen so many things that were just wrong. I couldn't understand it. Laruna and her goons. The kids in Sprig training. The two who'd tried to kill me. The White Rider. *Slavery!* I was still getting my head around that one, too. And now this Valdeg was here to kill us. For what? I didn't even know why. To keep control of the black market?

Forget anger. I was getting pissed. So far, I'd just been reacting. Even coming on this mission, I'd been reacting to the situation as we went. Following the plan. Being cautious and doing the next thing in front of me.

Maybe it was time to be a little more like Nora and go on the offensive. And I didn't mean on a small scale like when we'd scattered those horses. I'd been too nice for too long and there were too many people out there who didn't deserve nice. And too many who were getting crushed beneath their boots. Shéna and her people. Farukan and his family and all the rest of the *Rorujhen*. People enslaved. People killed. People like Tarana. Like Kirsat and Kooras.

I knew we had cruelty and injustice and the same kind of insanity back on Earth, as they had here. But I wasn't *on* Earth anymore. I was here. And here I wasn't just some high school kid. Here I could make a difference. I remembered when Shéna had taken on the new purpose of being strong for the future of her people. It felt like I was doing the same thing now. There were people here that deserved a better life; they deserved to be fought for. And I was going to do it.

"Someone's trying to get past the shale," Mooren's voice broke into my thoughts.

I got up and went to stand beside him.

"You see him?" He pointed.

I searched but couldn't see what he was talking about.

"Let your eyes unfocus," he told me, "and then just be alert for any movement."

I tried it and after about a half a minute, a motion drew my attention. I looked at the spot and saw a distant figure trying to come up along the far edge of the shale.

"I see him," I said. "Nice trick!"

"You could probably also see him by looking with the *Ralahin*." He smirked.

I should have thought of that.

# CHAPTER EIGHT

## MIRA

*W*e watched as the figure slowly went up and then started across the top of the loose shale. He'd come maybe thirty yards when he took a step and the shale shifted under his weight. His arms flailed for a few seconds while he tried to catch his balance, but the extra motion was too much and more of the slope began to slide, faster and faster, carrying him with it. He tried to jump past the moving section and sank up to his knees, causing a new section to start sliding, throwing him onto his side. He cried out as he fell, then he was tumbling in amongst the rocks.

He ended up at the bottom of the slope, about two thirds of the way across, half covered in loose shale. At first, he didn't move, and I wondered if the slide had killed him. After a few minutes, I saw a leg shift, then an arm. He struggled to get up but couldn't. I could hear him calling out to the others, but it became obvious that none of them were coming for him.

"Cover me," I said to Mooren.

"What are you doing?"

I didn't answer, I made my way toward the fallen *Urgaban*. As I got closer, I could see that his right leg was broken, and he had cuts and scrapes all over. He didn't notice me coming until I was getting close. He drew a knife from a sheath at his waist and his eyes followed my progress.

I looked down at him. He seemed young.

"Do you want my help?" I asked him, speaking in Urga.

"I thought you'd come to finish me off."

I shook my head. "I'll help you, if you swear on your life you will not harm me or any of my people."

He looked at me, as if trying to decide if I was telling the truth.

"If I wanted to kill you, I'd just do it. I wouldn't need to trick you," I said. "It's your call, but you know none of your friends are going to help you."

"They aren't my friends," he said sullenly. "Alright, I swear." He tossed his knife away.

"Any other weapons?"

"Bow. Quiver. Up there someplace." He nodded up the slope.

"Alright," I told him. "I'll only warn you once. If you try anything, you won't live to regret it. I won't hesitate."

"You already have my oath."

I took his hands and pulled him to his feet. Then I helped him hobble toward the bottleneck. He couldn't put any weight on the broken leg. It was awkward because of the height difference. He was too short to get his arm over my shoulder, he had to reach across to hang onto my opposite shoulder with his right hand, and I had to hold him with my left. It was slow going, but I wasn't going to try carrying him outright.

Once I'd gotten him through the bottleneck, Mooren and one of the *Urgaban* took him from me and brought him to the center of camp near the cook-fire. I watched as Mooren went about setting his leg and cleaning his injuries. He sucked his breath sharply between his teeth when Mooren set his leg. He wasn't much more than a boy. His eyes flicked all over camp, taking everything in. They lingered over the food.

"What's your name?" I asked him.

His eyes swiveled back to me. "Javen."

"I'm Raven," I told him. "I imagine you're hungry. Your people probably haven't had much to eat in a few days."

"They ate." He no longer met my gaze.

"They?"

He nodded once.

"Not you?"

He hesitated, then shook his head.

"Why not?"

He just shook his head again, his mouth in a hard line.

"How long since you've eaten?"

He shrugged. "Four days."

"Why not?" I asked again.

"Couldn't." He raised his eyes to mine, and I saw grief there. And anger. "I won't eat horse."

That was how they'd fed their people. They'd started eating the horses. It wouldn't be my first choice either, but if it was that or starvation, I knew I would do what I needed to survive. Not with a *Rorujhen* of course, that would be like eating people. But regular horses? They're animals, right? Like cows? Of course, they were much more beautiful than cows. Should they be exempt because of their looks? I shook my head, dismissing the unanswered question. I didn't want to get into philosophy today.

"I take it you're particular about your food?" I asked him.

He looked at me like he didn't understand the question.

"Horses aren't food. I don't care about food." His eyes were on the ground.

"You like horses." I thought I was understanding him now.

He nodded once.

Mooren had finished bandaging Javen's injuries and assigned one of the *Urgaban* as a guard to watch him.

"Get him some food, please," I said to Sharuza, who was working on something at the stove over the fire.

Javen accepted the plate with reservations. He held it under his nose and took a whiff. The expression on his face changed to

64

wonder. He took a small bite and his eyes closed. He took another small bite, and I could see him working it around in his mouth, savoring it and chewing it slowly.

"I was wrong." He looked at me. "I do care about food."

Sharuza laughed and went back to her cooking.

"I thought all *Urgaban* were famous for their cuisine and appreciation for food," I told him.

"Not where I eat," he said, taking another bite.

"Is Valdeg planning to attack tonight after dark?" I asked him.

He shrugged, still focused on his food. "Don't know. Probably." He took another bite. "Seems like he has it in for you guys."

"What about you?" I asked. "You're working for him. You came after us."

He shrugged again. "It's just work."

"Aren't there other jobs?"

He shook his head. "Not much. Gotta take what you can get."

"This kind of work can get you killed."

"So can starving." He set aside his empty plate.

"Do you know why Valdeg wants to stop us?"

"What do I care about rich people fighting?"

His answer made me pause.

"We want to open up trade," I told him. "This would create more jobs. A lot more jobs over the next few years. You're contributing to your own problem."

He thought for a moment. "Maybe. But work next year won't feed you now."

There was nothing I could say to that.

"Is that how it is for all of them over there?" I asked. "They're fighting us because they needed a job?"

"Some. Mostly mercenaries, but a lot of them have families. Some don't. Some don't care about the job as long as they get to hurt someone."

"Maybe we can talk them into quitting."

He shook his head. "They took the job. They'll do the work, so they get paid."

"What about you?" I asked him. "You took the job, too."

"They left me out there," he said. "They didn't do anything to help. Besides. They ate the horse."

That seemed to settle matters for him.

"Why do you like horses so much?" I could feel the magic of the pendant working to relax his walls, to build up his willingness to share.

"When I was about seven," he began, "my mother took us with her to the hills north of the city to gather wild vegetables, me and my brother Zivak. Never did know who my father was, it was just us. She was still young. People who knew her still talk about how beautiful she was. A lot of men wanted her, but she just wanted to be left alone to raise me and Zivak. Well, that day, three of them followed us.

"Out in the hills, they caught up with us. One of them grabbed her. Zivak pulled his knife and stabbed him in the leg. The guy screamed. He drew his knife and slashed Zivak across the throat. My mother went crazy, hitting and clawing and screaming. I tried to help, but I got hit.

"When I woke up, the sun was setting. Standing above me was this horse, it was nuzzling my face. I sat up and he backed away, looking at me. It was a stallion. Then he reared and I could see the sheen of the sunlight off his coat. Everything was tinged in red and gold. He started running and his herd was there, they ran around me, past me. I could see Zivak. And my mother. I wanted them to see the herd too, but they couldn't see anything anymore. I watched the herd run off and wished I could run with them through the night. Across the plains, far away. I wished I could be free, like they were."

I doubted he would have shared that with me if I hadn't been wearing the pendant. The spell didn't coerce; it wouldn't change someone's mind or their nature. The spell only made it easier to say things that were risky to say. Still, I was touched.

"Have you ever seen a *Rorujhen*?" I asked him.

"What's that?"

"*Farukan? Can you hear me?*" We'd been testing how far apart we could be and still be in contact.

"*I hear you,*" his answer rumbled.

"*Would you come over here for a moment, please?*"

Javen was still looking at me, his question unanswered. It wasn't long before Farukan's heavy step could be heard, and felt, as he approached. Javen turned his head and his jaw literally gaped open when he saw Farukan.

"Javen," I said, "This is Farukan. He is a *Rorujhen*."

Javen slowly recovered from his shock. He turned to me and awkwardly got to his hands and one knee, with his other leg in a splint.

"Master Raven," he said, "I know you have no reason to trust me, I have been helping your enemy. But mostly, I was a groom. I take care of the horses. I beg you, let me be a groom for this magnificent creature. I swear to you I will never hurt him or betray him or you. He will be my life."

"*Farukan, can you look into his mind? Can we trust him? Is he telling the truth?*"

Farukan looked at Javen, and I could tell he was focusing his mind on him, reading him. After a moment, Farukan stepped lightly forward to Javen and reaching down with his nose, nuzzled him gently on the neck.

"Get that leg healed, Javen," I told him, "and then I think you have a new job."

Mooren had gone back to where he could look over the approach to the bottleneck, a cup of coffee in his hand. He glanced at me when I walked over to join him. Sabela was sitting nearby, sharpening a dagger.

"Are you sure you can trust him?" Mooren asked me.

I nodded. "I'm sure."

I heard the question in his silence as he looked out over the field.

"I have a little secret," I told him. If I hadn't already had his attention, that would have got it. "Maybe I should say the White Riders have a secret, and I've decided I don't need to keep it. The *Rorujhen* are telepathic. They can speak mind-to-mind with their riders."

"They can speak?" His head swiveled to me. Sabela had stopped sharpening her blade. "They're intelligent? Sentient?"

"And enslaved? Yes."

Sabela's breath whistled slowly out through pursed lips.

"That's contrary to the *Ashae's* official position on slavery," he told me.

"Maybe that's why the White Riders keep it a secret," I said. "They breed them, and then they hold the families hostage to make them obedient."

"The White Riders are one of the oldest *Ashae* traditions. If this gets out, there will be a lot of repercussions."

"You mean *when* this gets out. Once I make sure Farukan's family is safe, I'm going to blow this whole thing wide open."

He stared at me for a moment, then started to chuckle.

"What's so funny?"

"Rispan was right," he said.

"About what?"

"About you always managing to find trouble and being right in the middle of it."

I scowled at him but didn't dignify his comment with a reply.

"Anyway," I went on, "*Rorujhen* can also look into someone's mind. It's against the White Riders' rules of course. But I'm not Farukan's master, I'm his partner. I asked him to look into Javen's mind to see if we could believe him. That's how I know we can trust him."

He nodded, thinking. "I wonder if there are other ways that skill can be utilized."

"With our bond, we can communicate easily: words, concepts, emotions. But we don't know the range," I explained.

"With Javen, looking into his mind, he was standing right next to him."

"Good to know." He nodded. We stood for a few more minutes, saying nothing, enjoying the company. "It will be dark soon," he said, "but it will probably be several hours before they try anything. You might want to get some rest."

"Good idea. I'm a lot better at riding, but it still tires me out. Have someone wake me at midnight, or sooner if anything is happening."

I walked to the wagon and Réni and Shéna had wandered off someplace from the back steps. I closed the door and drew the curtains. The boots Gylan made for me felt wonderful to wear, but it was still nice to pull them off.

# CHAPTER NINE

## MIRA

*J*t seemed like only seconds later when a knock on the door woke me up.

"Yes?"

"It looks like they may be coming soon," one of Bavrana's guards spoke through the closed door. Réni and Shéna were both asleep, they must have come in while I was sleeping.

"Thank you, I'll be right there."

I pulled my boots on and stepped out of the wagon. It looked like Mooren had let me sleep past midnight. He was right where I had last seen him, and I went to stand next to him.

"Why didn't you wake me earlier?" I asked him.

"I knocked," he said. "When you didn't answer I figured you needed the sleep."

I looked at him suspiciously. "How loud did you knock?"

He just grinned and pointed across the field. "We saw some motion over there a few minutes ago. I think they're getting ready. They're probably waiting for the moon to set."

I glanced at the sky. Only the larger of the two moons was up, and it was just touching the nearby peak. Soon, the field would be in shadow.

"Still," he said, "the dirt here isn't dark by any means. They'll still stand out against it. We won't be able to see details, but we'll know where they are."

We quietly got all of our people in place. We didn't know for sure when they would come. It could be soon, or it could be hours. But if there was movement over there, it would probably be soon.

The shadow of the peak slowly made its way across the field approaching the bottleneck.

"Keep your eyes to the shadows," Mooren said. "If you stare at the light, it will take a few minutes for your eyes to adjust to the darkness."

I turned to make a joke to Sabela, but she wasn't where I thought she'd be. She usually stayed pretty close to me or Mooren. She was probably with Farukan.

I looked around, and I still didn't see Sabela. That wasn't like her.

"*Farukan?*" I called to him in my mind. I waited, but there was no response.

"I'll be right back," I said to Mooren. I walked toward where the horses were kept and tried again when I was closer.

"*Farukan?*"

"*Yes.*"

"*Have you seen Sabela?*"

"*She came to see me just before dark,*" he answered. "*She had become aware of my abilities. You told her?*"

"*Yes, her and Mooren. Do you know where she is?*"

"*I could not say for certain,*" his rumble told me. "*Would you like me to show you what happened?*"

"*Show me?*" What did he mean by that? "*Um... okay.*"

Suddenly my vision was split in two. I could see the night around me, but I also saw a different scene, and the sun had not quite set yet.

*I'm looking at Sabela as she walks toward me. She has a wry smile on her face.*

"*I hear you've been keeping a secret from me,*" she says.

71

*So many secrets. Which one does she mean? She steps closer and pats my shoulder, reaching up to do it. I know from her touch that she is not angry about the secret.*

"I guess I should start thinking of you as a person instead of an animal."

*Ah, Mira has told her. I feel afraid for a moment. Then I remember that I no longer serve the White Riders. They are no longer my masters. She stops patting my shoulder and goes to where she keeps her things. She has slept close to me since taking over for Rispan. I watch her wrap her boots and sleeves with some kind of brown cloth. She attaches another cloth that hangs over her shoulders and down her back, with a part that raises over the top of her head. I chuckle to myself. She is envious of a proper mane.*

"We'll talk more later, Farukan," *she tells me, smiling.* "I'm going to go take a peek at what the other side is doing. Maybe I can run their horses off again. They only have ordinary horses."

*Sabela walks away.*

The second vision faded, and I was standing where I had stopped when Farukan's memory came to me. I spun on my heel and went back to Mooren.

"Bad news," I told him when he turned at my approach. "Sabela went out to scout earlier and she's not back. She was going to try for the horses again."

"She's an exceptional scout," he said. "Maybe she just got stuck on the other side of them and had to wait."

"Maybe. Let's hope so."

The canyon fell fully into shadow, and I could see a darker line starting toward us from the far side. They were managing to be silent somehow, because I couldn't hear the sound of steps or gear clanking together.

Our strategy was the same as before. We waited until they were fairly close before we released arrows into them. We couldn't identify individuals in the approaching shadow, but they were close enough together that many of the shafts would find targets. The first volley struck, and surprised grunts could be heard, as well as the sound of a few falling bodies.

"Charge!" The yell sounded from somewhere in their ranks.

The dark mass surged forward toward the opening as the second and third volleys landed amongst them.

Veselek commanded two rows of guards with spears and shields at the bottleneck, and we had archers above to fire down into the enemy crowd. They had shields though and were able to block most of the arrows. The mercenaries clashed against our line and tried to break through, but our line was too strong, especially since we had the higher ground. They'd had the advantage of numbers, but we'd been able to nullify that. Or, Mooren had managed to nullify it by choosing the battlefield and getting everyone ready.

"Fall back!" one of them yelled.

The mercenaries disengaged and retreated across the field. Several shadows remained on the ground where they left their fallen.

I turned to Veselek, "Casualties?"

"We got off easy," he said. "We lost one, and several others have small wounds."

"Well done," I told him. I wasn't happy about the one death, but it could have been a lot worse. And it probably would have been worse if we hadn't had Veselek. He knew his business and had drilled his lines well.

"Movement," Mooren said. "It looks like they're coming again."

"Do these guys have some kind of death wish? They'll just keep losing more people."

The approaching line stopped about halfway across the field. They had torches this time, so they weren't trying for stealth.

"Gralbast! Raven!" a voice called out. "I think it is time we had a chat."

Gralbast stepped to my side, "That sounds like Valdeg."

"What do you want, Valdeg?" I called back to him. "Coming to say goodnight before going back to Pokorah-Vo?"

I could hear his chuckle before he responded.

"Raven, is it? No, I quite like it out here. But I would like to offer you a way out."

"I can't wait to hear it."

"Of course, you have been fighting for your lives," he said, "but it isn't your lives that I want. Leave the wagons and your weapons and you can go in peace."

"You had the numbers, and that wasn't enough for you. You lost your supplies. You couldn't keep track of your horses. And every attempt has just ended with you losing more people. And our way is pretty clear. We can move on, with our wagons, any time we want."

"A minor inconvenience. And you can't leave this spot without exposing your back to us. I have sent to Pokorah-Vo for more men and supplies, and you are stuck here until they arrive. In the end, you will lose."

"I have a counteroffer," I told him. "Leave now and we won't hunt you down like the rabid dogs you are and bury you in the ground."

"You are making a mistake." He wasn't laughing now.

"It's been known to happen. But not this time."

He signaled to someone behind him, and I could see three figures, two dragging forward a third between them. I reached out to the *Ralahin* so that I could see them better. It was Sabela.

"I believe this is one of yours," Valdeg sounded smug. "Accept my offer, and you can have her back."

With the *Ralahin* vision, I could See that Sabela was not in good shape. Her face was swollen and bruised. There were spots of blood on her body where they had evidently stabbed or cut her. I felt a rage building inside me. *I can't lose another one!*

Valdeg grabbed Sabela by her collar and pulled her from the two that brought her forward. She stumbled to her knees. I saw a knife in Valdeg's other hand.

"If you do not accept my offer, she will die slowly." With the point of his knife, he started slicing slowly down Sabela's left arm. She clenched her teeth from the pain but made no sound.

I didn't think. I just went. The *Ralahin* took me and suddenly I was standing in front of Valdeg, and my dagger had gone up under his chin and into his brain. I pulled it out and as he fell, he released Sabela. She fell forward and caught herself with her right arm.

The mercenaries were stunned, then they started to grumble and step toward me.

"Stop!" I ordered them. "You saw what I just did. Who wants to be next? Who can stand against me? I was trained by the Dark Blade herself!"

They froze in place.

"Valdeg is dead," I told them. "He can't pay you. Your job is over. Go back to Pokorah-Vo. I'll give you one packhorse with enough supplies to get you there."

There was a thunder of hooves and Farukan stood beside me. He reared and gave a deep, bellowing cry.

The mercenaries stepped back and started to move away.

"*I felt your distress,*" Farukan told me, kneeling down.

"*Yes, thank you.*"

I helped Sabela to her feet and we got to Farukan's back. He stood gently and I held on to her as he slowly made his way back to our camp.

# CHAPTER TEN

## RISPAN

*I* drifted up from a dream where I was trying to sleep but there was a sharp rock that kept poking me in my back.

"Stop thrashing about or you'll tear out the stitching!" The voice that came from nearby wasn't one I recognized, and my eyes snapped open.

The space I was in wasn't brightly lit, but I could see clearly that it was nowhere I'd been before. I was on one of a row of several short beds. Only some of them were occupied. Curtains hung between the beds. It looked like some sort of hospital or infirmary.

I started to sit up but gave up the effort when I felt a lancing pain in my side. I looked down to see a bandage wrapped around my stomach just below the ribs. That reminded me of the arrow I'd seen there. I must have passed out after getting into the sewer.

"Are you deaf or just stupid?" The voice sounded from my right, and I turned my head to identify the source. Two beds over I saw someone looking at me.

It was a man who stood at about two feet tall. His skin was a reddish brown, and his hair was green. His ears were pointed like mine, but a little larger in proportion to his head. *Ga-Né-Mo Ri.*

"Well," I gave him a lopsided smile, "I'm not deaf."

"Hmph." He apparently wasn't sure how to take my response.

"Might I ask how I came to be here?" I asked him. "And where exactly *here* is?"

"No!" he snapped. "Not for me to say. Not to be asking me such questions." His didn't sound like the same voice as earlier.

"And what of your name? May I ask that? I'm Rispan." My mouth felt like it had been stuffed with cotton balls.

"Rispan." He worked it around in his mouth. "Rispan, you are." He nodded. "I am Armin."

"Armin," I said to him, "I'm very thirsty. May I have some water?"

"My water?" He looked at me suspiciously.

"No, Armin," another voice said. "He doesn't want your water. Would you please go see if they need any help in the kitchens? They may have some snacks for you if you are nice and you help them."

"Snacks!" Armin turned and almost ran to the door at the other end of the room.

"Don't mind Armin," the voice said. "He had an injury when he was young, and it never healed properly. He's a bit simple." The figure stepped out from behind one of the curtains. She was another *Ga-Né-Mo Ri.* Looking back over her shoulder, she said, "Go ahead and finish the rounds. I'll take care of him."

"I still don't think he should be here," the answer came. This sounded more like the first voice I had heard. "It's too risky."

"Perhaps, Vahid," she sighed. "But that's not our call." She walked over to me and gave me a smile. "I'm glad to see you awake."

"That sort of implies you've been seeing me not awake," I replied. "How long have I been here?"

77

"You were brought in two nights ago," she told me. "Apparently you'd had an argument with an archer."

"I don't know if I'd call it an argument. But he did make a very pointed comment."

*Two days!* Mira must have left without me. She's too smart to risk staying. But knowing her, leaving would have been torture.

She went toward the head of my bed. There was a small table there I hadn't seen. It held a pitcher of water and a cup. She poured and handed me the cup. I took it thankfully and drained it. She took the empty cup and refilled it.

"You lost some blood," she said, "so it's natural to be thirsty."

I accepted the second cup. "Thank you." I drank this one more slowly. "I'm Rispan."

"Yes, I heard. I am Azadi." She looked at me critically. "We don't see many *Ulané Jhinura* here that haven't been slaves. You're no slave."

I shook my head. "I'm... not from around here. And," I added, "I need to be getting back as soon as possible. You are a healer?"

She nodded.

"Meaning no offense," I said, "do you not use healing magic?"

"We have very limited resources." She drew herself up. "We don't have instructors to teach magical healing. We make do as best as we can."

"Of course. I meant no offense," I assured her. "I was only asking. I don't know anything about you people or your situation."

"Understand this, Rispan-Not-From-Around-Here, just because we have helped you does not mean we trust you. Nor does it mean we will let you leave with the knowledge of this place."

"But that's not your call?" I asked.

She gave her head a single shake. "It is not."

"I take it someone else will be having a talk with me?"

"Yes." She nodded. "When you are healed more, we will—"

"I do appreciate your concern," I cut in, "but it's best to get this over with as soon as possible. I don't have a lot of time before I will need to go."

She pursed her lips. "Very well. I will see if I can expedite things. But you will still need to heal before you can go anywhere."

She moved the table around to the side where I could reach it.

"I'll have some food brought to you," she said, "and I'll find out about your interview."

Azadi was as good as her word. I was only halfway through a bland mushroom stew when I heard steps. I looked up to see Azadi and two other *Ga-Né-Mo Ri* come in the door and head in my direction.

Azadi opened her mouth to speak, but before she could say anything, one of the others cut in.

"It was the slavers who shot you, yes?" he asked. "They were chasing someone and then you landed practically on our doorstep. It was them?"

"Yes," I answered. "At least, they were chasing me. I assume it was one of them who shot me."

"And you are the one who stole the Princess from them? Yes?"

I stared at him. "Princess?"

He nodded.

"Um… What princess would that be?"

"Korashéna Ulané Sharavi," he said as though the answer were obvious. "Last of the royal line of Su Astonil."

"Ulané Sharavi?" I couldn't hide my surprise. "She said her name was just Korashéna!"

"Then you *did* steal her?"

"No." I shouldn't have let that last bit slip. "Look, I don't know who you people are. And I don't know anything about any princess."

"I am Kiarash," he said. "I—"

"*Rispan nya Su Lariano*," the voice booming in my head was strong. Almost overpowering. "*We are not your enemies, nor are we the enemies of Korashéna Ulané Sharavi. We are* Chados. *The resistance of Pokorah-Vo.*"

A three-inch long figure flew between the three *Ga-Né-Mo Ri* to hover in the air in front of them. It was a *Pilané Jhin*. I'd never seen one outside of their gardens. She appeared to be in her female cycle. The *Pilané Jhin* were alternately male and female and changed over a two-year period.

"The resistance?"

"*Yes. Those who have survived the destruction brought upon us by Arugak and his heirs.*"

I looked back and forth between all of them, my gaze settling back on the *Pilané Jhin*.

"You have no idea how happy I am to meet you." I grinned. "We have a lot to talk about."

I found out a lot of things as I recuperated over the next week and a half. The *Pilané Jhin* that had been talking to me in my head. That was Khuyen. *Pilané Jhin* tended to live for a very long time. Unless they were killed. Being so small made them vulnerable, and the reality was that not many died a natural death. Khuyen had been there back when Arugak had started burning all the *Pilané Jhin* and *Sula Jhinara* gardens.

Khuyen had been the queen for one of the *Pilané Jhin* communities in the old forest. When her garden was attacked, some of her people had rushed her to safety. The local *Ulané Jhinara* were already under attack, so in desperation she had gone to the *Ga-Né-Mo Ri* to ask for help. That's when she found out that the *Ga-Né-Mo Ri* had been the first to suffer from the *Urgaban*.

Pokorah-Vo had been built overtop the *Ga-Né-Mo Ri* city of Aganaté. The *Urgaban* hadn't realized that much of the city was underground. When it had become apparent that they couldn't fend off the *Urgaban*, the *Ga-Né-Mo Ri* had simply retreated below ground and sealed off most of the entrances. When most of their excavations mysteriously resulted in cave-ins, the *Urgaban* eventually gave up and focused on above ground construction. Most of Aganaté was still intact.

Her people slaughtered, Khuyen had taken to helping survivors from all races that Arugak and his horde had displaced. She had become the leader of the *Chados*: the Resistance. The *Ga-Né-Mo Ri* tolerated her use of outlying tunnels and caverns to provide shelter for those she brought in.

The *Ga-Né-Mo Ri* who'd been asking me all the questions was Kiarash. He'd been the one to find me when I passed out in the storm drain. He had also been coming by and keeping me company while I was healing. Most of my information had come from him.

"I know I've been plaguing you with questions, Kiarash," I told him, "but as you know, we didn't know anything about any of this."

He made a dismissive gesture with his hand. "Answering is easy enough. If you have questions, ask them."

"I get the idea that the *Chados* is a separate thing from Aganaté. But you *are* of the city and working with the *Chados*."

"Queen Jaleya and King Bardian don't really care what we do, as long as we don't put the city in danger. There aren't a lot of rules," he explained, "but if you are wise, you don't break the ones that are there."

"What do you think the odds are that they'd be interested in an alliance?"

"Between Su Lariano and Aganaté? An alliance would mean making the city known." He scowled. "Risky. We have everything we need."

"But you help the *Chados*."

"The Chados also stay hidden. Pokorah-Vo doesn't even know they exist. If you are looking for soldiers, my friend, you will not find them here."

I shook my head, "I'm not looking for anything in particular besides information. I'm just trying to get the lay of the land. Are there many *Ulané Jhinura* among the *Chados*?"

"Several hundred I should think," he answered. "Many of them born in the years since the destruction of Su Astonil. But as for *Ulané Jhinura*, there are many more who are slaves to the *Urgaban*."

"My queen needs to know about this," I told him, "and I can't wait much longer before I leave."

He nodded, thinking. "You still need to heal. But perhaps you could manage to travel."

"I'm sure that once my queen knows of the situation, she will want to communicate with the *Chados*. And with Queen Jaleya and King Bardian. She will want to help."

"That's a problem." He shrugged. "Once you have left Aganaté, you won't know how to return."

*"The solution for that is simple."* I hadn't noticed Khuyen coming in. I don't think she was being intentionally sneaky, she was just so small she was easy to miss. Until she spoke. *"Kiarash should go with you."*

Kiarash slapped his leg with a laugh.

"He would speak for you?" I asked.

*"He would not. But he could answer basic questions, as he has done for you. And he will know how to bring word back to Aganaté."*

I looked at him. "What do you think?"

He grinned at me. "All my life I have known nothing but Aganaté and Pokorah-Vo. To see your Su Lariano is a worthy adventure!"

*"When will you be ready to travel?"*

"I'm ready now," I told her.

Her laughter echoed in my mind. *"Tomorrow is soon enough. Kiarash, get any supplies you will need. It is a long way to Su Lariano."*

Kiarash made up packs for both of us and we started out early the next morning. No one came to give us a send-off. We just grabbed a quick bite and then he led off through the maze of tunnels. The last branch took us a long way with very little turning in the path.

We came to what appeared to be a dead end, but Kiarash worked some mechanism by the end and a chunk of rock swung away to reveal the sky just beginning to lighten. We stepped through and I looked around. We stood in a rocky plain outside the city on the south side. I heard a quiet thump and looked back. I knew the passage had been there, but there was nothing to indicate exactly where.

I adjusted my pack and put my back toward the rising sun.

"Alright," I said, "Let's head west and then look for a good place to cross the river once we are out of sight of the city."

"We should come to a foot bridge less than three days from here."

"That'll work." I nodded. We were almost two weeks behind Mira. She should be nearly halfway back to Su Lariano at this point.

The pack irritated my wound, but not too badly. We would just take it easy. We had five hundred miles to go, and I would heal as we went.

Toward the end of the third day, we came to the foot bridge. We crossed to the north side of the river and continued west along the road.

As the sun started to set, we saw a group of *Urgaban* coming down the road toward Pokorah-Vo. We hid by the embankment as they passed. I don't know if I'd ever seen a sorrier looking bunch. There were at least thirty of them, and they looked like they'd had a rough time of it somehow. They were on horses, and many of them were doubled-up.

"I wonder what happened to them?" I whispered to Kiarash. He just shrugged.

This close to sundown, they would likely stop shortly to camp, so we walked another two hours to put some distance between us. The pain from my wound had settled into a dull ache that greeted every movement like an old friend.

ADAM K. WATTS

Despite the distance we'd put between us and that party, we decided to go without a fire that night. We didn't know anything about them, and the extra comfort just wasn't worth the risk. Sunrise found us back on the move. I knew there were two routes back to Su Lariano. What I didn't know was which route Mira would take. I assumed she would go the same route we had used on the trip to Pokorah-Vo, but I didn't know that for sure.

I hoped to be able to tell from the tracks where the paths diverged which one they had taken. Even then there was no way we'd be able to catch them before they reached Su Lariano. Traveling by foot, we weren't moving any faster than they were. We'd likely be trailing two weeks behind them the whole way.

Four days later we arrived at the point the trail diverged. The tracks were an absolute mess. Weeks old wagon tracks went up both trails. On top of those were the tracks of boots and horses. Neither Kiarash nor I could sort out what was what.

"Let's head north," I said. "I know that's the usual route."

We made camp there for the night and headed north at first light. Less than two hours later, we noticed that the wagon tracks had gone off the path and into a small stand of trees. We glanced at each other, and I shrugged.

We followed the tracks to the trees and as we neared, I noticed that torches had been erected around the perimeter. They still stood, cold and dark. A search through the trees revealed wall-like barriers. They weren't very strong, so they wouldn't keep anyone out.

There had evidently been some kind of skirmish. There were bodies I didn't recognize. But whether they'd been from our caravan I couldn't say.

"That group we passed a few days ago," Kiarash said. "I think it likely they fought against your friends."

I nodded. "It definitely looks that way. At least they didn't look victorious, and they didn't have any of the wagons. So that's something anyway."

"They may not have been victorious," he cautioned, "but that doesn't mean they didn't draw blood."

That was something I didn't want to contemplate for the moment.

There was a seep where water formed a small pond in the woods, it wasn't much more than a large puddle. Several horses had found their way in. They were still saddled. At first, they shied away when I approached, but they relaxed as I spoke to them soothingly. Horses would improve our speed on the trail.

"I don't ride," Kiarash said as I led the three of the horses from the water.

"Don't worry." I winked at him. "I can lead your horse. You won't have to steer."

He didn't appear reassured.

Another important thing we discovered was that the wagons had turned back south. They'd gone the other way.

# CHAPTER ELEVEN

## RISPAN

*W*e were only a couple of hours in the wrong direction. Now that we had horses, would it be possible to catch up with the caravan? It looked like they had definitely run into trouble. What if they needed help?

"Let's try the other way," I said to Kiarash. "Hopefully, they're okay and we won't catch them. But if they're not okay, maybe we can get there in time to help."

"How fast are you planning to go?" He eyed the horses nervously.

"Relax." I grinned at him. "We can always tie you into the saddle. You won't fall."

"Wonderful."

Once I got him in the saddle though, it was looking very doubtful. His two-foot frame was just too small for the horse and the saddle. Even if I tied him to the saddle, it was going to be a problem.

"I don't see how we're going to do this," I said. "Maybe have you ride in a saddlebag or rig some kind of carrier for you."

"Just get me to the canyon," he told me. "Once we get there, I have another way."

I shrugged, "If you say so."

It was less than two hours to the pass entrance. The simplest thing was just to put him in front of me on my saddle. I still led the other two horses, though. Just in case. Our packs were tied, one each to the horses. It was a little awkward riding with him in front of me, but workable for the short distance.

"Stop here," he said as we entered the canyon.

I pulled up and he jumped down from the horse.

"Wait here," he told me. "Get comfortable. I could be an hour or two making arrangements."

"What arrangements?"

He just grinned at me and started climbing quickly up the south side of the canyon. I didn't know what he was doing, but I'd give him the benefit of the doubt.

"Fine!" I called up to him. "I'll just make camp for the night. It's getting a bit late anyway."

I climbed down from the horse and turned to watch him climb, but he was gone. I looked all over, above and below and to either side of where he'd been a moment before, but nothing. Maybe there was another secret entrance like the one we'd used to leave Aganaté. An entrance to what?

I passed the time by putting together a fire and broiling some mushrooms and vegetables. It was at least two hours after dark when I heard a scrambling nearby and looked up to see Kiarash walking towards me. If anything, his grin was even bigger than when he left.

"All set up!" he said.

"What is?"

"You'll see in the morning." Kiarash was almost skipping, he was so happy.

He was having fun with his secret, whatever it was. I guessed I'd find out in the morning.

"I made some dinner," was all I said.

"Ah, thanks! But I've eaten. I think I'll get some sleep. We'll likely have an early start tomorrow."

With that, he pulled out his bedding from the pack, set it out, and promptly went to sleep.

I'd picked up smoking a pipe from Gralbast. I filled a bowl and lit it, using a small stick from the fire. I sat for a while, listening to the night and looking up between the canyon walls to the stars above. I wasn't much for sitting around; I preferred to be doing something. But it was a pleasant night, and the smoke was relaxing.

I awoke the next morning just as the sky started to lighten. I brought some life back to the fire and started some coffee, letting it brew while I packed up my bedding. Kiarash got up just in time to help himself to the fresh coffee. We had a small breakfast and broke camp.

I looked at him expectantly, still waiting for him to tell me his secret. He tilted his head back and gave a piercing whistle. Then he simply stood there, waiting. It wasn't even a half minute before I saw something shoot by overhead.

A huge bird drew up to almost hover and landed on its feet. It was a raptor of some sort judging by its beak, maybe some kind of eagle. It was light colored on its underside and had gold and browns on its back and wings. It was huge, its eyes were on level with mine when it was standing. It also had some sort of riding harness at the base of its neck above the wings, and reins coming from a harness or bridle on its head. The feathers on its head escaped the harness to form a sort of mane. It looked at me with piercing eyes that were light grey with just a touch of blue.

"My ride is here." Kiarash flashed his grin. "We can go whenever you are ready."

"How did you…"

"Aganaté always had a *chabril* here," he said. "A sort of aviary or stable for the *reshan*. The *Urgaban* in Pokorah-Vo never knew about it, so it's been safe."

"*Reshan?*"

"These eagles," he explained, petting the one standing at his side.

"You know how to fly it?" I asked him.

"All scouts are sent here for the training," he told me. "It's one of our longest standing traditions. They are far superior to horses. You can travel further and faster. Though I suppose you might be a bit big to ride one."

I could see the advantage over regular horses, but over a *Rorujhén* like Farukan? I didn't see any benefit to arguing the point, though.

"Well, as long as it isn't going to eat you," I told him, "I suppose we can get started."

Kiarash grabbed the *reshan* by the shoulder and jumped up. The bird ducked its head to help him mount and launched immediately into the air. I climbed onto my horse and started up the canyon. Kiarash circled above on the *reshan*.

A few times that morning, I saw the *reshan* dive to the ground. I assumed it was hunting. I had to wonder how the *Ga-Né-Mo Ri* had domesticated the creatures and not been eaten. They were certainly small enough to make a meal for these raptors.

We made good time, only stopping at midday to rest and eat. As I'd suspected, the *reshan* had already eaten. It had also nabbed a couple of rabbits for us to eat as well. From his height on the *reshan*, Kiarash had a wide view of the area, and he could scout around to see what was ahead and behind.

Near the end of the third day through the pass, Kiarash came down early to land in the path just ahead of me.

"We've got trouble," he said. "We can't go this way."

"Why? What's going on."

"It looks like there was a fight. There are bodies of *Urgaban* and a few horses. It has drawn a pack of *jahgreet*."

We didn't have *jahgreet* in the forest around Su Lariano, but I knew what they were. They were like big cats, but with six legs. And while they could walk on six or four legs, they mainly walked on two legs. They were hunters, possibly the most dangerous predators in the world. They might not be able to flit, as Mira called moving with the *Ralahin*, but they were extremely fast. When they were hunting, they were silent. They were nearly impossible to see when they weren't moving. Once they were coming at you, you might be able to see them, but that was usually too late.

"Is there any way we can go around them?" I asked.

"Yes." He nodded. "Go back down the canyon and take the other road."

"It's that bad?'

"There's about eight in the canyon itself, and more up on the rim on both sides. I don't know if they are all the same pack," he said, "but there's no way you can get past them on the ground."

"*Zerg!*" All this time coming through the canyon was wasted. Plus going back. This would put us another week behind the caravan at best.

I was tempted to try to get a look at the *jahgreet*, but if they caught our scent, we'd be in trouble. In fact, we might already be close enough to draw their attention. They would probably prefer a live hunt to what they were eating now.

"It's a good thing you've got that bird," I told Kiarash. "Otherwise, we'd have been *jahgreet* breakfast tomorrow. Let's get out of here."

I turned the horses back down the way we'd come and Kiarash took to the air. We were way too close to them. We'd need to ride through most of the night to put some distance between us. We rode well past midnight before stopping to rest and then we were back on the trail before the sun was up.

I knew this was going to be hard on the horses, but from what I'd heard, even one *jahgreet* was hard enough to deal with. Even an *Ogaré* would hesitate against a single *jahgreet*, and they had thick, hard skin and stood over nine feet tall. We'd stand no chance at all against a pack.

*Jahgreet* didn't like large groups, so they would ignore something like the caravan. But an *Ulané Jhinura* and a few horses? Lunch.

I gave the horses a break as often as I could, but we pushed on into the next night as well. Kiarash had been keeping his eyes peeled, and so far, we were in the clear. By afternoon the following day, I felt like I was being watched.

At our next break, I mentioned it to Kiarash.

"It could be." He shrugged, helplessly. "These things are really hard to see from far away. I don't want to fly too close to the ground because they can also jump pretty high."

The long rides were wearying, and I still hadn't completely recovered from my injuries. Even so, it was rougher on the horses. By late afternoon, we came out of the canyon and headed north. I wanted to get to those trees before it got dark. Chances are, the horses we had seen there would stay close to the water. The more targets for the *jahgreet*, the more likely it wouldn't go for us.

We got there and I brought the horses to the seep so they could drink. I removed the saddles and packs so they could stretch and rest. As I suspected, there were several other horses there already. I gathered them up and removed their saddles as well. There was no telling how long they'd been out here, stuck in those things. A couple of them rolled in the grass, seeming to be very happy to be out of the saddles.

I looked over the area and found one dead *Urgaban* in the woods. In the plains to the north, I could see the dark shapes of a few more bodies. I checked them out and it looked like they'd been run over by horses. I was able to salvage a bow and some arrows, and I brought those back under the trees.

I checked all the gear and saddlebags and finally came up with a horse brush. After I gave one a quick brushing, the rest practically lined up for their turn. I only spent a few minutes on each one. I knew they needed it, but I couldn't spend too much time on them.

Kiarash came in and the *reshan* went up into one of the nearby trees.

"There's at least one still with us," he said.

"Are you sure?"

"We circled and looked around as low as I dared. He's out there."

"He?"

Kiarash shrugged. "Or she. I don't know which."

"We could try to just keep running," I said, "but it's hard on the horses and eventually this thing will attack. If we stay here, we can at least be ready for it."

"What are you thinking?"

"If we use the horses as bait, maybe we can ambush him."

"Have you ever fought a *jahgreet*?"

"No," I admitted.

"They aren't easy to kill. And hurting them only makes them angry."

"Lovely. Well, you're safe enough. They can't fly." I thought for a moment. "Okay, there's not much choice. I'm going to have to try to kill this thing. If it works the other way around, then I'll need you to go without me. Maybe you can catch the caravan. If not, you can just go to Su Lariano yourself. Ask to see Mira or General Dzurala. Tell them everything you can."

"What do you need me to do here?"

"You don't have a bow. How are you with spears? Something you can throw and stay at a distance."

He chuckled, "I'm not without resources."

He reached into the pouch at his waist and drew out a leather thong as long as he was tall with a sort of pocket in the middle. He took both ends in one hand. Then he bent and picked up a small rock, putting it in the pocket. He started spinning it around over his head and then released the rock. I heard a loud smack and turned to see a small branch falling from where it had snapped off a nearby tree.

"I just need a handful of pebbles," he said.

"I'm impressed," I nodded, "but can you do that from up a tree? Or while you are flying? You need to stay off the ground."

He glanced at the trees, studying them. Then he shook his

head. "No room to swing the sling in those branches. I can make up some short spears for throwing. From the trees or on the wing. Though with flying, I think I'd need a lot of practice with the sling or the spear."

I explained my plan, and we started getting ready. The *jahgreet* could come up on us at any time, so we kept a watchful eye. There was a small clearing around a dead *Jhiné Boré* tree. I gathered all the horses and picketed them together near the tree. Kiarash had shown me the length he needed for his spears, and I started in on cutting several and sharpening the tips.

Meanwhile, Kiarash took to the sky and hunted up a couple of rabbits. When he got back, we made sure they were both bloody and put one at the outer edge of the woods and the other near the horses. I wanted the scent of blood to put the *jahgreet's* attention where I wanted it. It would lead him to the horses, and a *jahgreet* would always prefer live prey. Hopefully, I could kill it before it hurt any of the horses.

We climbed two trees at the edge of the clearing that gave us two different views of where the horses were picketed. He had about a dozen spears, and I had the bow and a full quiver of arrows. I kept an arrow nocked and ready to pull. I sat on a branch with my back to the trunk of the tree, about thirty feet from the ground. We settled in to wait. From where I sat, I could just see the carcass of the rabbit near the horses.

Two hours later, I noticed that the rabbit was gone. When or how, I had no idea. I held myself very still, hoping I hadn't already given away my position. The horses started to get nervous, their eyes wide. They pulled on the pickets, but I had sunk them deep into the ground. They weren't going anywhere.

I still couldn't see the *jahgreet*. Something moved, but when I turned my eyes to look, I couldn't see where. It's like the *zergish* things were invisible.

A shrill roar sounded, and something launched off the ground onto one of the horses. I drew back the arrow and sighted in; I could see it now. It had its claws and teeth sunk into the horse's neck. Its back slightly toward me. I took careful aim and released. The shaft struck deep into its upper right shoulder and its head spun looking directly at me. It came in my direction, and I saw a spear just miss as I nocked another arrow. It was coming fast.

Another spear flew and this one struck the *jahgreet* in its lower right thigh, tripping it. But it got quickly to its feet and continued toward me. It leaped and landed on the trunk about halfway to my height. I took careful aim and released. The shaft sunk into the top of its chest, and it snarled at me. The thing glared at me and poised to leap again. I scrambled to get out of the way as it flew toward me. I lost my footing and fell, striking three or four branches on my way to the ground, trying to grab hold as I passed to slow my fall.

I got to my feet and quickly moved away from the tree, not turning my back to it for a second. My bow was gone, lost somewhere in the fall. I pulled my double-sticks from the carrying case I wore across my back. These looked standard, but I'd had them custom made. I pressed my thumbs into the recessed releases and gave both of them a flick. The about twenty inches of wood slid off to reveal the blades hidden within.

I wasn't really a swordsman or a fancy knife-fighter, but I could use these with almost the same technique as if they were sticks. I was going to need more than blunt sticks. The *jahgreet* jumped to the ground, it's eyes on me. I got my first clear look at it. Its color seemed to change to match whatever was close to it. It stood up on its hind legs, and even half crouched, it was taller than me. Its middle limbs were closer to the upper set than the lower. I could see both arrows, deeply embedded where they had struck, one in its right shoulder and the other into its chest at an angle. A short spear was all the way through its left hind leg above the knee.

It came after me. It was slowed, and I could tell it was badly injured, but it was still extremely dangerous. Even slowed, it had four uninjured legs and it was still fast. It was on me before I knew it. I blocked the swipe from its upper left paw, cutting deeply into tendons and muscles. I followed up with what would have been strikes to the head with sticks, but with blades it slashed across its face and one eye.

It snarled again and another spear struck, piercing all the way through its torso. It turned its head to look toward Kiarash. I didn't let the chance pass; I thrust with both blades up into its neck. One of the blades glanced off its jaw, but the left one sank deeply and came out at the top of its head, lodging in place. The *jahgreet* gave a shudder and fell heavily to the ground, wrenching the stuck blade from my hand.

Not taking any chances, I stabbed through the vertebrae at the base of its skull with my other blade. I needn't have bothered; it was dead.

"Are you alright?" Kiarash called down to me.

I just waved to him and nodded.

I'd survived, but it could easily have gone the other way. I didn't know how that thing could keep coming at me with all of those injuries. If Kiarash hadn't distracted it with that last spear, I probably wouldn't have lasted much longer.

I looked at the thing, where it lay at my feet. Even now, it was hard to see against the ground. I knelt and examined its short fur. It somehow refracted the colors from whatever was close by, like water, or how I had seen crystal take on the color of whatever light was on it. If the jahgreet was on green grass, it would be green, on brown dirt, it would be brown.

Kiarash had joined me.

"That was a close one," he said, "but you got it!"

"We got it," I corrected him. "I couldn't have done it alone."

"I've studied about these things," he said, "but I've never seen one up close before. I didn't know they changed color like that. No wonder they're so hard to see."

"Yeah." I nodded. "That's a handy trick to have." I looked at it again. "I wonder…"

I rolled it onto its back. In many ways it looked like a mountain lion, but the legs and shoulders were a little different, allowing it to easily walk on two legs. Standing, it was the size of a human. Or a *Loiala Fé*. The body seemed like a mix between humanoid and cat. It didn't quite have opposable thumbs, though the paws were elongated giving them long fingers that ended in deadly claws. And that fur.

"I think I'm going to take the pelt," I said. "I'm wondering what kind of cloak it would make if the fur can be preserved."

A movement from the *jahgreet* caused me to jump back. I looked at its face, but it was clearly dead. There was movement again from low on its belly. I looked closer and saw that there was some sort of natural pouch, and something was moving inside it. Cautiously, I lifted the edge of the pouch. When I did, a mewing sound came out. Kiarash and I shared a glance before I reached in and pulled out a kitten.

"A small one," Kiarash commented. "A runt. It will never survive without the mother. Best to put it down now."

Put it down. He meant, kill it.

"No," I said. "I can't kill it."

"Cruel to leave it."

"I won't leave it, either. I'll find a home for it."

Kiarash just looked at me, his eyes wide. Then he just shrugged.

# CHAPTER TWELVE

## MIRA

Sabela had passed out in my arms as we made our way to the bottleneck. We were almost there when she woke up, and she started to panic.

"*Easy little one, you are safe,*" I heard Farukan's rumble.

Sabela stopped moving. "Who — Farukan? Is that you?"

"*Yes. You are safe. We have you now.*"

"Huh. Wondered… what you… sounded like…" She shifted her head around to see my face. "Who's… Oh… Sorry, boss."

Before I could say anything, she passed out again. Once in camp, we laid her out on a blanket and Mooren started looking over her injuries.

"That arm is going to need stitches," he said. "So are a couple of these other wounds."

There was a gash running from her shoulder almost all the way to her elbow. Fortunately, Valdeg hadn't been cutting very deeply or she might never regain full mobility of the arm. As it was, she would have an ugly scar.

Sabela's wounds were mostly superficial, as far as we could tell, intended to create pain while not being life threatening. Besides her arm, she had other cuts on her body. There was bruising from being hit, and she probably had a concussion. We had no way to know how bad the concussion was, or if she had internal injuries.

I watched, feeling helpless, as Mooren stitched her up and bandaged her wounds. Afterwards, we moved her to my wagon. It was getting crowded in there, but I'd sleep on the floor if I had to.

She was the last of my friends who'd come with us that was still alive. Rispan was still out there, but I didn't know whether he was alive or dead. There was nothing I could do about him either way. But Sabela was here, and I could make sure she would be alright. But I was no doctor.

They didn't really have doctors here, not as I knew them. They had people like Mooren who could patch people up. And they had healers, who used magic to heal people. I could use magic, but I had no idea how to use it to heal. As soon as we got back to Su Lariano, I'd see what I could do to change that.

We broke camp the next morning after burying our one casualty. It was only a few minutes to the summit, and the way was all downhill after that. By now, I was more comfortable on Farukan's back than on the bench of the wagon.

Going uphill had been hard on the horses, but going downhill had its challenges, too. The teamsters had to constantly lean on the brake handles to keep the wagons from going too fast and overrunning the horses. Going down was faster, but we had to be careful not to go too fast. Early on the third day, we came out of the pass on the other side and turned north toward Su Lariano. From my understanding, it would probably be another four weeks from the pass. Maybe more.

On the second day, we came to a wide river. There was a stone bridge in place that made crossing a simple matter. The bridge gave plenty of room for flooding and had one massive support in the center. The whole thing looked like it had been there for a long time.

"Who built this?" I asked Gralbast.

"It's part of the coastal trade route," he told me. "It was

funded by villages and merchants alike. Hundreds of years ago from what I hear. Villages need goods, traders need to trade. This river was a big problem. Then someone got a bright idea and got folks together."

"It's that old and it's still sturdy?"

"Magically reinforced," he explained. "They didn't want to have to keep rebuilding it, so they really built it to last."

By the end of the week, Sabela was feeling well enough to ride on the bench of the wagon, though she didn't talk much. As long as she didn't move too quickly, she didn't get woozy. If she'd had internal injuries, we would likely have known by now, so I was relieved about that. The concussion was still a worry.

Three days later we came to a small stream and a village. We were merchants, so stopping to trade was expected. This was my first meeting with any *Loiala Fé*. As with all the races I'd met in the Daoine realm, they had pointed ears. But these were the first people that seemed to be the same height as people were back home on Earth. In fact, if it weren't for the ears, I might think I'd stepped back in time a few centuries to any European village. Both men and women seemed to grow their hair long, though the women's seemed to be longer. And they put more effort into keeping it together. Hair, skin and eye color had a lot of variety. They gave Farukan more than just a few glances.

We bought and sold some items, but one of the biggest sellers was from the stock of tobacco Bavrana had brought. I had another interest and was pleased to find out the village had an actual healer. I was directed to a little house at the edge of town. I walked up to the door and knocked. After a moment, a young girl answered.

"Hello." I expected someone older. "Are you Nadezhda? The healer?"

She crinkled her nose at me. "No, silly. I'm Abrina. Who are you?"

"I'm Raven." I smiled at her. "I was told I could find a healer here. No one said anything about a pretty little girl."

She just looked at me for a moment. Then she turned and disappeared into the house.

"Auntie," I heard her call out. "There's a crazy person at the door for you."

A woman in her thirties appeared, with a concerned look on her face.

"Can I help you?"

"I hope so." I smiled. "I was told I could find a healer here."

"Are you ill?" she asked.

"No, I'm fine. It's for someone else. Your Nadezhda?"

"Yes. And you are…"

"Not crazy," I joked. "At least I hope not. But they call me Raven."

She flashed an annoyed glance behind her and turned back to me.

"What is wrong with your friend?"

"She was beaten." Saying it, I felt my anger resurfacing, but I pushed it back down. "I think she has a concussion — a head injury — and she has knife wounds."

"How long has it been?"

"Almost two weeks."

"Abrina," she called over her shoulder, "grab my bag and come along." She didn't wait but ushered me to move. "Come on," she said. "Show me where she is."

We hadn't gone very far before Abrina was skipping along behind us. I led them to where we had pulled up the wagons on the far side of the little town, and into my wagon, where Sabela was resting. Abrina followed us in.

Sabela looked up at the sound of our step.

"Hi Sabela," I said. "I've brought a healer to take a look at you."

She relaxed back onto the bed as the healer approached her.

"I am Nadezhda," she said. "I will do what I can for your injuries."

I connected with the *Ralahin*, so I could observe everything she did. The first thing I saw was her using her vision to look into Sabela. I tried to do the same, but I didn't know what I was looking at or looking for.

Nadezhda motioned for Abrina to stand next to her.

"Look at her," Nadezhda told her. "Can you see it?"

Abrina studied Sabela for a long minute before answering.

"You mean her head, right?" the girl asked. "Not the rest. The rest is easy to see."

"Very good." Nadezhda nodded. "Now watch me closely as I try to heal it."

I was watching closely myself. This was something I wanted to learn. I could tell that Nadezhda was weaving the magic that was part of Sabela, using it to correct something, to somehow restore it to how it should be. But I couldn't tell how she was doing it, or how she knew what to correct or how it was supposed to be. Finally, she stopped.

Then she moved to the long cut on Sabela's arm. She removed the bandages and, taking a small knife from the bag Abrina had brought, she removed the stitches. I watched again as she used the magic to complete the healing. Slowly, the partially healed skin came together, leaving only a faint line where the wound had been. This was easier for me to understand. I could almost understand what was happening. She repeated the process for the other cuts on her body. When she was finished, she turned to me.

"She is sleeping now," she said. "There will be scars. Too much time has passed to prevent that."

"And her head?" I asked.

"It is good that you brought her to me. She may not have survived."

I felt my stomach clench up when she said that.

"She will live," she went on, "but I am only a village healer. I don't have great power or skill. There was only so much I could do. In time, she may fully heal on her own. But if you can, you should find a better healer for her."

"We're going to Su Lariano," I told her. "They have good healers there. But that is another three weeks away. Is there one any closer?"

She shook her head.

"We also have some other injuries around camp," I told her, "and one broken leg. All less than two weeks, same as Sabela."

I handed her a pouch of silver coins. She looked at it.

"It is too much," she told me.

"Nothing is too much," I said, looking at Sabela's sleeping form.

"She is your wife? Your mistress?"

"She is my friend. One of the few I have left."

"True friends are to be treasured." She nodded.

I thought about that after she left. *True friends are to be treasured.* I had found purpose in trying to make life better for people I didn't know. Would never know. It was one thing to look at these ideas about general injustice and cruelty. It was another thing to look at someone I know, someone who is close to me, and see them hurt or in danger. I knew that if I had to decide between Sabela and a stranger, I would pick Sabela. I also knew that wasn't necessarily fair.

As much as I loved Sabela, objectively, she wasn't any more valuable than any other individual in the world. But she was to me. She was my friend. But everyone was someone's friend, partner, brother, sister, parent, or child. If Nadezhda had to choose between Sabela and Abrina, I'm sure she'd choose Abrina. I couldn't fault her for that. Complete fairness, perfect justice — these things just weren't possible. We do the best we can do, I guess.

*True friends are to be treasured.*

They are. And I do. Even when they can be annoying or exasperating, like Rispan. I hoped he was okay, and I tried not to think that he might not be. I couldn't think that. It hurt too much to contemplate. But Sabela was going to be alright. And when we got back to Su Lariano, we'd get her to a better healer and make sure. Meanwhile, all this worrying and philosophy wasn't getting any onions chopped.

I found Gralbast and Bavrana.

"How soon can we be ready to move on?" I asked them.

They exchanged glances.

"We've pretty much finished here," Bavrana said.

"I can see you are anxious to leave," Gralbast told me, "but it is too late in the day to travel now. We can leave in the morning."

I nodded once. He was right. By the time we broke camp, we'd scarcely be out of sight of the town before we'd have to stop again for the night. We would leave tomorrow.

By first light we had eaten and were breaking camp. Not for the first time, I missed Rispan's scowling face as he would stumble for his morning coffee. I climbed onto Farukan's back and felt the support of his wordless connection as we headed north from the little town.

It was eighteen days later when we reached a fork in the road. The left branch would skirt around the forest and continue north. The other one went into the forest toward Su Lariano. Spring was turning into summer, and the shade from the trees was a nice change to the open sky we'd been traveling under.

Both Sabala and Réni seemed relieved to be back in the forest of Su Lariano. Mooren was simply attentive to our surroundings, as always.

Three days later, the road brought us through the outer village to the main gates of Su Lariano that waited a short distance beyond. I could scarcely believe we were back. It did feel a lot like coming home. Not *home*, home. Not to *that* family. But it was *a* home for me, and I did have a family of sorts here.

"We should make camp out here." Mooren indicated the open ground by the side of the road between the outer village and the city gates.

I had no sooner given the orders to make camp when a shout turned my head.

"Mira!"

I looked toward the gate and saw Mouse jogging toward us. I could see his eyes scanning our party.

"Mouse!" I called to him, leaping down from Farukan, a big grin plastered to my face.

Mouse stopped short, looking at me as I ran toward him. I saw his eyes grow wide as his confusion turned to surprise when he recognized me. Then I was hugging him. Yes, I was definitely happy to be back.

"How did you know we were back?" I asked him when we finally separated.

"Scouts had reported the caravan not long after you entered the forest." He grinned. "I've been on gate duty for more than a month, hoping to see you come in. We've known for a couple of days when you would get here."

"Yo, Mouse!" Sabela had joined us, and she gave him a hug, too.

Mouse looked past us, "Where's Rispan and the others?"

I froze. My whole body clenched up. I wanted so badly to just cry into his shoulder, and it took everything I had to hold it in. I opened my mouth, but no sound came out and I had to clench my jaws together to keep control of the torrent of emotion that threatened to break free.

"We got separated from Rispan when we left," Sabela told him. "We don't know about him."

*But we know about the others,* I thought.

*Tarana.*

*Kirsat.*

*Kooras.*

Mouse nodded slowly, reading between the lines from what hadn't been said, but not knowing exactly what it would be.

Suddenly, Neelu joined us.

"Welcome back!" she said, giving me a warm hug. "You look very different from when you left." She eyed me critically.

"Yes." I was glad of the distraction. With a small bow, I swept my hat from my head. "I am Raven, merchant, and captain of this caravan."

"I see," she chuckled. "I take it this will be an interesting tale." Then she stilled as her eyes found Farukan, who stood just behind me.

"Is that a *Rorujhen*?" she asked me.

"Yes," I told her. "This is Farukan."

"*Zergishti maloto, putri firgolo*," She cursed softly. "This can't be good."

I heard footsteps behind me and Neelu looked over my other shoulder. I turned to see Gralbast and Bavrana approaching.

"Neelu," I said, "this is Bavrana, leader of the Merchant Guild of Pokorah-Vo, and this is Gralbast, the merchant we met in the forest. My friends, this is Neelu Ulané Pulakasado, Princess of Su Lariano."

Neelu scowled at that last while Bavrana and Gralbast gave her a respectful bow.

"We don't need any of that if we're not in an official meeting," Neelu sounded annoyed, as she tended to be when reminded of her official position.

"As you say," Bavrana smiled. "We have brought—"

"Yes, yes," Neelu interrupted her with a wave as Bavrana had started to gesture to someone at the wagons. "You've probably brought gifts or something for the queen and whatnot. Well, it's appreciated, but it can wait. You," she said to Mooren, who had joined us, "Report directly to Dzurala for debrief." Mooren nodded and headed for the gates. Neelu turned to Mouse, "Stick Felgor, see to the caravan. Make sure they have everything they need and keep a general eye on them." He nodded and walked toward the wagons. "As for you three, the queen is waiting. It's not her favorite thing to do. So, let's go."

She turned on her heel and we followed her through the gates. I looked back to the wagons and saw Shéna's eyes, wide with concern and curiosity. I motioned her to quickly join us.

*"Farukan,"* I sent to him. *"Come with us. I want the queen to know about you right away."*

Neelu looked over her shoulder with surprise at the sound of Farukan's step.

"Farukan will be joining us," I told her.

She shrugged, not understanding but not interested in discussing it. Gralbast gave me a glance but didn't say anything either.

Shéna reached my side. I was tempted to take her hand in reassurance, but I knew she would not want to seem weak.

While the others studied our way, I was reminded of the first time I had made the trip down the long tunnel, over the stone bridge, and through the final tunnel that led to the throne room. When we entered the room, I spoke to Farukan again.

*"Wait here, please. I will call you when it is time."*

"Wait here," I whispered to Shéna.

Neelu led us to the midpoint of the throne room and stopped. I could see Astrina at the throne with a couple of people in front of her, but I had no idea what they were talking about. After a couple of minutes, the two bowed and stepped away from the queen. As they left, Neelu brought us forward.

# CHAPTER THIRTEEN

## MIRA

*A*strina looked at each of us in turn as we approached. At the bottom of the short steps at the base of the throne, Neelu motioned for us to stop. She continued on to stand next to her mother.

"This is Bavrana and Gralbast," she said. "He's the merchant we've heard so much about, and she is the leader of the Poko-rah-Vo Merchant Guild." Neelu then indicated Astrina, "This is Queen Astrina Ulané Poloso nya Su Lariano."

Both Gralbast and Bavrana performed bows accompanied by a "Your Majesty."

"Welcome to Su Lariano," Astrina said. She looked us over again. "I would make a wager, knowing my daughter as I do, that she brought you straight to me from the road without a pause for rest, refreshment, or preparation. And I'd add that she said anything but coming directly here could wait until later?"

Gralbast chuckled. "If I were the type to gamble, I think I would be very cautious in opposing you in a wager."

Astrina studied him for a moment, then turned to Neelu. "I see what Mira meant with this one. He'll need some watching. Mostly honest, but slippery."

This drew a guffaw from Bavrana that she quickly stifled.

"Forgive me, your Majesty," she said. "It's just that I've never seen Gralbast revealed so quickly or correctly."

Gralbast just looked back and forth with a mock, hurt expression on his face.

Astrina flashed a brief smile before continuing.

"Since you haven't had time to rest or refresh from the road," she said, "I'll cut right to it. You want to establish trade between Su Lariano and Pokorah-Vo, yes?"

"We do," Bavrana answered.

"And you are aware we already have a relationship with Laraksha-Vo?"

"Yes."

"So long as there is no conflict with our existing relationship," Astrina went on, "I am willing to grant trade access to the two of you. However, there are some conditions. First, the fact that I am only allowing the two of you from Pokorah-Vo at this time in no way should be taken to indicate you have exclusive rights, and I may extend this to other merchants of Pokorah-Vo at any time with no notice required to you. Understood?"

I could tell they weren't happy about that, but they agreed.

"Second, attacks on our people from Pokorah-Vo must stop immediately."

"Sadly," Gralbast sighed, "this is beyond our control."

"Explain."

"We are only of the Merchant Guild," Bavrana told her. "We do not govern Pokorah-Vo. We do not police the people."

"If I may," Gralbast cut in. "I am somewhat aware of the problems and the goals you have in regard to Pokorah-Vo. I share those goals. But they will not be achieved overnight. Our first king, Arugak, set a bloody example and his heirs have followed suit. King Vegak is not nearly as clever as his grandsire, but he is almost as bloody. There are many in the city that long for a change.

"Bavrana represents the Merchant Guild. I am no official representative. I speak as a citizen of Pokorah-Vo. It is long past time for a change, and I would welcome any assistance that Su Lariano, or even Laraksha-Vo, could provide. However, I can offer nothing beyond our shared goal of peace between our cities. We would stand on our own, as equals, and not become vassals or indebted. But know this, factions that profit from the current situation, and on slavery, are not limited to Pokorah-Vo."

Astrina nodded. "This is pretty much what I expected. I accept what you say, and for now, it will do. But this conversation has only begun." She motioned to an attendant at the side of the room. "Meanwhile, we can provide you with accommodations and refreshments."

They both bowed and were led away.

"Astrina," I told her. "I have someone else for you to meet."

She nodded and I turned, "Shéna!" I motioned her forward.

Shéna strode across the room with her head held high, proud, and strong. I knew her well enough that I could see the worry in her eyes, but she was determined to stand before Queen Astrina as an equal.

She stopped when she came to where I stood.

"Please forgive me for making you wait," I told her. "I thought it would be better if your meeting was not with the *Urgaban* present. I thought only to provide you a more private meeting and meant no disrespect." I didn't need to say this for Shéna, and she knew it. I was saying this for the benefit of Queen Astrina and Neelu.

Turning back toward the throne, I spoke formally, "Queen Astrina Ulané Poloso, Princess Neelu Ulané Pulakasado, I present to you, Queen Korashéna Ulané Sharavi nya Su Astonil, last of the royal family of Su Astonil."

Astrina almost jumped out of her chair in shock. "Last?"

She stood quickly and came down the steps to Shéna and wrapped her arms around her.

"Sister," Astrina said, stepping back from her. "I do not know your story, but I grieve for your loss. Will you accept the friendship of Su Lariano and the pledge that whatever the needs of Su Astonil, we will face them together?"

Shéna was at a loss for words, emotions threatening to overwhelm her. But she mastered them quickly.

"I accept both the friendship and the pledge, sister," she replied. "I could wish for nothing else."

"Arané-Li!" Astrina called. Then she turned to Shéna. "We will set you up with quarters in the royal wing and get you everything you need. We will have many long conversations, and plans to make, I am sure." Arané-Li had arrived. "Arané-Li, this is Korashéna'u nya Su Astonil. Please get her quarters in the royal wing and see that she needs for nothing."

"Of course," Arané-Li nodded her head.

"If possible," I said. "Could you put her close to me? Also, she has no friends here and no retinue, but she has grown close with Réni, maybe…"

"Say no more," Arané-Li smiled. "I will see to it." She turned to Shéna, "Majesty? If you would come with me, please?"

After they had left, Astrina turned to me. "That was not expected. What happened?"

"Too much," I told her. "Also, she was raised to think that Su Lariano had betrayed them. She knows the truth now, though."

Astrina seemed to almost take that as a physical blow, then nodded her head.

"Um… I have someone else for you to meet."

"I don't know how many more surprises I can take," she said, trying to lighten the mood.

I turned to face the door.

*"Farukan,"* I sent to him. *"It's time."*

# CHAPTER FOURTEEN

## MIRA

*F*arukan stepped forward in a slow prance, almost like he was dancing across the room. He reached where I stood and bowed, one front foot forward and the other tucked underneath.

"This," I told them, "Is Farukan, of the *Rorujhen*. I ask that you touch him to establish the bond so that he may be introduced to you and speak with you directly."

"Speak?" Neelu looked at me.

I nodded. They stepped forward and placed their palms on his shoulder.

"Farukan," I said. "This is Queen Astrina Ulané Poloso and Princess Neelu Ulané Pulakasado."

*"I am honored to meet you,"* Farukan's voice rumbled in our minds as he bowed his head.

"Welcome to Su Lariano, Farukan," Astrina seemed unsure of what to make of what she was experiencing. "Am I to understand that all *Rorujhen* have this ability?"

*"We do, your majesty."*

"But why have we not heard of it?"

*"The White Riders forbid that we reveal this secret. On pain of*

*death, we were not allowed to speak to any with whom we had not formed a bond."*

"Let's back up a little bit." Neelu held up her hand. "Mira, how is it that you have the mount of a White Rider?"

"We were attacked by a group of humans about a week before we reached Pokorah-Vo," I told her. "They were led by a White Rider."

"What happened to the Rider?" she persisted.

"I killed him."

"What? Do you know what kind of obligations come with that?"

I nodded. "A bit. I've been told."

"I don't think you realize how big a thing this is," Neelu told me. "It's not that uncommon for White Riders to fight each other and inherit the property of the loser. And they proclaim that anyone can challenge. But almost no one ever does and when they do, they never survive. Those they can't beat physically, they destroy with battle-magic."

"This one didn't get a chance to use magic," I said, "but I was told that at some point I have to go to the *Ashae* and claim my inheritance."

"You have a time limit," she told me. "We will speak of this later. We have to make plans."

"Farukan," Astrina asked, "Why did you stay with Mira after your Rider was killed?"

*"The laws of the White Riders are very explicit,"* Farukan answered. *"If a Rider is slain, we become the property of the victor."*

"Property?" Astrina asked.

"Slave," I told her. "The White Riders enslave the *Rorujhen*. They breed them and hold their families hostage for good behavior. I freed Farukan as soon as I found out."

"But," Neelu objected, "slavery violates the laws of the *Ashae*."

*"Only the White Riders know of the secret,"* Farukan explained. *"As far as anyone else knows, we are simply animals."*

"That's barbaric!" Neelu was angry. "That's no better than *Urgaban* slavers from Pokorah-Vo! This is an outrage!"

"Yes," I told her. "But remember, his family is hostage. I promised Farukan we would save his family before we revealed what we know. As far as anyone knows, I own him. But the reality is that we are partners."

"You're going to need a partner when you go to Shifara, the *Ashae* capitol," Astrina told me, "and you will need to start training in battle-magic or you won't survive very long after you arrive."

Astrina turned her attention back to Farukan. "Obviously, we have no knowledge of the *Rorujhen,* or your needs in terms of accommodations. But if we are to preserve this secret for now, we should continue to go with standard stables and grooms."

*"The physical needs of my body are not of any real difference from that of a horse,"* Farukan told her. *"The difference is our mind."*

"I have a dedicated groom for him," I said. Javen had taken over the duties full-time since Nadezhda had healed his leg.

That reminded me of Sabela.

"Sabela needs to see a healer. She has a concussion... blows to her head. There was a healer in the village to the south who did what she could, but she recommended that a better healer see to her."

Astrina motioned for another attendant and gave him instructions for getting a healer for Sabela.

"I know Mooren is debriefing with Dzurala," Astrina told me, "and you will do the same later. But for now, let's go to my private chambers and you can fill me in on everything that's happened since you left. Farukan." She looked at him. "I'll have someone take you back to the others if that's alright with you?"

*"Of course."* He dipped his head.

"Farukan," she added. "We are completely opposed to slavery. We will do what is necessary to aid you and your people with your plight with the White Riders."

*"Thank you, Your Majesty."* His head dipped again.

Once we were in Astrina's private audience room, we made ourselves comfortable and I went into the story. Mainly, I gave more of a summary than a blow-by-blow, and I didn't go into the details of what happened with Kirsat and Kooras.

"It sounds like you've been through a lot," Neelu said.

"And you handled things quite well," Astrina told me. "We will need to send you to Shifara soon to handle this White Rider inheritance business. This is not something that can wait."

"There's no way we can get her trained enough in battle magic before she has to leave." Neelu frowned. "She'll have to do training on the way. I think we should send Tesia with her. They already have a good relationship."

"Speaking of sending," I interrupted. "One thing we were missing on the mission was an actual healer. And we needed one. I don't want that to happen again. When we go back to Pokorah-Vo, we should bring a healer. I don't want to be in that position again."

"We can do that," Astrina said, "but you won't be going with them. Not until after you've finished dealing with this inheritance. That has to be top priority for you."

"But there's still so much to do in Pokorah-Vo," I objected. "We've only scratched the surface!"

"True." Astrina nodded. "But you also accomplished a lot. You brought us not one but two *Urgaban* allies. You brought us the last royal of Su Astonil. We have intelligence about our obstacles and possible allies."

"Shéna was all Rispan's doing," I said. "He's the one that found her."

"Even so." She smiled, "You led this mission and you and your team were successful."

"The ones who survived, you mean."

"Losing people, especially when you are responsible for them, is never easy." Astrina met my eyes. "This is a lesson that comes with leadership. I know you will carry this with you. It will make you a better leader in the future as long as you don't let the fear of losing people cripple you."

I shook my head. "No, I know that indecision can cost even more lives. We have an expression... He who hesitates is lost. But we balance it with another one... Look before you leap."

"What about these two *Urgaban*?" Neelu changed the subject, leaning forward intently. "How much do you trust them?"

"Gralbast is definitely in," I answered. "He wants what is best for his people, and he sees that as working with the rest of the world in mutual peace and prosperity rather than against it. He's a merchant, but deep down he's also an idealist. He sees himself as a patriot to his city, but not to its government."

"And Bavrana?"

"I don't know her as well." I thought for a moment. "She's a pragmatist. She knows that she can do better business with open trade, and open trade requires good relations between governments and acceptance and tolerance between people. Oh, that reminds me. She wants to partner with me in opening an *Urgaban* restaurant here in Su Lariano."

"A restaurant?" Neelu scrunched her face in confusion.

"Yeah. She has this idea that you can bring people together by getting them to like food." Neelu just gaped at me. "She has a whole strategy," I added.

Neelu shook her head. "She's either brilliant or crazy. Or both."

"Well, either way, she brought everything we need to start out stocking a kitchen."

"We have no laws prohibiting it," Astrina commented.

"She was worried that it might be better if a citizen of Su Lariano was one of the owners," I explained. "I wasn't really certain I qualified, but at least I'm not *Urgaban*, and that was another concern."

"There shouldn't be a problem with it," Astrina said. "You'll have to talk with Karméla. She oversees City Planning and Business. Réni can introduce you."

"Meanwhile," Neelu cut in. "We have bigger fish to fry. You —" The laughter that erupted from my mouth seemed to confuse her.

"I have no idea whether fish will be on the menu," I told her. "You'll have to ask Bavrana."

She scowled at me and continued. "You need to start preparing for being presented to the White Riders. It's possible you will face a challenge."

I tried to get serious again. "How likely is that?"

"Well." She thought for a moment. "They have never seen you fight. Never even heard of you. All of a sudden you show up claiming to inherit from a White Rider you killed in a fight they didn't even know happened. And you are human. I suppose it might be more accurate to say there is a slim chance you won't face a challenge."

"How serious would the challenge be?" I was worried I might have to kill again, though I suppose being killed would be worse. Or badly injured. But I'd rather not do any of that.

She shrugged, "It's probably best to assume the worst. The *Ashae* in general don't think much of other races, and that goes double for the White Riders. They'd probably do anything to keep a human from being one of them."

"Is there any way to avoid this?" I asked. "Do I have to go?"

"If you don't, it triggers a lot of things," Neelu explained. "Unless there is a family member to immediately take the place of a Rider, his family is slain because it is not known what secrets might have been shared. Their horses — their *Rorujhen* — are also slain. I had wondered why, but now I assume it's to also preserve secrets. And their land holdings and such are divided amongst the other riders. Most Riders have a family, this way they will have someone ready to bring in if one of them dies. Usually, they have a family before they are fully indoctrinated into the order."

"Wait, you mean the one I killed probably has a family?" I asked, "and they will lose everything when I claim it? Will they be killed? What if one of them is ready to join the White Riders?"

"I don't know everything about how they do things," she answered. "I think you can take them as your own family and protect them. There are advantages to doing that. But the point is," she went on, "no, you really don't have a choice. If you don't show, they will assume you assassinated the Rider and they will hunt you down to kill you and anyone that stands with you. You have to go to them. And you need to prepare for the challenge because not only are these among the most highly trained fighters in the world, but they also use magic to fight."

"Well, I'm completely screwed," I said. "I only beat the last one because he underestimated me. It was over before he could really try."

"Then don't make the same mistake he did."

"What do you mean?"

Neelu put her hand on my shoulder. "Don't underestimate yourself."

I thought about that as I went to see Dzurala to give her my report. Don't underestimate myself. Easy to say.

Dzurala motioned to the chair across from her desk when I walked in the room. She eyed me critically as I sat down.

"Your trip has changed you," she said.

I nodded. "I suppose so. It wasn't as easy as I thought it would be."

"It never is."

"I don't like having to kill," I told her.

"I know. And yet?"

"And yet I will do it to protect my people. My friends. My family." I thought about the people I had killed. "I don't feel guilty. I mean — I regret having to do it, but I don't feel guilty. Does that make me a bad person?"

"Not at all." She shook her head. "Ethics is about taking action which is for the greater good. You can look at just about any action — in one situation it is good and in another situation it is bad. Context is everything. If you are able to distinguish the difference, to know that you took the right action for the situation, then there is no reason to feel guilty. Failing to take the right action would be a reason to feel guilty. You're not a bad person Mira. Don't doubt yourself."

I laughed at that. "Did you just talk to Neelu? She just told me not to underestimate myself."

She gave me a look that was half smirk, half shrug.

I had a pouch over my shoulder, and I drug it around to the front. I opened the flap and reached in to pull out a stack of paper. I dropped it on Dzurala's desk.

"Here's my report," I told her. "I have detailed everything that happened on the mission up to last night, including all intelligence gathered in Pokorah-Vo. But it's not enough."

Dzurala just looked at me with raised eyebrows.

"We've just scratched the surface," I explained. "There are so many undertones in Pokorah-Vo. Alliances we can make. Opposition to identify. King Vegak will have to go; there's no way we can work with him. He will always be looking for how he can put a knife to our throats. We need to replace him with someone, but who? And the slavers hold a lot of power in the city, but we don't know exactly why."

"We will find out."

"Neelu says I can't go back until I deal with this White Rider stuff." I still wasn't happy about that. And the more I thought about everything that still needed to happen with Pokorah-Vo, the less happy I was.

"That depends on the timing. Either way, you will be gone for some time, and you will have to trust that we can move forward in your absence," Dzurala said, "and I don't mean to minimize in any way what you have accomplished."

"But who would be primary once I'm gone? I'm the one who is established as Gralbast's partner."

"You?" Dzurala smiled. "Or Raven?"

"What do you mean? I'm Raven."

She nodded. "Some of us know that."

"Ohhh, I get it. You mean we could pass around the persona as needed. Kinda like the Dread Pirate Roberts."

"Who?"

I shook my head. "Who would take over as Raven?"

"I don't know. We'd have to figure that out. But Neelu is right; until you handle the White Riders, you won't have time for anything else."

Too many thoughts were competing for my attention. "Do you know if there's been any progress finding out how Laruna learned to use portal magic?"

Dzurala looked at me for a moment, possibly deciding what she should tell me.

"We know that Laruna came to Su Lariano a dozen years ago," she told me. "She evidently came from Su Rané in the north. This hasn't been verified, but it is likely true. We know nothing of her training or history before she arrived here."

"And nothing in her rooms?"

"Possibly. We found some old texts and Tesia has been translating them." She tapped her fingers on the desk. "Evidently Laruna wasn't prepared when she left. We had guards in her room and a few days later she portaled in. She took one look at the guards and went right back out. That's when we searched again and found the texts hidden behind a panel in the wall. If there is anything in them about portal lore, Tesia will find it."

I shook my head. "I couldn't go home right now, even if we knew how. Not until after I deal with the White Riders. There's too much at stake."

# CHAPTER FIFTEEN

## RISPAN

*W*e spent the next two days resting after the hard ride from the *jahgreet* pack. I also did what I could to preserve the pelt from the one we'd killed. I tried to stay clinical about it but skinning the *jahgreet* and working with the skin was not an experience I enjoyed.

I'd never done it before, but I'd heard about it. Mouse had brought it up in passing and when he saw my reaction, enjoyed going over the fine details of every squeamish step. I wished the big lummox was with me so he could do it, but I was on my own.

"Not bad," Kiarash said when I laid it out for final drying. "It should stay soft and supple now."

"You know how to do this?" I asked him.

"Of course."

"Why didn't you say anything? I've never done this before."

"I know." He nodded. "I could tell. But you were doing fine."

"But I could have botched it!"

He shook his head. "I'd have said something if you were doing anything wrong. This way you learned better."

The fact that he was right only annoyed me more. I really didn't see why I needed to learn things like this if I had people around who could do it for me. I'd be happy to pay them. I'm more of a city guy. Camping and living off the land wasn't really my style.

The kitten was also taking up my attention. I wasn't sure what to feed it, so I started with broth. I found that it was able to drink from a bowl. It also seemed to like raw meat, and the *reshan* kept us in fresh rabbit. It got used to me quickly. It was only about eight inches long. The fact that it could eat meat made me think it might have been older than I'd thought at first. Maybe it was a runt, and that's why it was the only one left in its mother's pouch. If it had needed milk, I don't know what I could have done.

I had a length of cloth that I stained red from the berries of a bush growing nearby. The berries weren't edible, but I tied the stained cloth around the kitten's neck like a collar so I could see it easier.

My biggest worry was that the *reshan* would think that the kitten was a handy snack. Kiarash's assurances didn't make me feel any better when I could see the *reshan* watching the kitten intently.

"Are you going to name it?" Kiarash saw me looking at the kitten.

"I probably should. I guess the bird has a name?"

He nodded. "Naga." I saw the bird turn its head to look at him when he said its name.

"I don't know what to name it though," I told him. "I don't even know if it is male or female."

"Give it a female name." He shrugged. "If it ends up being male, just add something to the end."

"I could give it a mountain name." Those didn't always follow the standard conventions. But then I still had the question of male or female. I picked up the kitten and scratched under its chin. It purred softly. "I think I'll call it Bijoux."

"That's a good mountain name." Kiarash nodded. "And neutral."

We were back moving north the next morning. I wore a loose shirt with Bijoux tucked inside, and Kiarash flew overhead on Naga. We fell into a more relaxed pace than our mad dash out of the pass. The next three days were pleasant as the late spring wasn't too warm yet, and we still got some cool breezes coming down off the white peaks of the mountains on our left.

Looking through the haze to the east, I could just see the shadowy outline of the Great Mountains, even at this distance. Not much was known about what was beyond that range, other than it was the home of the *Rorujhen*. The range was considered impenetrable, but obviously the White Riders knew a way through. There was probably a route around the northern end by the coast.

I heard a roar and something large and heavy sounding struck the rocky slope to my left. I turned to look, but all I could see was dust and some sliding rock coming down on the further of two hills. I glanced around at the sky, but Kiarash must have been scouting ahead on Naga. My natural curiosity tempted me to investigate, but I decided not to waste time on any side adventures. I needed to get back to Su Lariano and let them know about Aganaté and the *Chados*. I was already so far behind Mira and the caravan it wouldn't surprise me if I came on them on their way back to Pokorah-Vo before I reached Su Lariano.

Then I heard a low roar, like something large was frustrated or in pain. Or both. Then I heard a sound that was more like a keening cry. Cursing, I nudged the reins to get the horse to head into the hills toward where I'd seen the falling rocks. If some creature was injured, I couldn't just leave it to die. I went cautiously though; I didn't want to run into another *jahgreet*.

Coming around the first hill, I looked at the bramble of bushes and shrubs. It looked like there was a darker shadow in one area, so I angled toward it. The keening sound had stopped, and I had nothing else to guide me. I thought I heard some movement and adjusted my direction. For just a moment, I thought I heard heavy breathing.

I got down from my horse and stepped into the bramble, going slowly and quietly so I wouldn't startle whatever was there. Then I was through the bramble, and I hadn't seen anything. The sounds I had heard made it seem like there had been something fairly large, it should be hard for it to hide. Unless it was another *jahgreet*. But what I'd heard hadn't sounded like a *jahgreet*.

I went back into the bramble and looked again. I spent several minutes searching with no luck. Well, I had tried. It was time to get back on the road. I turned to leave and saw a pair of eyes watching me through the brush. These weren't the eyes of some large creature though. It was a person.

"Hello," I said. "It sounded like there was an injured animal in here. Did you see anything?"

I took a step toward the eyes, and I saw a panicked look come across them and she took a few steps away from me. I could see now it was a she. It didn't appear she had any clothing. I stopped moving.

"Don't worry," I told her. "I won't hurt you. Are you alright?"

She looked at me very intently for a moment, her head cocked slightly to the side. Then she seemed to relax a little. I stepped toward her slowly.

"My name is Rispan." When she didn't say anything, I went on. "Do you speak the common tongue? Do you understand me?"

When I got a better look at her, I could see she had been wounded on her left side just below the collar bone. She still hadn't said anything; she just watched me.

"Come with me." I motioned with my hands. "Let's get you some clothes and we can take a look at that wound." I took a few steps in the direction of the horses and motioned for her to follow. She hesitated, but then came along. She looked like a *Loiala Fé*, but a little smaller. She was just a bit too tall to be *Ulané Jhinura*. But something about her made me think she wasn't either one. Though I didn't know *Loiala Fé* that well, so I couldn't be sure. Her features were... stunning.

I took my pack down from the horse that had been carrying it and pulled out a spare set of clothes. I handed them to her, but she looked like she didn't know what to do with them. I tried to use hand motions to show her, but in the end, I had to help her into them. She looked at what I was wearing and reached out her hand and peeled back the edge of my shirt slightly and inspected it, then at the shirt I had put on her. She examined the clothes she was wearing, running her hands over them as if experiencing something new. Then she stopped and looked back at me expectantly. Her eyes were a striking blue, and the edges of the irises were tinged in amber.

I took down a waterskin and held it out to her. She looked at it and then back to me. Who was she that she didn't know what clothes or a waterskin were? I took a drink to show her and then held it out again. She took it from my hand and sniffed it. Then she put it to her mouth and tipped it back, swallowing gulp after gulp until I thought she would try to drain the whole thing.

"Hang on." I reached to pull it back. "Not so much at one time."

I sat her down on a nearby rock and took a look at her shoulder. It looked like she had been stabbed with something and the wound was fairly deep. She'd been holding her left arm still and had winced when I'd raised it to put her arm in the shirt sleeve. We didn't have much in terms of medical supplies, but I was able to clean the wound and put a bandage on it.

I felt Bijoux moving under my shirt. He slept a lot. She saw the movement and her eyes locked onto the spot. I reached into my shirt and pulled the kitten out. Her eyes narrowed as I gave Bijoux a few scratches under the chin. I held Bijoux out to her, and she gingerly took the kitten from my hand, looking back and forth between me and the kitten. Then she lifted Bijoux and tilted her head back, mouth wide.

"No!" I grabbed Bijoux from her. "No eating! This is Bijoux!" I tucked the kitten back into my shirt.

I put my pack on the same horse that carried Kiarash's. We'd split them up over the two spare horses to minimize the load on each. I climbed up on my horse and motioned for her to get on the other spare. She reached up with her right hand and tried to get up, but when she had trouble, she instinctively tried to catch herself with her injured left and cried out.

Cursing myself, I got down from my horse.

"Sorry," I told her. "Let me help you."

Once I'd gotten her safely into the saddle, I climbed back onto my own mount and led the two other horses back to the road. I made early camp late that afternoon and it wasn't long before Kiarash and Naga landed nearby, startling my guest. She jumped to her feet in alarm.

"It's alright," I told her. "He's a friend. This is Kiarash."

"And who the *zerg* is she?" Kiarash asked.

She pointed at Kiarash and then to her mouth.

"No, you can't eat him either." I hoped she understood me. "We'll eat something soon."

"She thinks I'm dinner?" Kiarash didn't look amused. "Who is she?"

"I came across her this afternoon," I told him. "She's been wounded, and —"

"Wounded by who?"

"I don't know. There was no one else around and it seems like she can't talk." I turned back to her. She was watching our exchange and seemed to be relaxing. "I think she's hungry though. I'll get a fire going, I'm sure you brought some rabbits."

She watched me curiously as I stacked wood for a fire. I'd never learned magic like Mira did, so I always used a flint to get the fire going. She laughed at me when I sparked the flint and blew to try to get a flame going.

"What's so funny?" I frowned at her.

I didn't expect her to answer. But she did get up and walk to the pile of kindling I was working at. She bent low and, pursing her lips, blew onto it. As her breath came in contact with the wood, it immediately ignited.

Kiarash stopped what he was doing and stared, his eyes wide.

"My friend," he said. "Whatever you do, do not make her angry." At my look, he went on. "Do you not know what she is? She is *Darakanos*. She is a dragon."

I looked at her, confused. "She's not a dragon, she's some kind of *Loiala Fé*."

"*Darakanos* can change their form," he told me. "You didn't know that?"

Now that he mentioned it, I did recall hearing something about it, but I'd never believed it.

"I didn't think there were any *Darakanos* in these mountains."

He scowled at that. "It *is* unusual," he said, "but no one tells a dragon where they can or can't live."

I started to laugh and realized he wasn't joking. I glanced at her and saw that she was watching us.

"Does she understand what we're saying?" I asked Kiarash. "She hasn't said anything."

"Dragons are very different from other races," he answered. "I don't know how they communicate. It's probably best to assume she can understand us to some degree."

I turned to meet her gaze. "Do you understand me?" She just looked at me, unblinking. "If you can understand me, please nod your head." She cocked her head to the side, studying me. Then she moved her head up and down.

I pointed to myself, "Rispan. Kiarash." I pointed to him. Then I pulled the kitten from my shirt, "Bijoux. Naga," I indicated the *reshan*. Her eyes had followed me through the introductions. Then I pointed to her.

She looked at me for a moment, then slowly nodded her head. Suddenly, my mind was overwhelmed with a flood of images, emotions, and concepts. The onslaught was overwhelming, and I fell to my knees. The pressure lessened and it no longer felt like an assault on my mind. A single concept seemed to come into focus, and I struggled to translate it into words. It coalesced into something more succinct.

"Genevané," I said. The presence was gone from my mind, and I looked at her. "You are Genevané."

She considered me for a moment, then nodded her head.

"It's a beautiful name," I told her.

The smile spread on her face like the sun parting the morning mist.

Kairash got busy cleaning the rabbits and before long we had them cooking over the fire. I'd come across a patch of peppers the day before and helped myself, so we roasted some of those as well. The sun had set before we were ready to eat.

Genevané was very interested in the rabbits but looked doubtfully at the peppers. She followed my example of taking a bite of rabbit and immediately taking a bite of a roasted pepper. I assumed that, as a dragon, she wouldn't have trouble with spicy food.

I wasn't wrong. She grinned and took another double-bite. The peppers were a bit hot for me, but not enough to blow the top of my head off, and they were very tasty.

"Where are your people?" I asked her. "Your family?"

She just looked at me and chewed her dinner.

"Where do you need to go?"

There was still no answer from her. So, I just shook my head and brought out Bijoux to feed him.

A concept came into my mind with that thought. The only thing I got from it was that it was female. Genevané was looking at me.

"Female?" I asked her. "Bijoux is female?"

She just smiled and went back to her rabbit.

Bijoux also liked the rabbit, but one sniff of the pepper was all she needed, and she turned her head away, refusing to taste it. Maybe *Jahgreet* didn't eat plants. I bunched some spare clothing around Bijoux that she could snuggle into as a bed for the night.

Kiarash chuckled.

"What?"

"A *jahgreet* AND a dragon." He shook his head. "Only you could have this happen. I can only wonder what's next."

I scowled at him and went about getting things ready for sleeping.

The gear that had come with the horses had blanket rolls tied behind the saddles. I laid one of them out near the fire for her to sleep on. I hoped the smell wasn't too bad. The survivors we'd seen on the road didn't look to be the most hygienic people I'd ever seen.

I pointed to the bed, "Genevané, this is for you."

She stepped forward and touched the blankets. Then she laid down and fell almost instantly asleep.

"She must have been tired after her day," Kiarash said.

I looked up at him and froze. *How could something so big be so quiet?*

"Kiarash?"

"Yes?" He glanced at me and turned back to removing his blanket from his pack.

"Remember when you said you could only wonder what would be next?" I asked, looking over his shoulder. "Don't move quickly. Because it's here."

He looked back at me, and then his eyes got big as they looked past me over my shoulder.

*Zerg!*

Before I could say anything, a half dozen huge figures stepped out of the darkness and grabbed us. I was picked up as if I weighed nothing. In no time at all, all three of us were sitting on the ground with our hands and feet tied. In the firelight, I could get a better look at what they were. These were *Ogaré*. We didn't know a lot about them; they were a solitary people that usually kept to the high mountain peaks. I'd never seen one in person, but they were the only race I knew of that stood nine feet tall. I would barely come up to their waist.

One of them came to us and squatted down to look into our eyes. I could see the thick, heavy skin that covered him. *Ogaré* were very fierce, and their skin was so tough it was like armor all by itself. He grunted when he saw Genevané's eyes. He stood up and pointed to her.

"This one," he said.

"Why have you attacked us?" I asked. "We've done nothing to you."

He looked at me. "Make your case to the Justice. I will not hear your words."

Genevané looked furious. She drew a deep breath and blew the air back out at him. Some of his clothing sparked and caught fire. He casually slapped her to the ground and then patted out the flames. *Ogaré* were immune to heat or fire.

We were each picked by an *Ogaré* and thrown over its shoulder. They set off into the night, their steps quickly eating ground and elevation as we climbed into the mountains.

I kept getting flashes from Genevané. Pain, anger, grief, frustration and apathy all battled for supremacy. But none of it made sense. I remembered the last time I got hauled away over someone's shoulder. There was no way Mira would be coming along to save me this time.

# CHAPTER SIXTEEN

## MIRA

"Y ou've got to make the barrier solid," Tesia told me. "That's the only way to be invisible to the lightning. Otherwise, it will find you. If you are fully connected to the *Ralahin*, it will *probably* keep it from killing you. But you have to perfect the barrier to really be protected. And you *have* to be able to do two things at once."

I frowned in frustration, letting go of my *Ralahin* vision. We'd been at this for hours. I had worked on magical defenses with her before, but that was against physical weapons. Physical weapons were much easier to fend off. I rubbed my palm where the electrical attack had just zapped me. It's a good thing she was going easy with me, or I'd have been fried. My shields were fine until I tried to do something else at the same time. Like lighting a candle with magic.

"I know," I told her. "Electricity can get through a very small path."

She cocked her head and thought for a moment. "Yes, I suppose that is one way to think of it."

Her response surprised me a little, like she was missing information. Then I realized this magical lightning attack was the first use I had seen of electricity since I got to this world. And while the attack could be powerful, it wasn't very refined.

"Maybe if I understood the attack better," I suggested. "Can you show me how to do it?"

"Alright." She nodded. "I think you could use a rest from barriers anyway. First, we need a target —"

"Got it!" We were in the practice room in the Royal Wing and there were a number of weapons and things. I grabbed a wooden shield with a metal rim and leaned it against a wall away from anything else.

"Yes," she said. "It is a lot easier to use something metal as the target."

"That's because metal is a conductor," I told her as I went to stand next to her.

"A what?"

"A conductor." At her flat look, I went on. "A conductor is some kind of material that allows the easy flow of an electrical charge. Like the lightning — that's an electrical charge."

"That's an interesting view of it."

"In my world," I explained, "people don't use magic. At least, none that I know of. All of our devices are powered by electricity."

"But if you don't use magic, how do you create the lightning?"

"There's different methods for generating electricity," I said. "Have you ever walked across the carpet and gotten a little shock from touching a metal object? Like a doorknob?"

"Yes." She nodded.

"Your feet on the carpet built up a charge, and then it's released when your hand was close to the doorknob. Anyway, how do you do it with magic?"

"Alright," she said, raising her hand. "Watch me."

I opened my *Ralahin* vision, and the room came alive with magic.

"I connect with the magic, and I envision it transforming into lightning," she said. I could see and feel the buildup in her hand. "And then I focus on my target and push the lightning to it." Electricity shot from her hand to the shield.

"That's all?" I asked.

"All?" Her eyebrows lifted with the question. "It's not as easy as it sounds. The lightning is very difficult to control; it can have a mind of its own. It can go where you don't want it to if you can't control it."

I could see how that might happen. The lightning was just launched in the direction of the target and if there was a better ground nearby, it would hit that instead.

"Yes, sorry. Could you do it again please?"

I watched as the charge built up in her hand. She was using magic to pull in a flow of electrons. At the same time, I could see her creating a negative charge at her target, a spot on the shield. Then she gave a magical push, physically aiding the concept with a motion of her hand, and the lighting struck the shield.

I nodded. "How fast can you do it?"

She raised her hand and electricity immediately shot to the shield, which was starting to crack and twist. I was still able to see the same process as before, it just happened much more quickly. I got another shield and put it about fifteen feet from the first one. Tesia watched me with a look of curiosity.

"Can you do it again, please?" I asked. "Same target?"

She launched the electricity again. This time, as it neared the target it turned sharply and struck the second shield.

"Yes!" I shouted.

"How did you do that?" she asked.

"Well, I could see you created a negative charge in your target. I just gave it a better path! I put a channel from in front of your target to the other shield. Electricity will always take the path of least resistance."

"But the other shield was further away."

"It doesn't matter." I shook my head. "Okay, let me try it."

I raised my hand and pulled in the flow of electrons.

132

"Don't hold it too long," she cautioned.

I wasn't worried. I put my attention on the shield and the path between my hand and the shield, creating a negative channel to pull the flow of electricity. Then I let the flow go. The bolt flew from my hand in a straight line and struck the shield.

"How did you make it fly so straight?" Tesia asked.

"I didn't just focus on the target," I explained. "I created a path."

I raised my hand to try again, then I paused. Why did I need my hand? I was creating the negative channel all the way across the room. Did the positive channel need to start close to me? I lowered my hand to my side and focused on the two shields. After a moment, a flash of lightning flew from one to the other.

"How did you do that?" Tesia's eyes were big.

Instead of answering, I tried something else. I thought of images I had seen of circuit boards and diagrams. I remembered how the conducting wires would often travel around different things on their way to the next connection. I looked at the two shields and tried again. This time, the electricity shot up from the first shield, across the wall between them, and then down into the second shield.

"I think I see part of what you are doing," Tesia said. "You're using one shield as the point to create the lightning."

"Right." But that got me thinking, too, and I had another idea. This time, instead of starting with a shield, I just picked a point in the air and sent the charge to the first shield."

"Wait," Tesia said. "I didn't see how you did that one."

"Since we're using magic to generate the electricity," I explained, "we don't really need a physical object as the starting point. We are still just creating a flow of electrons. Using our hand, or another object, just helps to give us a focus for a starting point. But we don't need it."

I went to stand near one of the shields.

"Let's try this again," I said. "Go ahead and send one at me like before."

She nodded and I got ready. As soon as I felt her start to build charge, I created a channel from in front of me to one of the shields. Her bolt flew along the channel to strike the shield.

"That's amazing!" Tesia grinned. "I thought I was supposed to be teaching you!"

"And you know what?" I said. "I could also send it back to you instead of to the shield."

She laughed, "That would certainly catch your enemy by surprise. But you still need to be able to keep your shield solid while you are doing something else."

Shield. Right.

Light the candle. Put out the candle. Keep the shield going.

I frowned, thinking about the process. The problem was that the shield took so much concentration to hold up. The moment I started thinking about anything else, it would start to falter. I formed a shield around myself and looked at it with the *Ralahin*.

I could see the flow I was directing to form the shield. I saw the magic going into it. Why did I need to keep the flow going once it was formed? I looked more closely and could see that the magic was dissipating; it flowed into a hard ridge, and then flowed out of it.

*If I could lock that down somehow—*

As soon as that thought came to me, the dissipation stopped. The shield was suddenly larger and thicker since my flow into it kept going. I eased off and found a way to sort of tie it off. Then I stopped the flow. The shield was still strong, and it took no thought or effort from me.

Tesia shook her head. "Yes, that's a more advanced way to handle the shield. I was going to teach you that later. For now, I was trying to get you to be able to focus on two things at once."

"Well." I smiled. "At least I'll be able to keep the shield up now."

Tesia waved her hand, and my shield was gone.

"You were saying?"

*That* was disappointing.

She laughed at my expression. "Don't worry, you are doing very well."

"But you made my shield go away with no effort at all!"

"That was just because of your knot," she told me.

"My knot?"

She nodded. "If you don't want someone to be able to easily unravel a standing spell, you need to tie it off with a more difficult knot. And as you know, there are different kinds of magic. Shields still use a form of the *Ralahin*. But offensive magic is very different. You will eventually be able to weave different forms together. For example, create a standing ward or shield that contains an attack for anyone that tries to break it. And shields don't have to be untied; they can be broken."

That's when we shifted our focus to breaking shields. This was basically just battering it with powerful attacks until it crumbled. At first, I envisioned it like pounding away with a baseball bat. Then I tried envisioning a huge axe. This worked better than the bat. Then, instead of one axe, I envisioned more like a wheel, like a great machine turning a wheel with a dozen axe blades, striking one after the other without letup until the shield shattered.

Tesia nodded in approval. "It is not only raw power that makes one formidable as a mage, but innovation. You do have raw power, but it is your innovation that is your true strength. You think of things in new ways; you think of new applications."

That made sense. And I knew I had a big advantage in that. I loved movies, and not just the old black-and-white classics. I also loved to watch action movies, and sci-fi, and movies with magic. Plus, I read a lot. I'd seen so many ways of doing things, it gave me more ammunition for ideas.

The trick was figuring out how to make those ideas come to life.

That evening, Gylan came by my rooms to see me.

"Gylan." I motioned for him to come inside. "It's been a long time! It's good to see you."

"And you as well." He smiled. "How did those boots work for you?"

"They're wonderful! Thank you so much!"

"Ah, I am glad." He nodded. "I wanted to get a look at you for sizing for the next project."

"What next project?"

"I am to emulate the armor of a White Rider for you," he said.

"Emulate it?" This was the first I had heard of this.

"Yes. I have been provided the armor of the Rider you defeated. This will serve as a model."

"I suppose I'm going to need it when I present myself to the Riders."

He nodded. "As I understand it, you would normally wear the armor of the one you fought, but it won't fit you. I have been instructed not to take the old armor apart, so I imagine you will bring it with you."

"So, you make armor as well, then?" I asked him.

He nodded. "I do all sorts of leather work. I can make you armor that will be comfortable yet will be hard enough to repel any blade."

"I appreciate that." Images flashed into my mind of armor I had seen on women in computer games. "Um… It's not going to be… skimpy, is it?"

"What do you mean?"

"Well, it's going to cover my whole torso, right?"

"It wouldn't be very useful if it didn't," he answered. "Of course, there are openings. Like under the arms at the shoulder."

I nodded, remembering my fight with the Rider. His first serious injury had been there. But my second serious blow had not been.

"When I fought him, I was able to stab through his armor with my knife pretty easily."

He blinked at me. "May I see your knife?"

I'd been warned about the daggers broadcasting their presence like a beacon. Shielding the daggers from being so magically visible was one of the first things Tesia had taught me when we'd started our lessons with the *Ralahin*. Since the daggers were also designed to cut through spells, that warding had to be replaced occasionally. As long as they were in their sheaths, they were magically invisible. I handed him one of the daggers and he looked at it closely, then nodded as he handed it back.

"A few things," he said. "This blade is very strong, and it is extremely sharp. Much sharper than most blades you would fight against. Also, it is magically reinforced to assist in cutting through resistant material. Even the best leather armor would have trouble with a blade like this. But I will do what I can to make yours as strong as possible." He winked, "Maybe I'll have my daughter add some magical reinforcement."

That would be good. I was sure Tesia could manage that.

He looked me over for sizing. I was wearing one of the sets of leather clothing I'd gotten from Felora, and it was fairly snug.

He nodded. "Very good. I'll get right on it. Do you want any decoration?"

I started to say no, then I thought of the raven pin that Rispan had found for me. I showed it to Gylan.

"If it would be possible to work something like this in?" I asked him. "If not, that's okay. I don't really need decoration."

"I'm sure I can manage something." He smiled. "These are very auspicious. Or ominous."

"Ravens?"

"We call them *balangur*," he said.

"*Balangur?* I haven't heard that word before."

"*Balangur* represent hidden things. Hidden knowledge. Hidden pathways. But it can also mean bringing hidden things to light or opening hidden ways." He shrugged. "There are many meanings associated with the *balangur*. Anyway, I have your measure. I'll get started on your armor."

"Thank you, Gylan. Say hello to Felora for me."

After Gylan left, I looked at the raven clasp Rispan had found for me and started thinking about ravens and the significance they had on Earth. Evidently, they had special meaning here as well. When I looked at the clasp, I realized there was something familiar about it. I picked up my daggers and looked at the hilts.

The daggers were identical except that one was worked with black on part of the hilt, and the other with white. As I looked at the black design, I realized it was a stylized bird — a raven! It was looking at the raven from the back, and the wings were wrapped around the hilt with the bird looking back over its shoulder. The way it was done, in with all the filigree, I hadn't noticed before. I guess I'd been looking too closely to see the overall pattern. Now that I was looking for it, it was pretty obvious. I checked the other dagger, and it was the same thing. Was there such a thing as a white raven?

What was the word for a lucky coincidence? Serendipity? It was pretty cool that I had taken my second name as the same thing from my mother's daggers.

I spent the next couple of weeks working intensively with Tesia on battle magic. Electrical attacks were the easiest for me; the other attacks were trickier. One was pulling moisture out of the air to form ice shards to send at your opponent. But if you do that very many times, you'd run out of available moisture. Another one that was hard for me was to use compressed air as an attack. The idea was to create a thin edge that would slice or puncture, but all I managed to do was a broad, blunt-force attack. That could work for knocking someone off their feet, or magically kicking a door in. I could also move air around or use air to move other things.

Sabela was almost back to her old self. The healers had worked with her daily the first week until they were satisfied she would make a full recovery. I had been very relieved to hear the news.

Mouse was staying in my spare room when he was on his days off. Surprisingly, he was also a huge help in getting the restaurant up and going. We had settled on naming it the

Raven's Nest. Bavrana and I had gone to see Karméla, and it turned out there was a good-sized space available near the Dancing Peacock. Bavrana and I would not be able to always be around to run things, and the *Urgaban* chef, Jakeda, was strictly focused on the kitchen.

Mouse expressed an interest and I'd given him the go-ahead. He'd taken on the responsibility with gusto. He spent all of his free time at the restaurant. He'd even enlisted help from Arané-Li, the royal Chamberlain, to make sure it would be appropriate to serve the elites of the city. Mouse still had his duty shifts with the City Guard, but his main focus had become being manager for the Raven's Nest.

Bavrana and I were satisfied it was in good hands. Not that we'd just dumped all the decisions on Mouse; it was still primarily our vision, or Bavrana's vision, and Mouse was turning it into a reality. His experience in the mushroom farms also gave him a good background to help Jakeda to connect with high quality sources. Bavrana was working closely with him every day. We had already announced the grand opening, to be held in another week, and even Queen Astrina had accepted the invitation.

I didn't know how they were spreading the news, but I was hearing talk of it almost every day now when I ate in the dining hall. There was an *Urgaban* dessert unique to Pokorah-Vo that would bring out a flavor in a particular kind of mushroom that it reminded me of apples, and it was prepared with a crunchy, crumbly coating. It was served like a kabob and was almost like apple-cobbler on a stick. We'd had people pushing carts through Market Square selling them at low prices to get interest going for the *Urgaban* fare of the Raven's Nest. It was working.

I snagged one of our samples on the way after a long day drilling with Tesia. It was wonderful. Mouse saw me as soon as I walked in and flashed me a big smile. I'd been checking in every other day or so.

"Everything is on schedule," he said. "We've been getting so many reservation requests, I had to go to Karméla for permission to add extra tables in the space outside the front door."

"She agreed?"

He nodded. "Just for the Grand Opening. But reservations are booking up for the rest of the month."

"Well, if it isn't the Raven herself!" a voice called as someone stepped out of the kitchen.

"Bavrana!" I grinned. "Judging by all the reservations, this was a brilliant idea you had."

She shrugged. "I have my moments. The main things to finish up are the decor and training the staff. Grangor has given us temporary use of Ergek and Shaluza. They got pretty familiar with a lot of Jakeda's creations on the trip."

"Oh, right!" I said. "I was going to ask you how your meeting with Grangor went."

"He's alright," she answered. "He was a bit standoffish at first. His assistant was much worse."

"Assistant?" This was news to me.

She nodded. "Some kind of junior ambassador. She only recently arrived from Laraksha-Vo. Her name is Yarmilla."

"I haven't met her."

"I think Grangor expected everyone from Pokorah-Vo to be murdering thugs, but he's come around. Yarmilla..." She shrugged. "Let's just say there's still work to be done there."

"I bet Grangor is starting to appreciate that the situation with Pokorah-Vo is a lot more complex than we thought."

Bavrana nodded. "But that's Gralbast's business. I'm just looking for a way to ease integration to maximize trade. More profits that way."

"Or maybe you just don't want to step on his toes?" I asked.

"I'm no revolutionary. I'm just a merchant."

"How are you and Gralbast getting along these days?'

This was the first time I'd seen an *Urgaban* blush.

"We get along just fine. Why wouldn't we? Now, I need to check with Jakeda about something." She turned and hurried toward the kitchen. I chuckled and she scowled at me over her shoulder as she disappeared through the door.

"It sounds like you guys have everything under control," I said to Mouse.

He nodded, "I can't wait until we open the doors. Rispan's going to love this place!"

His smile disappeared as soon as the words left his mouth. I felt my stomach drop out and my face locked down, hiding any emotion.

"I'm sorry," he said. "It's just…"

"I know." I put a hand on his shoulder. "There's still hope." I forced a smile. "That brother of ours is probably just busy causing trouble for someone. He'll show up any time."

He nodded. But I could see the doubt.

"Alright," I told him. "Let me know if you need anything."

I had to get out of there before I lost it. I walked briskly through Market Square and headed for my rooms. I knew that with how slow travel was on this world, that things could easily get delayed for weeks, even months on a long trip. At the same time, I was terrified that I'd never see him again.

*Rispan! Where are you?*

# CHAPTER SEVENTEEN

## RISPAN

*I*t was hard to tell how fast we were moving, but *Ogaré* could take huge strides. From what I could see from my position, we were ascending quickly. It's not that the *Ogaré* were particularly fast in their movement, but they were relentless, and they didn't slow or pause.

Maybe if I could move like Mira, I could have done something when they grabbed us. She was also really good at talking her way out of things. Of course, I was pretty good at that, too. But not like Mira. The *Ogaré* went on and on for hours. I was tired and wished I could sleep, but it was far too uncomfortable and had way too much jostling to be able to sleep. We just had to ride it out.

As the sun began to rise, our captors stopped in front of a large hut. From my understanding, their communities didn't really have towns. They simply set up homes in the vicinity of each other. They had a main person, like a chief or a mayor. If they needed him, they went to his house. For legal issues, they went to the home of the Justice. From what they had said the night before, I guessed that's where we were now.

We were put unceremoniously in the bare space in front of the hut.

"We call for justice!" It was the same one that had spoken the night before.

After a few moments, the door to the hut opened. A gnarled *Ogaré* stepped out and looked over everyone in front of his house. He ran a hand through his wiry hair with a sigh. He sat down on his porch with his legs dangling off the edge.

"What is your grievance, Chevis?" the Justice asked.

"Blood!" Chevis answered.

"Whose blood is shed?"

Chevis motioned for a young *Ogaré* to step forward. I could see he had bandages on his chest and shoulder, and on one of his arms.

"Gaetan has been attacked!" Chevis proclaimed. "Three days ago, by a *Darakanos!* That *Darakanos!*" He pointed at Genevané.

The Justice looked at Genevané. Then he looked at me and Kiarash before he turned his attention back to Chevis.

"And these others assisted?"

"No," Chevis answered. "She came upon them yesterday and —"

"If they did not assist, then they are dismissed from this trial. Release them."

Chevis bristled at that, but Kiarash and I were freed from our bindings.

"What is the damage?" the Justice asked.

"Gaetan's shoulder was deeply injured," Chevis said. "He may never regain full use of his arm. His scars will be lifelong."

"What was the provocation?"

Chevis looked at Gaetan and then back at the Justice. "None. He was simply climbing the peaks."

"What says the accused?" asked the Justice.

Everyone looked at Genevané. She made no reaction.

"The accused offers no defense," the Justice said, "Therefore—"

"Wait a minute!" I jumped up. This wasn't justice. This was a joke. "First of all, they already wounded her with a similar injury. Do you deny that?" I asked Chevis.

"That is true," he said, "but that was in defense."

"Secondly," I turned back to the Justice, "she doesn't even know what you're saying. Dragons communicate mind to mind, not through words and language."

That much at least I'd been able to figure out in my short time with Genevané.

The Justice shrugged. "Our minds are impervious to the thoughts of others. They can neither read our minds, nor attack us with theirs."

"No one said anything about attacking," I objected. "You're about to render sentence on someone that doesn't even know what she is being accused of, and you call that justice?"

"We cannot have attacks on our people. If she does not understand, she can at least serve as a warning to others."

"I will speak for her!" I told him. "It isn't perfect, but I can understand her to a degree, and she seems to be able to understand my intent when I speak to her."

"Very well," he sighed. "Ask her if she injured the boy."

I turned to her. "Genevané." She looked at me. "Did you injure this person?"

She looked at Gaetan. I could see anger in her expression. And grief. She nodded.

"There we have it," the Justice said.

He continued speaking, but I couldn't hear his words as my mind was flooded with images... a nest... Gaetan climbing a slope... rocks, sliding and falling... a nest... an egg... grief... rage... loss... despair...

"... as we cannot have our people attacked without consequence, even by dragons, it is the judgement of this court that the accused—"

"Wait!" I interrupted.

"Now what?" The Justice looked at me.

"We call for justice!" I proclaimed.

He rolled his eyes. "You can wait until this matter is settled. Now—"

"We have a prior grievance!" I interrupted again.

"I am losing my patience," he said. "What is your prior grievance?"

"Infanticide."

All heads turned toward me when I said it.

"What is your evidence?" The Justice asked me.

I turned to Gaetan. "Three days ago, you were climbing the peaks, right?"

He nodded.

"There was a small landslide, yes? You knocked some rocks loose and it caused a slide. Right?"

He shrugged. "So? It happens. What of it?"

"What of it? You were above a nest, that's what. A nest with an egg three weeks short of hatching. And you killed it. In your negligence, you murdered her child."

I heard a soft keening and turned to look at Genevané. Tears were streaming down her face, she had her arms wrapped around herself, and she rocked back and forth. I wanted to go to her and take her in my arms, but I had to get this settled first.

"We demand justice!" I shouted.

"Gaetan," the Justice spoke. "What say you? Was there a nest?"

"I don't know!" he protested. "Maybe! I saw something down below, but what do I care if there was a nest?"

Chevis fell to his knees, "My son, what have you done?"

"The dragon's grievance has precedence," the Justice said.

"What?" Gaetan looked to his father and then back to the Justice. "But I didn't do anything. I was just climbing!"

Chevis got to his feet. He pulled a knife from his belt and held it by the blade. It was huge; for me it would have practically been a sword. He kneeled in front of Genevané and extended the hilt toward her.

"I didn't know. I grieve for your loss," he said. I could see

145

tears in his own eyes. "I ask that you take your vengeance upon me rather than my son. Please. Do not take my son."

Genevané looked at me and I repeated what he had said. She took the knife from his hands and stepped forward. She pointed the knife at his throat, and he looked at her, unflinching. He gave her a single nod. Genevané turned the knife. Grabbing the blade with her other hand, she snapped it in half and dropped the pieces in the dirt. She fell to her knees, weeping. Chevis wrapped his arms around her and held her while she cried.

I had wanted to do that for her, but now it was too late. I was angry for a moment, but let it go. That was alright; it should have been me, but as long as she was getting what she needed.

"Do you call for blood?" the Justice asked.

I didn't need to look at Genevané to know the answer. "We do not. Blood will not change anything."

"Very well," the Justice answered. "However, we cannot have our people acting irresponsibly without consequence. I will think on this and give sentence for Gaetan shortly."

With that, the Justice climbed to his feet, went into his hut, and closed the door behind him.

After several minutes, Genevané pulled back from Chevis and wiped her eyes. She walked over and put her arms around me, squeezing me in a tight hug. Why did she do that?

*Thank you.*

The message came through clear and strong. Then she let go and started walking away from the hut.

"Wait!" Chevis called. He turned to me. "Tell her, we will take you back to your camp, but we need to hear the judgement first."

I passed it on to Genevané, but she just shook her head. She turned to leave again when the door of the hut opened and the *Ogaré* Justice stepped back out, holding a staff in his hands with some sort of crystal set at the top. Genevané paused to wait.

"As has been said," the Justice spoke. "Blood and vengeance will not restore what was lost. Nor does the accused seem to have any repentance or sense of responsibility for the consequences of his actions. It is therefore my judgement that Gaetan will serve this *Darakanos*, and stay with her faithfully, until such time as she can forgive him for his actions."

"Stay with her?" I couldn't believe what I was hearing. "That's torture for her! He would be a constant reminder!"

"Perhaps," the Justice said. "Yet she will live with her pain either way. She can only escape her pain if she can find forgiveness for him. If he can earn it, it will free them both."

I was dumbfounded, and I couldn't think of anything to say to him.

He raised his staff and closed his eyes. The crystal started to glow. He opened his eyes and gestured towards Gaetan with the staff, and even I could feel the magic.

"It is done," he said. "Gaetan. I have laid the spell of your sentence upon you. Wherever you are, you will know where she is. You must serve her until she forgives you, at such time the spell will be released. You will not be able to rest if you are not in her presence or seeking to aid her or do her bidding."

Gaetan gaped at him. Then his eyes narrowed. "Yeah? And what if she dies?"

"You'd better hope she doesn't, because if she dies, from that time you will never know a moment's peace or rest until the day you die."

"What if... What if she kills me?"

"She has already refused blood and vengeance. I suggest you give her no reason to reconsider."

"I don't understand," Gaetan turned to his father. "I didn't do anything wrong!"

Chevis slapped him across the face, knocking him to the ground. Gaetan looked up at his father with disbelief.

"You killed her child!" he roared. "It is only by her mercy you breathe! At least you have a chance for a life, which is more than you gave to her child." Chevis dropped his head. "But your life will not be here. Maybe one day. If she can forgive you."

Genevané looked at me, her expression asking what was going on. When I explained, her expression turned to horror. She turned and fled the clearing.

Gaetan's face took on a pained expression. Without a word, he broke into a jog and followed her.

Chevis grabbed me, holding me in his arms as he started after Genevané and Gaetan. He called out orders to the other *Ogaré*. Over his shoulder, I saw one reach for Kiarash, but he held up his hand to stop him. Kiarash gave a shrill whistle and I saw a shadow pass overhead and Naga landed for a moment and then was flying again, Kiarash on her back.

Going back down was much faster than coming up had been. Despite their huge strides, the *Ogaré* weren't able to catch up with Genevané. But then, she *was* a *Darakanos*, so she had a lot more physical abilities than it appeared. I'd bet I could make a killing setting her up for arm wrestling matches until word got out.

The ride down was also more comfortable for me. Chevis hadn't just tossed me over his shoulder like a sack of mushrooms on the way down. He actually carried me in his arms. It might not be the most dignified way to travel, but within a couple of hours we were back at our camp.

Genevané looked up from where she sat by the fire when we got there. She had Bijoux in her hands and the kitten was luxuriating in the petting and attention she was getting.

Gaetan had arrived just before us, his breathing still ragged from his flight down the mountain after Genevané.

Kiarash was already there and had the fire going. He was pouring fresh coffee for himself. He looked at us and motioned to the pot.

"There's likely spare cups in any of the saddlebags," he said.

Good point. We really hadn't dug into them to see what all we'd inherited from the previous owners of the horses. We lucked out and a quick search turned up three cups. I didn't know how clean they were, so I gave them a rinse. I tossed a cup to Chevis. I tossed one to Gaetan as well, trying to keep my face as neutral as possible. None of us were thrilled by his presence. I poured a cup for Genevané and handed it to her. She smiled and took a sip. She nodded and took another.

I noticed that as she looked around, her eyes avoided Gaetan's direction. Maybe that was how she was going to deal with him. Just ignore him. That was only going to work for so long, but this was something she would have to work through. I didn't envy Gaetan, either, but I felt no sympathy for him.

"May I ask where you are going?" Chevis spoke over his coffee.

"Well," I answered, "Kiarash and I are on our way to Su Lariano. We only met Genevané yesterday. I don't have any idea what her plans are." I looked at her as I spoke. "Of course, she is welcome to come along with us if she wants."

She met my eyes for a moment and then she turned her attention back to Bijoux and her coffee.

"I don't know why she hasn't shifted back to her dragon form," I said.

"The wound, maybe," Kiarash guessed. "From what I understand, it's easier to shift out of dragon form, stashing the extra body mass in some magical pocket, than it is to change back and pull all that back into the world. And with that wound, it could be too difficult."

"Hm," I mused. "You'd think it would be the other way around, that it would be easier to revert to their normal form."

He shrugged, "Maybe both forms are their normal form. Like sitting or standing for us. Both are normal, but it can be easier to sit down than to get back up. I'm no expert though."

"Are we just going to sit here talking and drinking coffee like nothing's happening?" Gaetan demanded.

"You don't want coffee?" I shrugged. "Don't drink coffee."

"Father." He turned to Chevis. "There has to be some way to break this bond. I can't just follow her around everywhere like a lost lamb."

Chevis shook his head. "You can no easier find a way to break the bond as you could find a way to restore what you destroyed."

"Destroyed? But—"

"Gaetan!" Chevis silenced his son. "At this moment you are fortunate that she cannot see your thoughts. But if you continue with this nonsense that you did nothing wrong, at some point she will see your words in their thoughts." He indicated me and Kiarash with a motion of his cup. "If she decides to take vengeance on you, no one will be able to help you. Mind your tongue!"

I could see the anger and the rebellion in Gaetan's eyes, but he stopped talking.

"She may continue to travel with them as she heals, or even after," Chevis went on, "or she may not. She may return to her people. She may travel across the sea. She may choose to live in the icy peaks of the Great Mountains as a recluse. Wherever you go, whoever you meet, remember that you represent the *Ogaré* and our clan. Do you hear me?"

"Yes, father," Gaetan's eyes were on the ground.

"Do not dishonor us."

We heard a sound and looked up to see another of the *Ogaré* arriving. It was a woman, and she carried a backpack and had an enormous walking stick in one hand. She took the backpack off as she approached Gaetan.

"I packed what I could for you, my son," she said. She set the pack and the walking stick near him.

"Mother, I—" He couldn't meet her gaze. "I didn't mean to do anything, I—"

"You may not have had malicious intent," she said, "but the results of your actions cannot be denied. We must accept responsibility for our actions and their consequences. Always. Even if those consequences were unintended."

"Yes, mother."

She gave him a hug and stepped back. "I hope I will see you

again one day," a single tear traced its way down her cheek, "but every day I will think of you and hold you in my heart."

Chevis set his cup down and walked to stand next to Gaetan. He put his massive hand on the boy's shoulder.

"Make us proud, son. Be the *Ogaré* we know you can be." Chevis turned his head to look at me and gave me a nod. Then he and his mate turned and walked back toward the mountain.

# CHAPTER EIGHTEEN

## MIRA

*A*fter breakfast, I headed to the Royal Practice Room where Tesia and I had been holding our daily training sessions. I'd been spending a lot of time in that room, since I worked with her during the day and most evenings I would go back for physical training. I needed to get better with the longsword of the White Riders. There was no question in my mind that I was going to need to be at the top of my game when I faced the White Riders.

When I got there, Tesia wasn't alone. Gylan and Neelu were there with her.

"Good morning, Mira," Gylan said when I stepped in. "I hope you don't mind my intrusion, but I wanted to show you your armor."

"Come see it!" Tesia was excited. "It's beautiful!"

I walked over to the table where the pieces were laid out. I'd only seen a glimpse of the Rider's armor in my wagon, but there seemed to be more to what I was seeing here.

"I took some liberties," Gylan was saying, "so there are some differences to the armor you inherited."

"I don't really know anything about armor," I told him. "Would you mind explaining it to me?"

"Of course!" he said. "First of all, regular leather armor isn't very protective. Layered cloth armor, a gambeson, works a lot better. But the Riders use leather armor that's been hardened into a protective shell using a special white resin, and that's even better. So, we have a hard breastplate and backplate here." He pointed. "This alone can be as strong as mail armor. I have used similar hardened leather for the pauldrons, here, to protect your shoulders and upper arms. And bracers to cover your forearms. But I was worried after our last talk, about the weak points under the arms. That's why I have the pauldrons fixed to a gambeson that you will wear under the chest and back plates."

That made sense. Especially in view of how I'd killed that Rider.

"As you can see," he went on. "I maintained the white color for all the big pieces of hardened leather, I brought black in for the gambeson and some of the other pieces."

I saw what he meant. Even the white pieces were trimmed in black. And there was a sort of skirt of overlapping pieces that would cover much of my thighs, each a few inches wide, that alternated black and white. I could also see that he had added some kind of artwork to the plates, and I looked closer.

"Ravens!"

"Yes." He nodded. "The *balangur*. I used variations of some classic designs."

The breastplate and backplate each had two large ravens, *balangur*, one on the left and one on the right. The ones on the back were viewing the ravens from behind, kind of like how they were on the hilts of my daggers. The ones of the front were viewing the ravens from the front in similar positions, wings up away from the body, but not like they were in flight, more like they were ready.

"This is beautiful work!" I told him. "How do I put it on?"

"It can be worn over your shirt," he said, "but it doesn't need to be. Do you want to try it on now?"

I didn't need to be asked twice. I'd long since gotten over any shyness, so I pulled off my leather shirt, leaving just my sports bra.

"You should be able to get into this by yourself, but I'll help you for now to get the idea."

First, I got into the gambeson. The pauldrons on the shoulders would tighten down, but only after I got the plates on so they could slide under the edge of the pauldrons.

"You can wear the plates without the gambeson and pauldrons," he said, "so you have options for when you don't need everything."

"Sometimes, armor is worn for show or to deliver a message," Neelu told me. "Other times, you need full protection."

The sleeves of the gambeson cloth ended just under the edge of the bracers that wrapped all the way around my forearms.

The hardened leather greaves went on my shins. The skirt I had seen belted around the waist on the bottom of the chest and backplates. The gambeson also hung underneath it.

"I thought this would be a lot hotter to wear," I said.

"It would be," Tesia grinned, "but I imbued it with a spell that would help maintain your body temperature, and even wick away any sweat. I also reinforced the armor and put in resistance to heat or cold."

"You know," Neelu commented, "This is better than any of our existing armor. This is truly a work of art."

"The final touches," Gylan said. He pulled out a jet-black cloth and attached it above my shoulders. "The Riders attach a white cape," he said, "but I thought you would like this better."

"You're right." I nodded.

"Your daggers." He picked them up from where I'd put them when I took off my shirt. "They will slide into place here."

He'd designed the breastplate to hold my daggers in place over my right hip.

"Your longsword will hang here on your left," he showed me, "and lastly, there are these."

He handed me a pair of gloves. I pulled them on, and they fit perfectly. They were black, except for the underside of the palms and fingers, which were white. The leather over the knuckles was hardened. They had cuffs that extended several inches past my wrists.

"There's a light helmet, too," he said, "and it's padded and reinforced."

"Gylan, Tesia." I looked back and forth between them. "I don't know what to say. I knew I'd need armor for the Riders, but I never imagined it would be like this."

Gylan grinned, "I'm glad you like it. I'll let you get back to your training."

"Thank you, Gylan!" I gave him an awkward hug before he left.

"Are you ready for today's training?" Tesia asked.

"Sure," I answered. "Just let me get this—"

"On, no." Neelu grinned. "You need to get used to wearing it. And you need to get used to fighting with weapons while you are fending off magical attacks. That's why we're both here."

The look on her face told me that she was planning to have some fun at my expense. I was definitely going to need to keep the armor on today.

After lunch it was even worse. They brought Mooren in. Neelu came at me with a staff, Mooren used his *shyngur*, and Tesia attacked me with magic. And I was using the longsword, which I was still trying to learn.

I was pretty good at using a style of staff fighting where I worked the staff from one end with both hands. I was able to incorporate a lot of that technique with the longsword. At first, I was afraid the longsword would be hard to use because it was heavier than a one-handed sword. Since I was using two hands to hold it, it was no problem. The longsword I had inherited from the White Rider was made for an *Ashae*, so it was even longer than a regular longsword but still shorter than the staff I was used to. The practice sword I was using was created to the same scale, weight, and balance, but I wouldn't have to worry about cutting anyone.

Neelu kept getting faster and faster while Mooren attacked with his *shyngur,* and Tesia would move around to throw a magical attack at me from behind or the side or from anywhere I wouldn't expect it.

I held onto the *Ralahin* vision without even trying at this point; it was just *there.* I was able to sense Tesia's attacks even when I didn't have line-of-sight.

"Move faster!" Neelu yelled.

Neelu was so fast, even without flitting. She was using the *Ralahin* to assist her speed, but was using standard *Ulané Jhinura* techniques. She hadn't used the "Neelu flit" against me yet. Suddenly she was behind me, and I felt the impact of her staff on my ribs hard enough to break bone if I hadn't been wearing armor.

I feinted a strike at Mooren and spun to launch at Neelu. She was already coming at me again though, and my strike shifted into a block. I saw Mooren coming at me again and took three steps back to keep both of them in view. Tesia sent a lightning bolt at me, and I redirected it to the ground in front of Mooren's feet. Neelu was gone from where she'd been an instant before, and I swept my sword behind me and felt it make contact. Then I flitted to stand behind Tesia, my practice sword resting on her shoulder.

Neelu laughed. "Nicely done!"

"Does that mean we can take a rest now?" I asked through ragged breath.

"Yes, I think we can call it a day. Besides," she said, "Don't you have something to get ready for this evening?"

She was right. Tonight, would be the opening event at the Raven's Nest.

"You know," she went on. "I think at this point we can say that my geas to you has been fulfilled. You have learned to fight, and you have learned to flit."

"But I'm not nearly as good as you!" I objected.

She shook her head, smiling. "*That* wasn't part of the deal."

"I know." I laughed. "I've learned all of that and more. Thank you, Neelu. And thank you too, Tesia, for all the help learning magic."

"You've only scratched the surface with magic," she said. "There is more studying in your future."

"But not today." I laughed. "I'll see you all at the Nest tonight, right?"

"Of course!" Neelu smiled. "Even my mother will be there! She's cutting the ribbon."

I headed back to my rooms and took a long shower to wash away the sweat and loosen my muscles. In keeping with the theme of the Raven's Nest and my persona as Raven, tonight I would dress in my all-black leathers, with a black cloak and the audacious hat Rispan had picked for me. One addition would be the gloves I'd just received from Gylan; they'd be tucked under my belt.

Not a lot of *Ulané Jhinura* knew me — Not taking the entire population of the city into account. A number of the higher-ups knew me, and of course everyone I'd trained with or had duty with. The persona of Raven would be a good one to use to draw attention. My job was to be gregarious and flamboyant and give the people of Su Lariano a non-*Urgaban* face to alloy the entrance of an *Urgaban* business into the city.

As Raven, I would be the public face of the restaurant. In return, I got a full partnership. That partnership also allowed the business to have a more diverse ownership, which was another strategic idea from Bavrana. Fully dressed for the part, I headed to Market Square.

Neelu mentioned that Astrina would be cutting the ribbon. I'd asked at one point if there was going to be a ribbon-cutting, but apparently this wasn't a concept known here. Bavrana liked it though and immediately started to incorporate it into her plans. A wide red ribbon was stretched across the front of the restaurant. I ducked under and went in the door.

There was a short counter just inside and a small waiting area. The room beyond was essentially divided into four areas. To the left was the bar. In the center were tables for diners. Beyond the tables was an open area for dancing with a small stage for live music. To the right were a few alcoves that allowed parties to either look out over the room and watch the performance or close off the space to provide them with more privacy. The best one of these was permanently reserved for any member of the Royal household. This is where Astrina's party would be seated tonight, or any night they came to the restaurant.

Mouse was sitting at a nearby table, wearing his finest clothes. He looked up when I walked in, and I joined him. He'd been granted several days of furlough to handle the opening.

"I feel like I should be doing something," he said, "but everything is in place and ready to go. Jakeda is running the kitchen like a precision drill-team. All the food prep is done. Our staff is trained and ready to start. We're just counting down until time to open."

"Are you nervous?"

He looked at me like I was crazy, and then started laughing. It was so loud and uncontrolled that it was contagious, and I started laughing with him. I didn't know what was so funny, but we couldn't stop, and I could barely breathe.

"What's so funny?" I gasped out between breaths as we started to slow down.

This just launched him into another fit of hysterical laughter.

"Nervous?" he managed to get out. "Why — what's to be nervous about?" He couldn't catch his breath. "It's only the queen! And every other important person in the city!"

It took a few minutes before we could settle down, and I had to avoid looking at him.

"Hooooooooo." I breathed out, finally getting control. "Okay, that's the last time I ask *that* question."

This brought another round, but more subdued.

"Mouse." I put a hand on his arm. "You guys have got this. You have a great team here ready to make everything happen. The menu is incredible. Plus the decor — the fusion of *Urgaban* and *Ulané Jhinura* styles is masterful. This is going to be awesome!"

As the hour got closer, wait staff started to show up to get ready. We were to have a brief ceremony to cut the ribbon at the end of the dinner hour. It was timed that way to allow people to get ready after their daily work or duties.

A crowd had started to gather outside, and everyone was taking their places. Finally, it was time. First, Astrina addressed the crowd. Bavrana and I stood to one side, Neelu and Grangor to the other side.

"Good evening, people of Su Lariano," Astrina smiled out at the crowd. They cheered in response, and she waited until she could speak again. "I know you are hungry, so I will keep this short. Raven's Nest is not just a restaurant, it is a beginning. It is the start of a new era of peace and prosperity between *Ulané Jhinura* and *Urgaban*. This doesn't mean that all problems will just go away. Raven's Nest is not a cure-all. After all, it's just a restaurant. But it's not *just* a restaurant. Raven, a citizen of Su Lariano, and Bavrana of Pokorah-Vo have come together to bring you true wonders to delight the palate. It is their spirit of cooperation which we hope will bring all of our peoples together."

I looked out over the cheering crowd and smiling faces. With the extra tables, we could serve about two hundred people. We had also paid to distribute complimentary beverages and snacks from carts around Market Square. There were at least five hundred people gathered around.

As we started to move into position for the ribbon cutting, I saw a different kind of movement at the far end of the crowd. Someone was shoving past people and trying to run through the throng.

"As we cut this ribbon," the queen was saying, "we open more than merely the doors to this establishment."

Something about the figure was familiar. I had split my attention between the figure and the queen, slicing the great red ribbon with an oversized pair of shears.

The figure was waving its arms and shouting something, and I couldn't make it out. Then I heard one word.

"Assassin!"

I quickly seized the *Ralahin* vision and looked around. Everyone was smiling and shaking each other's hands. Grangor smiled and stepped towards Astrina. Something was wrong. With the *Ralahin* vision, Grangor was not right. As he neared Astrina, I saw him slide a knife into his hand and he lunged forward.

# CHAPTER NINETEEN

## RISPAN

*B*ijoux was growing fast. When she gets much bigger, I wouldn't be able to keep her under my shirt anymore. Already she would tend to poke her head out so she could look around as we rode. She was also eating more and more, and that must have helped her growth spurt. Of course, I really had no idea how fast *jahgreet* were supposed to grow. Bijoux had made friends with Genevané and tolerated Kiarash, but Gaetan had made no effort to become acquainted with her.

Gaetan was *Ogaré*; he was huge. How someone could avoid seeing him for so long was beyond me. But Genevané managed it. Day-in, day-out as we continued north. It was as if he didn't exist for her. Gaetan didn't talk much, either. This made the days more than a bit awkward, but eventually we got used to it. With his stature and stride, it wasn't difficult for him to keep up with the horses.

Genevané hadn't let me know how long she was going to stay with us. Her shoulder seemed much better. Evidently, dragons were fast healers. She stayed with us, which I was glad for, but I still hadn't seen any clear signals as to what was on her mind. I was usually pretty good at knowing what was in a woman's head, but she was hard to read, and that made me hesitate. She had gotten better at communicating with me and understanding what I was saying when I spoke to anyone. But she didn't seem to be the talkative type.

The days wore on uneventfully and we finally started to angle west as the mountains to our left fell away into gently rolling hills and oak trees. Soon, I would be back in Su Lariano.

Kiarash landed in front of us on the trail only halfway through the afternoon.

"There's a camp ahead," he told me. "There are a couple of *Ulané Jhinura* there. It looks like the site has seen a lot of previous use."

I nodded. "I know the spot. Only two of them?"

"From what I saw."

"Were they wearing uniforms or something like that?" I asked.

"No." He shook his head. "Nothing particular. And definitely not alike."

"Alright. Let's approach quietly and see what we're dealing with. We can't assume they're friendly just because they're *Ulané Jhinura*. We're no more perfect than anyone else."

When we drew close to the camp, I dismounted and handed Bijoux to Genevané. I didn't know what we were facing and didn't want the kitten distracting me. Leaving the others behind, I crept forward through the trees. I came upon the camp sooner than expected; I thought I had stopped further away. When I looked, I only saw one person fiddling with a fire. No one else was in sight. I could see several horses though, both for riding and for carrying the packs I saw sitting nearby.

I started to inch forward for a better view and felt something very sharp and pointed press against my back.

"Hold it right there," a voice said from behind me. I froze in place. "Got him!" he called out.

The *Ulané Jhinura* at the fire got to his feet with a grin. "I knew there was someone out there."

"Move forward," the voice at my back told me, "and go slowly or I'll make you into a pincushion."

I slowly made my way to the fire, the point of his sword a constant pressure on my back. It had already cut into the skin, and I could feel blood start to drip down from the wound.

"Now sit down slowly," he said when we reached the fire, "and keep your hands on your knees."

"Who are you?" the other one asked, sitting across from me, "and what are you doing here and why were you trying to sneak up on us?"

"I'm nobody. Just a hunter," I told them. "I didn't know who was down here, so I thought it would be better to get a look first."

"Hunter, eh?" He looked at me. "Where's your bow?"

"I use traps. For the pelts."

"You said hunter, not trapper. I don't see no pelts, either." He eyed me suspiciously. "Where are they?"

"You think I'm stupid?" I asked him. "I tell you where my pelts are, and you'll probably just steal them and sell them yourself. Not going to happen."

He chuckled, "You're not a very trusting sort, are you? Maybe because you know what you'd do in our shoes, eh? Kill the trapper and steal the pelts? Maybe that's how you got them in the first place. You don't look like a trapper to me."

He stood up. "I guess we better tie you up for now." He pointed at his companion. "Shok here is a pretty good tracker. Quiet on his feet, too. But you found that out already." He grinned. "He could follow your trail back to wherever you have your pelts. If we cared about them."

"You don't care about money?"

"I didn't say that, boy." He chuckled. "Stealing pelts is small-time. We're in the big-time now, eh, Shok?" He winked at his companion.

Shok just looked at me like he was still ready to stick me with his sword.

"Big-time, huh?" I was intrigued, but not for the reasons I would let them think. "Maybe you've got room for one more. I knew a guy once." I made up the story as I went. "Pickpocket. He ended up working as a spy for the queen. Easy work and it paid big."

"Ha!" he jeered. "Your friend's going to need to find a new boss, soon."

"Why's that?"

"That's the problem with bosses." He was definitely amused by his own wit. "The minute they stop breathing, they stop paying."

"Queen Astrina'u is dead?"

"Not yet." He winked. "But it won't be long now."

"Serves her right." I nodded. "I always thought she was a pretty smug old bitch."

"Got that right!"

"That's gotta be hard to pull off though," I mused. "Poison?"

He was still suspicious of me, and his eyes narrowed. Then he glanced at the sun, lowering in the sky. "I s'pose I can tell you. Nothing anyone can do about it now. They're going to drive a knife through her shriveled heart. And all nice and public, too!"

"No way," I scoffed at him. "She always has guards around. No one could get close with a knife. Especially not in public. Maybe if they found a way to sneak into her room and wait. But in public? She's too well-protected. You're putting me on."

"They could if they was already close." He gave me a knowing look. "If they looked like somebody friendly. Why do you think we're sittin' out here? They'll sneak out here after and we'll take them north."

"I still don't buy it." I shook my head. "I'm no assassin, but that sounds like suicide. Even if they succeed, they wouldn't be able to sneak away. And she's never in public anyway. Maybe somebody is putting you on."

"You think yer pretty smart, eh?" He glared at me. "You ain't been in town in a while, have you? There's a big to-do going on today."

*Today?*

"Something about opening a restaurant selling a bunch of that grubby *Urgaban* mess," he went on, "but it'll look like an *Urgaban* killing her. We got war coming, boy!"

They must be opening that restaurant Bavrana wanted. And they had someone close to kill the queen. When? I sent a plea to Genevané, hoping she would be able to receive it. It was just a burst of emotion, desperation, need, urgency.

"It sounds like the plan is all worked out," I said.

"Aye." He nodded. "But I still don't trust you. And I'm talking too much. I think we're going to need to take care of you. Permanent-like."

"So." I grinned. I leaned forward, bringing my hands together. "You don't want to make me a partner?" I kept throwing knives on my firearms under my shirtsleeves. Shifting my position had put them in easy reach.

"I'm Rispan," I told him. "What did you say your name was?"

"Rugan," he answered. "But—"

"I said keep your hands on your knees!" Shok growled at me.

Just then, we heard the sound of heavy steps and cracking branches coming quickly through the trees. Both of them turned to look in the direction of the sound. I took the opportunity and put a knife into Shok's neck, and he fell to the ground. Rugan reached for his blade, but I put a knife to his throat and his hand stopped moving, his eyes were very large.

Gaetan burst into the clearing and looked around.

"Thank you, Gaetan." That was a perfectly timed distraction. I turned back to my former captor. "Who is the assassin? What do they look like?"

"I don't know!" His eyes shifted between me and the blade. "They never said!"

"You seemed to know a lot." I pushed slightly with the blade. "You expect me to believe you don't know that?"

"They had to tell us that much to get us to believe they could do it," he licked his lips, "but they wouldn't say no more."

Kiarash landed with Naga and was looking back and forth between us. Then he wasted no time in producing some rope and started tying Rugan's hands behind his back. I was glad Rugan had never got around to tying mine.

"When will it happen?" I asked him. "If you lie, I will slit you open from bottom to top."

"There's some kind of opening ceremony," he said. "End of the dinner hour. You're too late. There's nothing you can do."

Genevané stepped into the clearing and stopped. Seeing me, she walked forward.

There had to be something I could do. I looked at Kiarash. Maybe he could fly on Naga and get there in time. But no one knew him. Even if he could arrive before it happened, it would take too long for anyone to believe him and do anything. I looked at Genevané. What about her? Could she carry me in dragon form?

"Genevané," I said to her. I tried to keep my thoughts focused and clear. "This is an emergency, or I would not ask. Can you carry me to Su Lariano in your *Darakanos* form? Please!"

Most of Su Lariano loved our queen. There was never a question that she cared about the people or that she was putting their interests first. It would be a crushing blow if we lost her.

Genevané carried Bijoux to Kiarash and handed her to him. At first, Bijoux fought it, but Genevané put her hand on Bijoux's head, and she settled down. Then Genevané stripped off her clothing. In a moment, she was no longer a woman, but a huge dragon. Blue and gold scales glistened in the light of the setting sun. Even in dragon form, she was beautiful and magnificent.

I turned to Kiarash, "Follow behind."

Gaetan was gingerly picking up Genevané's discarded clothing.

"Can you bring that with you, please?" I pointed to Rugan. Gaetan nodded.

"Alright," I said to Genevané. "Try not to drop me." She seemed to be amused and lowered her head for me to climb on. Wait until Mira sees this; she thought Farukan was big!

Words formed in my head from Genevané, "*Hold on!*"

With that, she launched into the air.

The view from above was different from anything I was used to. I could understand why Kiarash was so happy to have Naga. I wasn't able to really appreciate the experience though; I was too worried that we might not be there in time.

With long sweeps of her great wings, Genevané pushed us forward and the trees rushed by below us. In the distance, we could see the mountain that housed the city of Su Lariano. I sent her a mental image of the front gates. She sent feelings of assurance in return and my connection with Genevané was stronger than ever.

I didn't know the exact time, but I was afraid we were already into the dinner hour. Every second as we drew nearer to the city gate was excruciating. Finally, Genevané was landing in front of the gates. I could see the alarmed guards preparing to fend off an attack. As we landed, Genevané shifted back to her other form.

I ran to the guards, yelling to them, "I'm Rispan with IIB! Sound the alarm! There is a plot to assassinate the queen! Notify General Dzurala!"

Genevané, nude, was right behind me.

"She's with me!" I yelled. Then I was off and running with Genevané on my heels. "We have two more coming!"

I went down the tunnels and made my way toward Market Square. I wished I could flit like Neelu or Mira. But I couldn't move faster than any other *Ulané Jhinura*. I didn't even know where in Market Square they would be. That wasn't a problem though, because once I reached the Square, I could see the gathering of people. Maybe I was in time after all!

I headed for where everyone seemed to be focused. Someone was saying something, and the crowd was cheering. I thought I could recognize some of the people at the front.

"Mira!" I shouted, trying to push my way through the crowd. "Neelu!"

The crowd was too loud. One of the people at the front was wearing a big black hat. Mira! I kept pushing forward, waving, and calling to her.

"Mira! Mira! There's an assassin!"

The figure that must have been Mira seemed to respond. I could see her turn and look around her. I was closer now and I could see the queen. Suddenly, Mira was gone from where she'd been standing. Then she was standing in front of the queen pushing someone away and toward the edge of the crowd. I just got through the front row, when people started moving forward to go in the doors to the restaurant. They hadn't seen what happened.

The person Mira had grabbed flashed between two images. One was Grangor, and the other was one I didn't recognize; it settled on the second one. I could see one of Mira's daggers embedded in the assassin's chest. Neelu and Mooren were rushing toward her, apparently the only ones who had noticed. The assassin fell and Mira turned. When she did, I saw the assassin's blade lodged in her stomach. She fell to her knees as Neelu and Mooren reached her. I got there right behind them.

"Rispan!" Mira grabbed me and pulled me close. "I was so worried! Um… Who's your naked friend?"

A couple of the guard detail had evidently seen Neelu and Mooren rush to Mira and had followed them.

"We need a healer!" Neelu shouted to one. "Quickly!"

"See?" Mira said to Mooren. "It's not me. He's the real trouble magnet."

Then her eyes closed.

# CHAPTER TWENTY

## RISPAN

*I* could see she was still breathing, and my moment of panic passed. It seemed like aside from Neelu, Mooren and the two guards, no one else realized what had happened. Genevané standing naked by the line seemed to draw a number of curious glances as they walked by. It served as a good distraction though and none of them noticed Mira or the fallen assassin, though they were well off to the side. Genevané in turn was shifting her attention to all of the people around us. I wondered what kind of experience the flood of minds would be for her. One of the guards had gone to get a healer. The other took off his jacket and handed it to Genevané. She looked at me.

I nodded to her, and she put her arms through the sleeves. It was a little small, but it would do for now. She turned her attention back to the people in front of the entry.

A unit of guards was pushing their way through the advancing crowd. People were being let into the restaurant, but they hadn't formed a line outside the door, so it was a jumble of bodies, all focused on the entry. Neelu motioned to the guards when they got to the front.

"We had word there was an assassin after the queen," he said. From his breathing and the sweat of his face, I could tell he'd been running. "But there was confusion on where to send aid. Word went to the palace and the throne room. Guards were dispatched, but minutes were lost before we were directed here."

"It's not your fault, Tree," Neelu told him. "The queen is inside. She is safe."

He looked at Mira, all in black. "Is that the assassin?"

"No," Neelu told him. "This is the queen's savior." She pointed, "*That* is the assassin. Please have a couple of your men go to the queen. The rest should remain here to block the view."

The earlier guard had returned with a healer.

"That was fast," Neelu said to him. "Well done."

"Healer Lacela was waiting to get in," he answered. "I recognized her from — it doesn't matter."

Lacela was already crouched next to Mira and focusing on her. She reached for the dagger and with excruciating slowness, began to pull it out. She got it halfway and paused.

"I have to heal each part as I draw the blade," she explained, taking a breath. "The blade is preventing her from bleeding too much. If I just pull it out, she will die. But this is very tiring for me."

"You can do it though, right?" I asked her.

She nodded. "I have been trained for this. Now, let me focus."

She put her attention back on Mira and continued the process.

My lungs felt on fire, and I realized I was holding my breath. I felt a hand on my shoulder and looked up. It was Genevané. She was flowing support and assurance to me. Her strength helped to calm me down. I nodded thanks to her and turned back to watch Lacela.

Finally, the dagger was all the way out and Lacela staggered to her feet.

"It is done," she said, "but the healing is not complete. She is not stable. I can do no more without rest. She can be moved, carefully. And she needs to see another healer right away."

"Thank you, Healer Lacela," Neelu said to her.

Lacela looked embarrassed. "I am only a student," he said, "and I assist at the hospital. I did not mean to deceive you, but there was no time."

"You did well," Neelu assured her. "You will be commended to your instructor."

"Did you see what happened?" I asked Neelu.

She shook her head. "I only saw that Mira seemed to be pushing someone away from my mother. I didn't realize what was happening until it was over." She looked at the body of the assassin. It was a *Loiala Fé*. "I didn't see this person anywhere near, though."

"That's because he didn't look like that," I told her. "He looked like Grangor."

Neelu's eyes widened. "Then where is —" She turned to the guard in charge of the detail. "Send a unit immediately to Grangor's quarters! He may be in danger or injured!"

We waited while additional healers were brought in, with a stretcher. The crowd before the entry had thinned to almost nothing as they had made their way into the Raven's Nest. The healers were just lifting the stretcher when Mouse came out.

"Mira." He was smiling. "Where are you? The—" His expression changed when he saw the stretcher. Shéna had come out right behind him. Her eyes lit up when she saw me, but then she looked at Genevané and then back to me. She turned and went back inside.

"What happened?" Mouse asked.

"Mira saved the queen," I told him. "That's what happened."

Mouse's eyes got very big. Then his expression shifted again. "Rispan! You live!"

Suddenly his arms were around me and I could barely breathe.

"Let me go you big oaf!" I pounded on his back. "I'm happy to see you, too."

He gave another squeeze which I thought was going to break ribs before he let me go.

"She thought you were dead, you know," he told me. "She never said it, but I could see it in her eyes whenever someone spoke your name."

I could easily imagine what she'd been going through. I'd just had a taste of it myself, thinking she was going to die in front of me. And if Lacela hadn't been so close, that's probably what would have happened.

"We almost lost her," I said to him, shaking my head. "Almost."

Mouse looked torn as he watched the stretcher move away, glancing back in the restaurant. I noticed that he was dressed finer than I'd ever seen him.

"You're all dressed up," I commented.

"I'm the manager," he said, distractedly, his eyes still on Mira.

That explained his look of indecision. "Don't worry, brother," I told him. "There is nothing you can do for her. Take care of the restaurant.

Another group of guards was approaching. Among them I could see Kiarash. Gaetan's immense form dwarfed them all. Gaetan immediately stepped forward and put Genevané's clothes on the ground in front of her. Without looking at him, she stooped to pick them up and quickly got dressed.

"Sorry for the delay," Kiarash said, pushing his way through the guards. "We had to see to Naga. And turn over our prisoner. And these," he gestured to the guards, "weren't sure we were really with you."

"More friends?" Neelu asked.

"Well," I grinned at her, "let's just say I have a tale to tell."

"Don't you always?" She arched her eyebrow at me.

Dzurala stepped out of the restaurant and saw us standing around. Then her eyes fell on the dead assassin.

"Felgor," Neelu said to Mouse. "Give my apologies to the queen. I will not be able to join her after all."

"I think that includes me," Dzurala put in. "Though I was very much looking forward to the meal." She looked at the group of us, her eyes lingering on Genevané. "Shall we go to my office?"

"I'll see that food is sent for all of you," Mouse said. "I promise you won't go hungry." He winked at me. "For you and your friends, too."

We all followed Dzurala to the IIB offices. Once we had arrived in the waiting area outside her office, she turned around.

"I don't mean to be rude," she said, "but if you don't mind, I would like to speak with Neelu'u and Rispan privately first. You three can relax here. I don't think it will be too long before Felgor has sent food from Raven's Nest."

Kiarash jumped on a nearby couch with a grin and put his feet up. "Fine by me! I can use a rest after this day."

Gaetan was already having trouble in the room with the ceilings not being built for his height. He squatted and sat down against one of the walls.

Dzurala turned to her aide, who sat at a desk near the door to Dzurala's personal office.

"There should be some food coming soon," she told him. "Meanwhile, please see to the needs of our guests."

Dzurala turned and went into her office, motioning us past. She gave a surprised look when Genevané followed me in.

"I'm sorry," Dzurala said to her, "but this is to be a private conversation—"

"It won't do any good," I cut in. "Genevané can read our minds from the next room."

"I see." Dzurala scowled and closed the door behind us.

We all took a seat, Dzurala behind her desk.

"Can we start with what just happened?" she asked.

"I think I'd better let Rispan tell it," Neelu said.

I shrugged. "There was an assassin. He used some kind of spell to look like Grangor. I was able to warn Mira in time and she stopped it. But she was injured in the process." I thought back over what I'd seen. "I think she must have flitted between the assassin and the queen. She was one place, and then suddenly she was next to the queen and pushing the assassin away."

"She must have practically impaled herself on the assassin's blade," Neelu commented. Then she looked at Dzurala, "I sent some guards to check on Grangor."

"How did you know to warn her?" Dzurala asked me.

"Oh, I'd found out about the plot at the trader camp in the forest," I explained. "There were a couple of guys there waiting to take the assassin and whoever north."

"So, our assassin has confederates in Su Lariano?"

"That's what it sounded like." I nodded. "As soon as I found out, I came as fast as I could. Fortunately, Genevané helped."

Dzurala blinked for a moment before speaking. She glanced at Genevané and back to me. "She is *Darakanos*, yes?"

I nodded.

"And she… When you say she helped…"

"She gave me a ride in her dragon form," I said. "Otherwise, we'd never have made it in time."

"And you asked her to do this for you?"

"Yes." I nodded. "We didn't have much time. She didn't seem to mind. Why?"

"What do you know of *Darakanos*?" she asked me.

"Nothing really," I said. "Just that they don't speak like we do. They communicate mind to mind. And even that's not with words, it's… different."

"*Darakanos* are extremely private," Dzurala told me. "Asking her for that level of what they would view as physical intimacy is akin to a proposal of marriage. And her agreement would be taken as her response. The act itself would be the consummation of that agreement."

"*What?*" Panicked, I jumped up from my chair. "I'm married?"

I looked at Genevané. She just looked back at me with wide, unreadable eyes.

Truth be told, I knew I had been developing feelings for Genevané. I was enchanted from the first time I saw her. But marriage was something else altogether.

"Genevané," I asked, "Are we married?"

"*You have to ask?*" The thought came to me very clearly. Dzurala's surprised reaction told me she had heard it, too. "*Did our bonding flight mean that little to you?*"

"No! I— Wait, how are you communicating so clearly with me now?"

"*All those people at once. All those minds and their thoughts. It allowed me to absorb your language in a way that would not have been possible otherwise.*"

"That's great!" I said, "I—"

"*You are changing the subject!*" Her face was like stone.

"I think you've met your match, Rispan," Neelu had an evil glint in her eye as she said it. "Literally."

I gasped for words like a fish out of water, but nothing came to me.

Genevané stood stiffly and stared at me through narrowed eyes. Then she fell into a fit of laughter, and it washed over me as she looked at me with what seemed like affection.

"*No, dear one,*" she said, stepping closer to me. "*We are not married. I fully knew your intent when you asked for my help. You were honorable at all times.*"

"Rispan was honorable?"

I ignored Neelu's question.

"It's not that I don't care for you—" I started.

"*I know.*" She smiled. "*And I care for you.*" She put her hands on my face and kissed me briefly on the lips. "*But we have different paths; we are not to be mates.*"

She turned and started for the door.

"You're leaving?" Things were suddenly happening very quickly. "But why? And what about Gaetan?"

Her head dropped for a moment. *"He is my burden to bear."* Then she looked back at me. *"But know this Rispan nya Su Lariano, we are not bonded in marriage, but we ARE bonded, me to you and you to me. I will see you again. And..."* I felt an intensity take hold of me. *"You owe me a debt!"* The intensity fell away, and she glanced at Neelu and Dzurala. *"This is an interesting city, and you have interesting friends."* She turned and went through the door.

She snapped her fingers at Gaetan. He looked up at her, surprised. She motioned him to follow. He scrambled to his feet, and they went out the door and disappeared down the corridor.

"Rispan, close the door please." Dzurala's tone was softer than usual.

# CHAPTER TWENTY-ONE

## RISPAN

*A*s I closed the door, I felt like the bottom had dropped out of my stomach. These last few weeks on the road with Genevané had been very different for me somehow. Now that she'd left, I knew I would miss her. I'd never felt such loss before. That brought me up short. Did I love her? I didn't know. Maybe so. But it didn't matter. Like she said, *we have different paths. We are not to be mates.* I sat heavily back in my chair.

"Are you ready to continue?" Dzurala asked me.

I blinked at her, focusing back on the matter at hand. "Yes. Sorry."

"Alright," she said. "Those were the specifics of what happened today. How about we go to the beginning?"

"I'm guessing you already got reports from Mira and the others?" I asked.

She nodded at that.

"And I'm assuming that Korashéna came back with them?"

"You mean Korashéna Ulané Sharavi nya Su Astonil?" she asked with an arched eyebrow.

"Uh, yeah." I nodded. "I heard about that later." Her bland expression told me I needed to stay focused. "Okay," I said. "Then I'll fill in the missing pieces, and there are a lot of them."

I started going through everything that had happened since I'd left Korashéna with Mira and Gralbast. When I got to the part about Kiarash, Dzurala interrupted.

"Are you telling me we have an ambassador sitting in our waiting room?"

"Ambassador?" I blinked. "Kiarash? No. Khuyen specifically said he had no official voice and was not a representative. More like a messenger, I guess. But he was there for the rest of the story, so we might as well let him in."

She considered that for a moment and nodded.

I stood and opened the door.

"Kiarash?"

His snore from the couch sputtered and he sat up.

"Huh?"

"Do you want to come in?" I asked him.

"I'd just started in on a nice little nap," he stretched, "but I suppose I can sleep later."

He shuffled into the room and found a seat.

"This is Kiarash," I said. "Citizen of Aganaté and a member of *Chados*, the resistance of Pokorah-Vo. He's also the one that got me to a healer after I'd been wounded. I may not have survived otherwise."

Kiarash made a dismissive gesture.

"Kiarash, this is General Dzurala. She runs our Investigations and Intelligence Branch. And this is the Princess, Neelu Ulané Pulakasado nya Su Lariano."

Kiarash jumped out of his chair at that and tried to decide if he should bow or kneel.

"Oh, sit down." Neelu laughed. "We don't need to be so formal. Call me Neelu."

Kiarash breathed a sigh of relief and sat back down. The chair was tall for him, so he had to hop a little to get into it.

"Neelu can be much more relaxed than you'd expect from royalty," I told him.

"Don't be cheeky," Neelu said to me. "I told him *he* could call me Neelu. I've never told you that."

"As you say, Neelu'u." I bowed my head, my cheeks burning. I'd been thinking of her as Neelu for some time now. I wasn't sure when that started, but I'd need to watch my tongue. Sometimes I had the distinct impression she would be happy to cut it out.

While we were filling them in on the rest of what had happened, the food arrived from Mouse. We paused while it was laid out in front of us. The odor was mouthwatering. Especially after the weeks of camp food. The taste was beyond anything I had experienced before.

"I think this restaurant is going to do well," Neelu said after slowly savoring a bite.

We eventually resumed our tale. Once we had finished, Dzurala turned to Kiarash.

"Would you mind sitting with some of our analysts and answer questions about the situation in Aganaté and Pokorah-Vo?"

"Seems like that's what I was sent for," he answered, "but I only know what everyone there knows. I don't know any secrets or private things."

"Of course." She nodded. "We would very much appreciate whatever you are able to tell us."

"I'd like to check in on Naga, though," he said. "I'm worried about her. No offense, but I'm not sure how familiar your folk are with taking care of *reshan*."

"Lengel!" Dzurala called. Her aide stuck his head in the door. "Kiarash here would like to check on his *reshan*. Could you see that someone assists him with this?"

Lengel nodded.

"Also," Neelu added. "He'll need to see Arané-Li about getting quarters in the guest wing, and someone to show him around."

"Of course," Lengel answered. "If you would come with me, please?" he said to Kiarash.

"You've certainly had a time of it," Dzurala said once they'd left, "and you've brought us vital information."

"Mira was right." Neelu grinned at me. "You're the one that's the trouble magnet."

"Hey," I objected, "I don't *make* the trouble. I just find it."

"Oh?" She raised her eyebrows with the question. "You never make trouble?"

I started to answer, but she went on.

"And remember, it's not a good idea to lie to your Princess."

A knock sounded on the door, saving me from any more embarrassment.

Lengel stuck his head in.

"General," he said. "We have a unit here reporting from checking in on Ambassador Grangor."

"Very well," she answered. "Send them in."

Lengel opened the door all the way and made a motion toward it with his hand. Four guards entered with a female *Urgaban* between them that I didn't recognize.

"This is an outrage!" she was saying. She looked at Dzurala and Neelu. "I demand to be released at once! I am an ambassador!"

"I am sorry for any inconvenience Ambassador Yarmilla," Dzurala told her. "Please allow me to extract an explanation from our guards so that I can adequately chastise them for their error."

"Release me at once!" she demanded again. "As long as they will be punished, I don't care about the details."

"Oh, it's no trouble at all. Just a moment please." Dzurala turned to the ranking guard. "Report."

"General." He nodded. "When there was no response at Ambassador Grangor's door, we entered. I am sorry to say that he is dead. We found this dagger in his neck." He placed it on Dzurala's desk. "There was also a dead guard in his room, one from his personal detail. Ambassador Yarmilla was also present. This empty sheath on her belt." He set the empty sheath next to the dagger and it was a clear fit. "She was also writing this letter." He handed a paper to Dzurala.

Dzurala took the letter and began reading it.

"That is a private, diplomatic correspondence," Yarmilla objected. "You have no right to read it!"

Dzurala ignored her and kept reading. Finally, she looked up and handed the letter to Neelu. I could see Neelu's anger build as she read.

"This letter says that you witnessed Grangor being murdered by *Ulané Jhinura* guards!" She glared at Yarmilla. "And that it was by my order after I killed my own mother to seize the throne!"

Yarmilla was silent in the face of Neelu's rage.

"Yarmilla," Neelu went on. "Your status as ambassador is hereby revoked! You are under arrest. You are a traitor to your people and a murderer!"

Yarmilla tried to object, but Neelu gave her no chance.

*"You will pay for your crimes."* The menace in her voice was beyond anything I had heard from her before.

Yarmilla collapsed into the arms of the guards.

"Take her to a cell," Neelu ordered. "Then submit a full written report from each of you."

Neelu continued to fume after they had left. Then she looked back at the door.

"Lengel!" she called.

Lengel put his head in again.

"Please send for Duskovek," she said to him. "He's the captain of the *Urgaban* guard detail. Make sure he is protected!"

"I can't believe Grangor is dead." Neelu shook her head. "He was annoying, but he was of good intent. He had done much to cement relations between our governments. This could have destroyed everything!"

"Imagine if they'd managed to assassinate the queen,"

Dzurala reminded her. "Making it look like it had been Grangor."

Neelu considered that for a moment. "There would be war. No question."

It wasn't long before there was another knock on the door and Lengel stepped in.

"Neelu'u," he said. "Duskovek is here."

"Please see him in," she answered.

"What's the meaning of this," the uniformed *Urgaban* demanded. "Am I under arrest?"

"No, Duskovek," Neelu told him. "The guards were for your protection."

He saw the look and her face, and his protests died. "What has happened?"

"Too many things," she sighed. "Please have a seat."

He sat uncomfortably in the chair vacated by Kiarash.

"First," Neelu told him. "There was an attempted assassination of Queen Astrina'u. It failed. To anyone watching, it would have been apparent that it was carried out by Grangor."

"What?" He jumped up from his chair. "Impossible! He would never do such a thing!"

"I know." She nodded. "It was illusion. They replaced Grangor at the ribbon cutting with an assassin who was spelled to look like him."

"Replaced him? But— Where is the real Grangor?"

Neelu looked at him and I could tell he was afraid to hear the answer.

"Grangor is dead," she told him. "As is the guard that was with him."

Duskovek sank back into the chair, eyes unfocused. Then he looked back at Neelu.

"How did this happen? Who is responsible?"

"Yarmilla."

He started to object but seemed to think better of it.

"You have evidence, I assume?" His voice showed that he was not doubting what she had told him.

"She was caught in Grangor's room," she told him. "Her dagger is there," she pointed, "and she was writing this." She handed him the letter.

He read the half-written letter, his face like stone.

"On behalf of King Karugan and Queen Nazreela of Laraksha-Vo," he said, putting the letter down on the desk, "I swear we had no knowledge of this and completely disavow these actions."

"There is no question of that," Neelu assured him. "Whoever is behind this wants war between our people. None of us want that. I know that Grangor trusted in you implicitly, and that he often confided in you."

He nodded. "We had worked together for many years."

"You are also the senior representative of Laraksha-Vo here," she pointed out. "You must take over as ambassador."

He looked up, startled.

"At least for now," she told him.

He nodded again. "I'm sure they will send someone more suited once they know what has happened. Wait." He looked up again. "You said, whoever is behind this. You think there's someone else? Someone put Yarmilla up to this?"

Neelu glanced at Dzurala before going on. "At almost every turn, someone has tried to prevent Su Lariano from forming relations with *Urgaban*, whether it was Pokorah-Vo or Laraksha-Vo."

"How big do you think this is?"

"You know we sent a group to Pokorah-Vo, yes?"

He nodded.

"They were ambushed by a group of humans led by a White Rider."

Duskovek let out a long breath.

# CHAPTER TWENTY-TWO

## MIRA

*I* opened my eyes to find I was lying in my own bed in my room, which was confusing. Then I remembered. There was an attack, and I was wounded. What else had happened?

"Astrina!" I tried to sit up, but a pain in my stomach stopped me short.

"She's fine."

I looked for the source of the voice to see Rispan sitting in a chair near my bed. He was back. I recalled more of the scene with the assassin. Rispan had been there.

"Rispan! Where have you *been*?"

He just grinned at me. "Miss me?"

"You jerk!"

"The one and only." His grin just seemed to widen.

"You can be so annoying sometimes."

He shrugged. "But that's why you love me."

"Probably." I scowled at him. "Now get over here and give me a hug before you really annoy me."

He laughed and came to the bed to give me a hug. He was careful to keep it to my shoulders. It still hurt, but I didn't care.

"I was worried about you," I told him when he stood back up.

"Me?" He shook his head. "I was more worried what would happen with you and Mooren without me around to chaperone."

My face felt hot. "I don't know what you're talking about."

"Oh, please," he said. "If that's true, you're the only one."

"Wait, didn't you show up to the Raven's Nest with a naked woman?"

"What can I say?" He shrugged. "I'm irresistible." He was trying to keep it light, but I could tell it was anything but.

"Do you want to talk about it?" I asked him.

He shook his head. "She was a dragon, a *Darakanos*. But she's gone now."

I knew better than to push him. He would reach out if he needed to.

"What is *that*?"

Something had moved under his shirt. Then a furry head poked up above the middle button, which was the top one he was using.

He reached in and pulled out a large kitten. No. Not a kitten. Some kind of cub. And it had six legs.

"What is it?"

"This is Bijoux," he told me. "She's a *jahgreet*. An orphan, like us."

"What's a *jahgreet*?"

"They're one of the deadliest predators we have here," he explained. "I almost didn't survive her mother. Fortunately, I had some help."

I looked at him. He seemed a little thinner than when I'd seen him last. But more wiry. Tougher. I *had* been worried about him. Neelu and Tesia were good friends. And Sabela and some others from our unit. But Rispan and Mouse were my family here.

I still missed home. My real home back on Earth and my family there. But with the distractions of the day-to-day challenges here, I thought of them less and less. I could tell a lot had happened with Rispan since I'd seen him last.

"We have some time," I told him.

He raised his eyebrow, as if in question. But he knew what I meant. He nodded and sat back down. His story was one surprise after another. When he got to the part about Jhuyen, the pixie queen, talking in his mind, I knew how he must have felt.

"That reminds me," I told him. "I meant to tell you. Farukan? He's intelligent. And telepathic. He can talk to you. But we'll talk about that later. Your story first. Go on."

He blinked at me for a moment to process that before continuing. There were parts of his story where he didn't look me in the eye. I could tell he was focused on the memory in his mind. He had just gotten to the part where he was trying to signal to me about the assassin when someone else came into the room.

"You're awake." It was Shigara, Astrina's chief healer. She glanced at Rispan and then focused her attention on me. Then she looked back at him. "You are tiring her out. She needs rest. Come back later."

"I'm alright," I objected. She turned an arched eyebrow at me. "Really," I said. Her expression didn't change. "Well, maybe I'm a little tired."

"Don't argue." Rispan smiled at me as he rose from his chair. "That's almost everything anyway. Get some rest."

"She should be healed enough to get out of bed tomorrow," Shigara told him.

Rispan gave me a wave and went out the door.

I looked at Shigara. There was a lot about magical healing that I didn't understand.

"How come using magic to heal — Why isn't it instant?"

She looked at me like I was crazy. "You have quite an imagination," she replied. "Next you'll be asking why you can't breathe dirt."

"But I've seen it heal cut skin, and—"

"How quickly healing can be accelerated depends on the

complexity of the injury, the delicacy of what was injured, and a number of other things I am not going to go into. Rest."

"Fine." Maybe if I just closed my eyes for a minute, she'd be happy.

I opened them again when I heard voices from the front room. I was going to ask Shigara who was here, but she wasn't in the room. Did I doze off?

I tried sitting up again, and I didn't get the sharp pain I'd felt the last time I tried it. I pulled back the covers and threw my legs over the side of the bed. I slid my weight forward onto my feet and stood up. So far, so good. A robe was hanging from a hook on the wall nearby and I wrapped it around my body. I felt a dull ache as I walked to the front room, but that was pretty good, considering.

"Hey there." Neelu smiled up at me from where she sat at the table with Tesia and Rispan having coffee. Rispan didn't appear to have Bijoux with him. "Shigara said you'd probably be up and around sometime today. How are you feeling?"

"Better than I expected this soon," I told her.

"We were going to come by yesterday," Tesia said, "but when Rispan told us how Shigara had run him off, we checked in with her instead."

"That was yesterday?" That explained why I was feeling so much better. I didn't even remember falling asleep. I sat down at the table. Looking at Rispan, I thought about our conversation.

"I'm guessing you've heard all the news from Rispan?" I asked Neelu.

"Yes." She nodded. "He had quite an adventure."

"There's so much happening in Pokorah-Vo," I told her. "I know I have to deal with the Riders, but I really think I should make another trip. Dzurala said it might depend on the timing?"

Neelu thought for a moment. "It's a long trip," she told me. "Even longer from Pokorah-Vo. I just don't see it. If anything happened to delay you, you'd end up having to leave Pokorah-Vo in the dead of winter to make the deadline. Even traveling on horseback without wagons." She shook her head. "You'd be better off trying to go to Shifara first, and then get to Pokorah-Vo before winter sets in. It doesn't do any good to go to Pokorah-Vo and leave before you have time to do anything."

That made sense.

"Alright," I agreed. "Then I should probably start for Shifara as soon as possible."

Tesia laughed, "You're still healing from a knife in your stomach, and you want to rush off and fight a White Rider? Has anyone ever suggested you might not be quite… rational?"

I sent her a mock scowl.

"I didn't mean I should leave *today*."

"Right." Neelu gave an exaggerated nod. "You couldn't *possibly* want to leave before tomorrow."

"You know I haven't had any coffee yet, right?"

Neelu lifted her hand to indicate the pot. I reached across to pour myself a cup.

"We should just figure out a plan and be ready for when I can go," I said after taking a sip.

"What's to plan?" Neelu shrugged. "We get you as ready as possible, and you go. You finish and head to Pokorah-Vo."

"I'll go with you," Tesia said. "That way we can continue your studies as we go."

"There you go. You can bring a scout with you. They can bring Tesia the last bit of the way here on your way back to Pokorah-Vo," she looked at me, "and I'm pretty sure Mooren won't let you go without him."

I didn't know why she was grinning so much when she said it.

"And Rispan," I said, moving on. "He's annoying, but he's resourceful. I'll want him with me, too."

"And Mooren." Rispan sipped his coffee.

"We already said Mooren." I scowled at him.

"Did we? My mistake."

"Just a small group then. Right?" I asked. "We won't need anyone else?"

"No fancy chefs this trip I'm afraid," Neelu said.

"*That's* disappointing," Tesia joked.

"I'd like to bring Kiarash, if he's interested," Rispan said. "He's handy to have around." He looked at Tesia, "He's not much of a cook though. Sorry."

"I read Mooren's report of the mission," Neelu said. "He mentioned your nice little speech to scare off those *Urgaban*. Trained by the Dark Blade herself, huh?"

"The scary story was just begging to be used," I laughed. "I couldn't help myself."

"I don't know." She shrugged. "You're probably scary enough on your own now. I doubt you need the help. After that trip, people will think twice about attacking Raven's caravans."

"I hope so," I said. "I wouldn't want to have to go through that every time."

She shook her head. "You won't have to. You made your point. Word gets out."

"What about the Pokorah-Vo caravan?" I asked. "It should wait for me."

"Send Réni and Sabela," Rispan suggested. "They can handle it between them until you get back. And they'll have Gralbast to help. By the way," he added. "I checked out the Raven's Nest last night."

"Yeah? What did you think?"

"I'd already had a sample of the food, which was incredible. But the place is pretty nice, too. Great ambiance. It has a distinct *Urgaban* feel, but with a grounding in *Ulané Jhinura* fundamentals."

"That was all Bavrana and Mouse," I told him.

"Yeah." He shook his head. "Talk about hidden talents!"

"Alright." I put my cup down. "I guess it really is pretty straightforward then."

"Yeah." Rispan grinned. "All except the part where you

beard the White Riders in their own den. That part's still a little sketchy."

"You don't have to tell me that twice," I shook my head, "but worrying about it won't change anything. Besides, with what they've been pulling with the *Rorujhen*? They deserve whatever we can do to them."

"Wait." Rispan looked up. "What?"

"They've been hiding that the *Rorujhen* are actually sentient, intelligent creatures. The Riders threaten their families if they let anyone know they are telepathic. They basically capture and breed them as slaves."

Rispan looked like he had a bad taste in his mouth. "No wonder the slavers in Pokorah-Vo have so much power. The White Riders are supposed to be the executors of justice in Daoine. If the White Riders perpetuate slavery themselves, they'll not only turn a blind eye, but they will probably help them."

"It's a wonder that slavery was ever outlawed by the *Ashae* at all." Neelu nodded.

"This has *got* to stop!" I could see Rispan's fury rising.

"Hey," I said to him. "That's the plan. Once we get Farukan's family to safety, we're going to blow the lid off this thing."

"Once the Riders lose their power," Neelu added, "The other slavers will lose their support and start to fall. It's just a matter of time."

"They need to pay," he said through gritted teeth. "Every last one of them."

"I understand." I nodded. "They—"

"You *don't* understand!" he snapped.

I was shocked by the violence in his words. Something else was going on.

"Tell me."

He opened his mouth to speak and clamped his jaws again in rage. He looked back and forth between us, and his eyes settled on the floor as he forced his breathing to be slow and even.

"You know I'm an orphan," he said. "I told you they found me wandering in the forest when I was younger, and that I didn't remember anything from before that."

I nodded.

"But I do remember some things. Just bits and pieces. I remember my father's face. Staring at the sky. His skull bashed in and bloody. I remember a cage and not being able to get out for days. Trapped and hungry and cold. And I remember my mother getting me out of the cage. Telling me to run. That I should hide if the slavers came looking."

"What happened to your mother?" I asked him.

He gave his head a small shake. "I never saw her again."

"Do you remember anything else?" Neelu asked him.

"No." He looked back up at us. "I've never told this story. That memory was all that I had of her. I think I felt like I would lose that bit of her if I talked about it. It was mine and no one else's. So, no. You can't understand why I hate slavers so much. Or why I want to put every last one of them in the ground."

Rispan stood up and headed for the door. "I'll go talk to Kiarash and see if he wants to come with us."

"Mira," Tesia said after he had left. "There's something else."

I looked at her, expectantly. "Go ahead." I was afraid to hear what she would say, but whatever it was, I'm sure I needed to hear it.

"Laruna's lore books," she said. "I was able to glean some information about portal magic."

I put my cup down again, splashing a little coffee onto my hand.

"Really? That's awesome!"

She shook her head, "Most of what I found is about creating point to point portals on one world, not for creating a portal to another realm. But there's more. Because time moves at such different rates between our worlds, creating a portal spell from our world to yours would take immense power. As you know, we have artifacts that were created expressly for storing vast amounts of power. I've taught you a little about how this is done. We have one here that is large enough."

"So, you're saying you can send me home? This is great news! How soon could we do it?"

"I would need to teach you the fundamental concepts," she said. "Because you would need to participate in the spell, but with a couple days of preparation, I'm certain we could do it."

I could be home in a couple of days! I would need to say goodbye to everyone, all the friends I'd made. I'd miss them, but I needed to get back to my family.

"Would I be able to come back and forth?" I asked her.

"Portals are one-way," she told me. "To come back here, you would need to create one by yourself, so we would need to take a little longer to train you more thoroughly on the process. And you would need a huge supply of magic to do it."

My head was spinning. I'd gotten so caught up in everything. Then I remembered my promise to Farukan. I told him I would get his family safe. I told him we would expose the slavery of his people. I couldn't just walk out on him. I couldn't betray him like that.

"I can't." It hurt me to say it, but I couldn't abandon him like that. What kind of person would that make me? "I have to keep my promise to Farukan. How can I put seeing my family over the lives of his?" I shook my head. "Teach me what you can, but I can't go home yet."

"I understand." Neelu put her hand on my arm. "When you first got here, I was very doubtful about you getting home. But now we have the way. Just be patient. You'll see your family again."

# CHAPTER TWENTY-THREE

## RISPAN

*I* was angry with myself for losing control. Especially in front of three of the people I respected most. Usually, I could keep my emotions at bay. If I was going to fly off the handle every time something happened, I didn't like I'd be in a constant state of hostility. That wouldn't help anything. I usually focused my mind on other things.

On the other hand, it did feel good to know that someone else knew my secret. It wasn't so much that it was a secret, just that it was private. If I couldn't trust those three with it, then I couldn't trust anyone.

Fortunately, none of them brought it up over the next couple of weeks as we got ready. I'd said all I needed to say. Now it was time to get back to taking care of business. I wondered off and on where Genevané had gone and how she was dealing with Gaetan, but that line of thinking wouldn't be productive either. That's something Mira and I had in common; we focused on what we needed to do. I'd also had a few conversations with Farukan and met his new groom, Javen. All that time I'd been grooming him, I thought he was just a really big horse.

I took the *Jahgreet* pelt to Felora and Gylan and asked about having it made into a hooded cloak. It seemed my treatment of the pelt had worked well; it was still supple and none of the fur had fallen out. The fur had also kept its ability to take its coloring from nearby objects. I also noticed that it tended to go black if there was limited light.

I'd had the same trouble spotting Bijoux, and I had to keep my eyes peeled for her red, ribbon collar so I could find her. She seemed to be amused by sneaking up on me.

I did talk with Kiarash about the plan to go to Shifara before returning to Pokorah-Vo and Aganaté, and he said he was in. That didn't really surprise me.

Meanwhile, rooms had been allocated around a common area for everyone in the caravan, plus Kiarash. Even those of us who had someplace else to stay tended to congregate there. The caravan would head back to Pokorah-Vo in a couple of days. "Raven" would join them later. I was talking about it with Sabela and Réni when Korashéna overheard. She mostly seemed to stop talking whenever I came in the room, but not this day.

"You aren't going back to Pokorah-Vo without me," she said. "I'm not going to hide here while my people need me. I will return with the caravan."

"Too dangerous," I told her. "You can bet they're still watching for you in Pokorah-Vo. You can't help your people if you get caught again."

"I met Kiarash," she said. "He told me about *Chados*. And about Aganaté. I can go to them; they've been living there in secret for generations. I will be safe."

"The problem is that only Kiarash knows how to get back into Aganaté, and he's not going with the caravan. He's coming north with me before we head back to Pokorah-Vo."

"Then I will go with you."

"That's too dangerous, too." I shook my head. "Besides, you'd just slow us down. Do you even know how to ride a horse?"

"Of course!"

I just looked at her. I was pretty sure that in her life as a slave in Pokorah-Vo she'd never ridden a horse.

"I've seen it done," she said. "How hard can it be?"

"Ask Mira about the first time she tried." I grinned. I remembered teasing her about how she walked for the next few days after her mad ride to save Mouse and me.

"He's right," Sabela put in. "It can be very tiring and painful to try to ride for very long if you don't know how."

"I'll just have to learn on the way." She said it like she was making a royal pronouncement, which I suppose she was. "I *will* return to my people."

She'd come a long way since I'd come across her in that slaver's shop.

"I'm not saying you shouldn't," I told her. "Just not yet. You can't go with the caravan, and I don't think it's a good idea for you to come with us to Shifara. You should stay behind for now."

"I am going. If you don't want to travel with me, maybe you should stay behind."

"What?" *Where did that come from?* "That's not what I said."

"Isn't it?"

"Hey," Mira had come in. "I only caught part of that. Shéna, were you saying you wanted to come to Shifara with us?"

"I must return to my people safely," Shéna told her. "Only Kiarash can get me into Aganaté. If he is going north first, I should go with him."

"Right." Mira rolled the idea around. "If you were to come with us, I don't think we should advertise who you are."

"She doesn't know how to ride," I objected.

"That's simple," Shéna said, ignoring me. "I'll pretend to be your maid."

"Are you sure?" Mira asked her. "I mean, you're a queen. Can you pull off being a maid?"

"This is crazy," I told them.

"I have been a slave all my life," Shéna said with a smile. "I think I know how to behave as a servant."

"That settles it then." Mira nodded. "We still have several days. You should get in some riding lessons before we go. It will make a big difference. Let's get you set up."

Mira and Shéna continued talking as they walked out of the room.

I turned to Sabela and Réni. I opened my mouth to make a comment about what had just happened, but the flat look Sabela gave me convinced me to keep it to myself. Sometimes, you have to talk to make women happy. Other times, talking is about the dumbest thing you can do. I turned and walked from the room while I still had skin on. If Shéna didn't care about the danger or the hardship of the trip, then that was on her.

On the day of departure, Neelu walked us to the stables to see us off. We had already said our goodbyes to everyone else.

There'd be no wagons this trip. We'd each have a horse, plus there were two packhorses with supplies and gear. Of course, Mira would be on Farukan. Naga was stabled in another area that gave her access to the sky, so Kiarash would meet us outside.

"I wish I was going with you," Neelu was saying, "but an *Ulané* in the group would just complicate things."

"I didn't know things could get any more complicated than they already were." Mira grinned back.

I looked around our group. Besides Mira and Mooren, the only one who would be used to travel was the one scout, Tabalin. I hadn't met him before, but he looked competent enough. I guessed Javen would be alright on the trail as well. Then there was Tesia and Shéna. This was going to be hard on both of them. I knew Shéna hadn't had it easy in Pokorah-Vo, but this was going to be different. We were starting our trip in the middle of summer, so cool breezes would be few and far between on the trail. We would probably arrive before it really started to cool down.

Mira towered over all of us from Farukan's back. Tabalin knew the way and led off. Javen brought up the rear, leading the packhorses. When we passed through the outer town, Gylan and Felora waved to Tesia and the rest of us as we rode by the shop. It was going to be some time before they saw their daughter again.

It was roughly seventeen hundred miles to Shifara.

Bijoux was growing really fast. She was already up to my knee when she was on all six legs. When she stood on her hind legs, she was above my waist. She was too big to ride inside my shirt, so she usually rode in front of me, laying on a blanket I set up for her. Mira had corrected me that Bijoux was a cub and not a kitten, but I figured that since she was a cat, either term should work. I didn't really care about semantics.

By midafternoon of the second day, we had left the forest behind and were making good time through the coastal farmlands. The mountain range that had fallen away to gently rolling hills to allow our passage east when we'd traveled to Pokorah-Vo rose again. It would eventually merge with the Great Mountains that divided our continent in half.

I was no farmer, but it looked like the winter wheat would be ready to harvest soon. We were more than halfway through summer.

"Do the *Ulané Jhinura* farm out here?" Mira asked.

Mooren shook his head. "Most of the farming is done by the *Loiala Fé*. We only farm the mushrooms and such. *Loiala Fé* farm pretty much everything else. Wheat, corn, vegetables, fruit, nuts. Even cotton."

"I imagine it's hard work," she said. "I don't know if I'd be happy as a farmer."

"*Loiala Fé* seem to like it well enough," Tesia spoke up. "At least, the ones who stayed here."

Mira looked at her. "As opposed to?"

"As opposed to the ones who didn't stay here." Tesia laughed. "When the *Tuatha De* left their realm, a lot of *Loiala Fé* went there to live. They were tired of the *Ashae* running every-thing here. They'd been pretty unhappy ever since they'd shown up and taken over."

"It sounds like there was a lot of moving around." Mira frowned.

Tesia nodded. "That was back when traveling between realms was easy. The *Ashae* came from the same realm as the *Tuatha De*. They left them and took over here. After the war with the Fomorians, the *Tuatha* ended up wanting to come here, but the *Ashae* wouldn't have it. They helped them find another place instead. By then the *Ashae* were very much established here. So, the *Loiala Fé* that wanted to be in charge of their own world moved to the empty realm."

"Sounds complicated."

"Well," Tesia told her. "It didn't happen as quickly as all that. But that's it in a nutshell."

Shéna had evidently made good use of her time to learn riding, because she was doing fairly well. She never complained, though in the evenings I could see from how she walked that she was feeling it. We'd brought a good bit of dried foods, but Naga brought us fresh meat every day. This was especially important for Bijoux; she would eat dried meat in a pinch, but she preferred fresh. She didn't seem to care much whether it was raw or cooked, but that might have been because none of our party was particularly skilled in cooking.

By the fourth day, we'd passed the last fields. This seemed to spark conversation about farms again, though I couldn't under-stand the fascination.

"Though the ground here looks like it was used for farming at one time," Shéna observed. "Did the soil become less fertile?"

"These lands are all very fertile," Tesia told her. "At one time this entire corridor was used for farming. But when the *Ashae* shut down travel between realms, there was less trade. Too many farms and not enough customers."

"It doesn't sound like closing the borders worked well for everyone," Mira said.

"From what I understand," Tesia told her, "It was really just the *Ashae* who wanted to do it."

"And they just forced it on everyone else?"

"They run things." Tesia shrugged. "They don't generally ask permission; they just announce."

"That sucks!" Mira said. "It's not right. Everyone should have a voice."

"That sounds like something Grangor would say," Tesia smiled. Then her smile faltered. "Would have said."

Conversation died down again after that. Shéna still hadn't spoken to me. It seemed like she was already angry with me in our last conversation, so it couldn't have been that. What it could have been though, I had no idea. She'd either tell me or she wouldn't. Two nights later she looked at me like she was going to say something, but then walked past.

Four days later, she approached me again. I was rolling out my blankets after dinner and she came and stood near me. I stopped what I was doing to look up at her.

"Rispan." She was looking past me, avoiding looking at me. "I've been meaning to talk to you."

"Yeah?" I went back to setting up my blanket. "What about?"

"I—" Her eyes fell to the ground. "I never thanked you."

I looked back up. "For what?"

"If it hadn't been for you," her eyes flashed to me for a moment before falling back to the ground, "I'd still be a slave."

"Oh." I nodded. "Right. Well, I was just in the right place at the right time. No big deal. I'm glad you got out of there."

Her eyes snapped up to me at that. "It wasn't just the right place at the right time when you ran off with that tracker and almost got yourself killed! You didn't even know me!"

"The tracker had to go." I shrugged. "Too dangerous for everyone to have it around. It was the sensible thing to do."

She shook her head. "The sensible thing to do would have been to leave me as soon as you knew I had the tracker."

"That didn't really seem like an option."

"You put everyone at risk," she said. "For me."

"I did what was right!" I told her. "I didn't do it for you. I did it because we can't give in to that kind of evil. I did it because I'd rather die than roll over and let evil win! Yes. I took a risk bringing you to my friends. But I knew if we moved fast enough, they'd be safe and then it was just on me."

She just stared at me. I didn't know why I'd exploded at her.

"Then you didn't free me because you wanted me?"

"No!" The question completely surprised me.

She nodded. "If you had freed me for selfish reasons because you wanted me, I could be flattered that you would take such a risk for me. But that you would take such a risk with no thought to yourself at all... This is the act of a truly noble soul."

She dipped her head at me and walked away.

Sometimes, I don't understand women as much as I think I do.

# CHAPTER TWENTY-FOUR

## MIRA

*a*fter the first week, we rode north through abandoned farmlands and occasionally the ruins of deserted villages. Orchards had grown wild, and grasses competed with grains for a foothold. The way itself was easy; it was just long. We had estimated that we would travel about two hundred and fifty miles a week. The whole trip should take just under seven weeks.

I'd never really connected with Shéna. On our last trip, she'd gotten pretty close to Réni and Sabela. I thought maybe we'd get to know each other better this trip, but so far, she'd been pretty focused on Rispan. Which made no sense to me since she didn't even speak to him the first week or so. They only spoke occasionally after that, but I would frequently see her looking at him. The aloof, superior expression seemed to come naturally to her, and I couldn't see through it. She could be infatuated with him or hate him, and I couldn't tell either way. Knowing Rispan, either one was a distinct possibility.

In the evenings, Tesia continued to work with me on my mage training. Mage was basically what they called anyone who could do more than just the simplest of spells. Battle magic was not simple. It was kind of strange to think of myself as a mage though. Of course, I'd heard the word before, but actually applying it to myself? That was different.

I guess I didn't think of myself as a fighter either, but if I was being honest, there was no way I could deny it. I thought back to Darek and some of the other "tough guys" back at my high school and had to chuckle. They didn't have a clue.

That started me thinking about Nora and my family again. I shut that down and turned my attention back to the road.

Rispan seemed more moody than normal, so he was less than his usual talkative self. Javen focused on the horses and Tabalin pretty much kept to himself. With Kiarash mostly in the air, that left me, Mooren and Tesia taking turns carrying most of the conversation. Except when Farukan made a mental comment. The first time he'd done that, I'd laughed at the reactions of the others. Eventually, they got more accustomed to his deep voice in their heads. Farukan didn't talk much, though, so he would still catch them off guard. Sometimes I wondered if he did it on purpose.

Tesia also talked with me about the theory she had learned on portal magic. It seemed like the most effective way was to have some sort of an anchor on each end of the portal. A physical anchor was best. This provided a focal point for each side of the doorway. Of course, for the starting point, the mage could use themselves as the anchor. Without a physical anchor, you needed to have a really clear mental image of the other end. That image needed to be strong enough to act as an anchor. It also seemed that portals were not two-way openings; you could only go through them in one direction. Travelling round-trip would require a new portal to come back.

"It's been difficult working from these old texts," Tesia said at one point. "They are from a time when the *Ralahin* was easier to access."

"It's harder now?" I asked her. "I hadn't heard that."

"I think it's been more pronounced the last few years," she

said. "The magic is there, but drawing it seems like going against the flow."

"But it's in everything. Why would it get harder to use?"

"I don't know," she shook her head, "but more mages have started to notice, and it's being looked into."

"That's something else I'm a little confused about," I said. "What exactly is a mage? Doesn't just about everyone use magic?"

"Most people can enact a few basic spells," she explained, "and anyone can activate a premade spell. A mage is someone who can create a wider variety of spells, and more complicated spells, from scratch."

It wasn't until almost our fifth week that we started to see fields that were actually being maintained, most of them with crops. I'm guessing we still had a couple of months before the big harvest.

"You should probably start wearing the armor," Mooren said that night. "We'll start running into people soon, maybe even another White Rider. You don't want to come across one while you are on a *Rorujhen* without your credentials on display."

That didn't thrill me, but I knew he was right. The weather was still warm, so I was glad that I would have magical temperature control built in, courtesy of Tesia. For now, I should be fine with just the breast and back plates. That longsword was attached to Farukan's saddle.

Mooren had been right, because the next day we started to see people in the fields. They didn't approach, but they saw us. I wondered if word would be sent ahead of us and, if so, whether anyone would meet us on the trail. The answer to that would become apparent a week later.

We came to a large town late in the afternoon. I had expected to see *Ashae* or *Loiala Fé*, but they were human. I was wary, because the only other humans I'd seen on this world so far had been trying to kill me.

"I don't know about you guys," Rispan said, "but I could use an ale and some food we didn't cook on the trail. Maybe even a bed if there's one to be had."

We didn't take much convincing. We dismounted in front of what looked like an inn.

"I'll stay out here with the horses," Javen said. "They probably haven't seen many *Urgaban* around here."

Kiarash landed Naga almost immediately.

"I don't know whose idea this was." He grinned. "But it was a good one!"

*"Please keep an eye, Farukan,"* I sent to him. *"Let me know if you see anything we should know about."*

I felt a flow of assurance in response, and I followed the others through the door.

Inside, there were tables with benches, a bar with stools, and in the back, there were stairs leading to a second floor. We found a table for the seven of us and sat down. Bijoux had jumped down and followed us in. She went under our table and peered out into the room through our legs. I was amazed at how quickly she had grown during the trip. If she stood on her hind legs now, she was nearly as tall as Rispan. During the days, she spent as much time running along beside us as she did riding with Rispan on his horse.

The man behind the bar gave us a suspicious look before saying anything.

"What can I get you?" he asked.

"Ale," Rispan spoke up. "And food if you have any ready."

"Still a bit early for food," the man said, "but it be ready soon enough." He filled seven mugs and brought them to our table on a tray. "Early for the waitress, too."

Rispan handed him a silver and the man dropped it in his purse.

"Name's Callum," he said. "Callum Barrach. I don't mean to be buttin' in, but we don't get many strangers through here. Leastways when they's not traders. You don't much look like traders if you don't mind my saying."

I shifted in my seat to face him and pushed my cloak behind my shoulders. His expression suddenly changed when he saw my armor, which hadn't been my intention.

"Begging your pardon." He started to back away. "I didn't mean no offense. Yer business is none o' mine. I'll make sure yer supper is coming right along!"

With that, he practically ran through the back door to the kitchen.

"That was weird." I frowned.

"White Riders are a pretty big deal," Mooren explained, "and wherever they go, they are judge, jury and executioner. And there's no appeal."

"You mean they're thugs and they terrorize everyone?" I asked. The more I heard about these Riders, the more I didn't like them.

"That's not something anyone would say out loud," Tesia cautioned.

Right. I'd have to keep hold of my tongue until we knew Farukan's family was safe.

"Though you're safe from immediate action," Mooren said. "Riders can do whatever they want to others. But with each other, everything has to go through their official channels. Still, you catch more bees with honey than vinegar."

I'd used that expression with Nora a number of times and she always hated it. It surprised me to hear it here.

"Fine," I answered. "I'll be nice. We do need to find out where to go, though. We still don't know exactly where to find the Rider Council."

"Maybe our friend Callum will be able to help us." Rispan smiled. "He seemed thrilled with the subject."

"The first thing you should do is present yourself to the *Ashae* Royal Court," Tesia said. "That way we establish that we are an official delegation from Su Lariano. From there, they'd be able to direct you to the Rider Council. But a little advance information wouldn't be a bad idea."

It was several minutes before we saw Callum again, and by then a few people had wandered in and were looking for him. Callum and a woman came in through the back door, bringing bowls of some kind of stew and spoons for everyone.

"Here you go," he was saying. "Sorry for the wait."

"Would you please have a bowl and a mug of ale sent to our groom?" I asked him. "He's with our horses out front."

He nodded and hurried away. He spoke to the waitress and went back behind his bar.

After Callum had served his other customers, I waved to him, and he hurried over.

"Is everything alright?" He sounded afraid.

"Yes," I told him. "Everything is fine." He looked relieved, but only slightly. "I was hoping you would have some information for us."

"I'll help any way I can," he said.

"Well," this time I hesitated. "I have only recently won the armor," I told him, keeping my voice low. "I've come to present myself to the White Rider Council. We assume it's in Shifara, but we don't exactly know."

Callum looked over his shoulder nervously and then back to me. "Yer better off running," he whispered. "Bury the armor and let the horse go if you have it. They'll never let a human wear the armor."

"That's not really an option," I said. He was clearly terrified. "I'm going to have to face them."

He nodded, not wanting to argue. "I don't know where they meet. But I can call them."

"How?"

"We can signal them," he answered. "They always say, if you need a Rider, send up a colored smoke and one will come if they're near. No one ever tries it though."

"Why not?"

"Better to sort it out yourself than have one of them come."

He looked around again as soon as the words were out of his mouth.

I looked around the table. "Do we want to wait? Or should we go ahead and make contact?"

"It wouldn't hurt to make contact," Tesia said, "so long as it doesn't keep you from Court."

"It might be nice to have an idea of the reception you'll be getting from the Riders before you go to Court," Mooren suggested. "I mean, we think we know how they will respond, but knowing for sure would help."

There were nods of agreement around the table.

I took a deep breath. "Callum, would you please send the signal?"

His face visibly paled, but he nodded and stepped away. A few minutes later, I saw him start a fire in the large hearth at the back of the room.

"Bit warm still for a fire. Eh, Callum?" one of the men at the bar spoke up over his ale.

Callum glanced at me, a question on his face. I nodded to him.

He threw a small bag into the flames. There was a brief flare of sparks and the rising smoke turned red. He didn't look at me as he went back behind the bar.

The man at the bar jumped off his stool, knocking it over.

"What have you done?" The man hurried out the front door. In a moment, everyone else had left as well.

It was only a few minutes before Farukan sent me a warning, *"A Rider is coming!"*

Not long after, an *Ashae* strode in the door. He was at least six and a half feet tall. He had platinum hair, like the other had. He also wore the same white armor. He walked straight to Callum.

"You have the gall to signal a Rider?" he demanded.

I stood up before Callum could answer.

"No," I spoke loudly. "I did."

The Rider's head snapped around and looked at me. His eyes narrowed.

"We've been expecting you," he said.

"Have you?" I arched an eyebrow at him.

"You were seen approaching. And your *Rorujhen* bears Vaelir's markings," he said. "You think it's a coincidence that a Rider was close by in a nothing town like this?"

"How would I know?" He was annoying me. "Maybe it's the only place they put up with your attitude." I was starting to sound more like Nora.

His eyes narrowed again, and his hand moved to the hilt of the sword at his waist. Callum's eyes got big, and he slowly sunk down behind the bar.

My eyes went pointedly to his hand and back to his face.

"Really?" I asked. "Is that what you were sent here to do?"

He looked at me, his eyes calculating. Then he took his hand off his sword.

"I am to bring you before the Council," he told me.

"And you are?"

"I am Niklos."

"Well, I hope you're patient, Niklos." I smiled, suspecting he was not. "The Council will have to wait their turn. We're on our way to the Royal Court. Besides." I looked to Tesia, hoping she would play along, "What's the requirement for seeing the Riders? How long?"

"One year," she supplied.

"Right." I looked back at him. "One year. We have several months yet before we are required to see the Council."

"No one tells the Rider Council or Master Dimétrian to wait!" He glared at me.

"Who?"

"Master Dimétrian." He looked like he expected me to know who that was. "Master of the White Riders."

"Oh." I shrugged. "I'll make sure the king and queen are

aware of your views," I told him. This guy was not a friend; I had to seem as strong as possible. "I summoned you—"

"You think I am here at your bidding?" He was furious.

I pointed at the fire. The smoke still burned red.

"I summoned you and you came along like a good little boy," I told him. "I did this as a courtesy. You can run along now and let the Council know I will be coming in due course."

I was starting to think it had been a mistake after all to send up that signal. If Niklos was any indication, we'd guessed right about the reception I was going to get. And something about his attitude and expression really got under my skin. I'd seen enough "badass bitches" in movies, that I could play the part fairly well.

"Didn't you hear me?" I asked. "You can leave now. You are dismissed."

His face was so red with anger, I thought his head was going to explode. But he turned and stormed out the front door.

Callum's head inched up from behind the bar and he looked around before standing up.

"I've never seen the like," he said. "You humiliated him!"

"You *were* pushing things a little," Mooren said.

"Nicely played, sis!" Rispan slapped my shoulder with a grin.

I let out a breath and sat back onto the bench.

Mooren put a reassuring hand on mine. Then he seemed to realize what he was doing and stopped, putting his hand back on the table in front of him.

# CHAPTER TWENTY-FIVE

## RISPAN

*W*atching Mira deal with the Rider was very satisfying. I knew talking to him like that had been difficult for Mira; that wasn't how she liked to deal with people. But some people needed it.

"That could have gone worse." I smiled and took another swallow of ale.

Mira scowled at me. "It could have gone a lot better."

I just shrugged. "Nobody died."

Shéna gave me a disapproving look. I still didn't know what to make of her and she wasn't making it easy.

"Do you think they'll try to stop me from getting to Court?" Mira asked the group.

"Unlikely," Tesia answered her. "You've made your intention clear. It would be risky for them to interfere."

"We still have, what, a week before we get to Shifara?" Mira looked at Tabalin.

He nodded. "About that."

"A lot can happen on the road in a week," I pointed out, remembering our trips to and from Pokorah-Vo.

"Yes," Tesia answered. "But we are getting into a much more

populated area. I'm not saying we should completely relax, but I think they'll wait."

*"Mira!"* Farukan shouted into our minds, and Mira was up and through the front door in an instant.

When I got out the door behind her, I saw that Niklos was holding Farukan's reins and Mira had the edge of one of her daggers against his throat. Javen was on the ground in front of Niklos, looking like he'd been thrown down. I heard a low growl and glanced down to see Bijoux standing on four legs and staring at Niklos with bared teeth. I still thought of her as a kitten, but she was also getting pretty scary.

"Take your hands off my horse," Mira's voice was hard.

"He's not yours unless the Council affirms your claim," Niklos answered.

"He's in my possession until the Council says otherwise," Mira's voice was hard. I hoped she was guessing right. We really didn't know the rules. "Lose the reins or lose blood. Your choice."

Niklos tossed the reins to Javen. "Enjoy it while you can," he said to Mira. "He'll be mine soon enough."

"Yours?" Mira stepped back from him.

"You might have been able to murder my uncle, or even to sneak up on me just now," he snarled at her, "but you won't steal my inheritance! You won't survive the challenge."

"I'll survive today," she said, "and you were just leaving."

Niklos glared at her. "Your time will come."

He had a horse nearby and mounted.

Bijoux moved to follow him as he started away, but I called her back.

"Did you notice he wasn't riding a *Rorujhen?*" I asked.

"Maybe they don't all have them," Mira guessed.

*"That is true,"* Farukan rumbled. *"Many White Riders must use horses. Capturing a* Rorujhen *is not easy, and often we refuse to breed in bondage. Though this is easier said than done. It is a symbol of some prestige among them to own a Rorujhen."*

"Javen," Mira said to him, "It's probably better if you stay with us. We're already a mixed bunch. Throwing an *Urgaban* in the mix shouldn't make a difference. I don't like you having to go up against someone alone."

It was a nice sentiment for general situations, but it was unlikely we would be able to travel around as a gang all the time once we got to Shifara.

Callum didn't have a lot of rooms, but it was the off-season, and he had enough beds for everyone. I couldn't help but notice that Mira and Mooren kept glancing at each other when the other one wasn't looking.

"You two want a room to yourselves tonight?" I grinned at them.

Mooren acted like he didn't know what I was talking about, and Mira looked more panicked than I'd ever seen her. If I'd said "boo" she probably would have run out into the street. It's these little moments that can make life so worthwhile.

Bijoux pulled a blanket onto the floor under my bunk and slept on it. The beds were nothing special, but they were a nice change after six weeks of sleeping on the ground. Javen preferred to stay in the stables with the horses. He was certainly very dedicated to them, especially to Farukan, and he wasn't very comfortable with people.

When we stepped out of the inn the next morning, a human woman was standing in the street. She wore plain leather armor. Her dark hair was shorn on the sides and the rest was gathered at the back of her head. She stood easily over six feet tall, and her hand rested on the pommel of a large longsword, which she held in front of her with its point down, on the ground.

"Saw you come in yesterday," she said. She was looking at Mira. "And I saw your sword."

"Um." Mira glanced at us uncertainly. "Okay."

"How well can you use it?"

Mira shrugged. "I'm competent with it. Why?"

"Competent?" She smiled. "We'll see. Show me."

Mira seemed confused for a moment, then realization showed on her face. "You want to fight me? Why?"

"I am Alénia," she said. "This," she lifted her sword, "Is what I do."

"You fight people?"

Alénia shook her head slowly. "I test people. I test myself. Any who use the longsword will face me eventually."

"Including the White Riders?" Mira asked her. "This was one of their swords."

"No. They do not honor the rules of the match. They use magic. That is not my way."

"You just wait here in this town for someone to wander through?"

"No," Alénia answered. "I roam the lands. I carry my home within."

"Look," Mira said. "I'm sorry, but I have nothing to prove to you. I'm not going to fight you."

Alénia looked at her for a moment before speaking. "You took that sword from a Rider?" She nodded toward the sword that was hanging from Farukan's saddle. Javen had brought the horses out for us.

Mira nodded. "I did."

"And now you will have to make your claim and face the challenge, yes?"

"Yes."

"If you cannot hold your ground against me," Alénia asked, "How do you hope to survive your challenge? Have you truly tested your skill with that weapon against an opponent who was a master at the longsword? And who was willing to hurt you?"

I could see Mira thinking that over and starting to waver. I didn't like it.

"Don't worry," Alénia said. "Unlike the Riders, I will not kill you. You have my vow."

"What if I kill you?" Mira asked her.

Alénia laughed. "If you kill me, I will rejoice in my death, that I have finally met a worthy foe."

"Fine." Mira said.

"Mira—" Mooren started to object, but Mira cut him off.

"She said she won't kill me."

"She didn't say she wouldn't injure you," I pointed out. "Or maim you."

"She's right." Mira had made up her mind. "None of you are a master at this weapon, and we've practiced hard, but none of you were really willing to hurt me. She doesn't have to hold back. And neither do I."

Mira took off her cloak and pulled her sword from the sheath. She stepped into the street, leaving some space between her and Alénia.

Alénia smiled as she stepped forward. "Be warned," she said. "If you use magic to attack or defend, my vow no longer holds, and you forfeit the match. This is to be blade against blade."

Mira nodded and brought her sword into position. Alénia had height and reach on Mira. Mira's blade, built for an *Ashae*, was just as long as Alénia's.

Alénia stepped forward, her sword flashing out. These weren't full attacks, but there was enough behind them that Mira couldn't ignore them as feints. Every parry Mira made gave Alénia more knowledge of what she was facing. Mira tried to do the same to Alénia, but Alénia reacted quickly, turning her own parries into an attack, pushing Mira back. Mira had heavily influenced her style with the longsword with techniques from the staff, using two hands from the end. As Alénia launched another attack, Mira set her sword spinning to create a defensive bubble around herself.

A look of confusion crossed Alénia's face as she examined this development. At first, she seemed unable to counter. As soon as Mira tried to use the momentum to strike, Alénia parried and came at Mira, positioned to prevent Mira from returning to her last technique. They continued for several minutes and sweat had started to run down both of their faces. Alénia was blazingly fast, and her blade suddenly flashed toward Mira's neck, and Mira was out of position to block.

*No!* I panicked, fearing the splash of blood.

Then Mira wasn't there. She had flitted behind Alénia.

"Magic!" Alénia accused as she spun to face Mira, her sword raised between them. "The match is forfeit! As is your life!"

Mira shook her head, tired from the exertion of the match. "I didn't use magic to attack or defend. And the match was already lost. Your blade was coming for my neck and my move was instinctive."

"I would not have struck you." Alénia frowned. "I would have stopped the blow."

"I believe you," Mira told her. "I didn't think. I reacted. But I also did not violate the rules as stated."

Alénia thought that over for a moment. "Agreed." She gave Mira an appraising look. "You lost," she said, "but you did well. I will travel with you. You need a guide, do you not? And I will instruct you on what you did wrong. One day, if you survive your challenge with the Riders, we may try again, and you will do better."

I wasn't sure this was a good idea, but Alénia shortly produced a horse of her own and refused to say anything else.

The road ran parallel to the Ashae River, which went all the way to the sea. Shifara was on the coast near where the river emptied into a delta. For the rest of the way to Shifara, we were able to find lodgings every night. Farming and fishing villages were frequent, and they earned their living supporting Shifara City and Shifara Castle. We crossed the river on a stone bridge as we turned westward to Shifara City.

The Riders were keeping an eye on our progress. We could see them watching in the distance at various times throughout the day, but they never approached us. They were too far away to tell if Niklos was among them.

We finally topped a low rise that gave us a view of Shifara.

Shifara City was a walled monstrosity of sprawling stone buildings. It had obviously been expanded a number of times, and there were places where old walls could still be seen inside the city. Beyond the city, we could see a causeway about a half mile long that led to Shifara Castle, which rose above the surrounding water, built onto an immense shoulder of rock. A seawall surrounded the entire area, with gates to the east and west to allow ships and fishing boats to travel to and from the deep seas beyond.

"Some of the guards are human," Mira commented as we approached the main gate to the city.

"That shouldn't surprise you," Alénia said to her. "There are plenty of *Ashae* in the military, but not many wouldn't have the connections to keep them off gate duty. Normally, they'd just let us pass, but the *Rorujhen* is going to upset them," she glanced at Bijoux, "and probably the cub as well."

As we got closer, the guards started to look more nervous. Their eyes were drawn to Farukan and Mira, but they kept returning to Alénia. One of them stepped forward to block our entrance.

"Alénia." He put his closed fist to his chest in salute. "Pardon my intrusion, but it is my duty to ask about your guests."

"Agrélian," she nodded to him. "This is an official delegation from the *Ulané Jhinura* kingdom of Su Lariano. They are to be presented at the Royal Court."

The guard nodded, and his tongue whetted his lips nervously. "And the *Rorujhen*?"

"That will be a matter for the Riders," she said. "Unless you would care to speak for them?"

Agrélian's eyes got very big, and he took two steps backwards.

"Not at all," he said. "I will escort you to the north gate. A moment."

There was a small corral and stable just outside the gate,

probably so that the guards would have horses available if needed. He quickly saddled one of the horses and led it out.

"They seem to know you pretty well," I said to Alénia.

"They have all faced me in combat." She didn't turn to look at me. "They know me."

Agrélian mounted and called to us.

"Please follow me."

He led us through the gate and into the city. Being raised in Su Lariano, I wasn't used to so much structure above ground. Pokorah-Vo hadn't been so bad because buildings there were rarely more than two stories. Shifara City had many buildings that were four stories or taller. I saw at least one building that was seven stories and I was relieved when we had safely passed it by. Buildings below ground were fixed to rock at both bottom and top, I couldn't imagine what kept these from falling over.

The street ran the long length of the city. Eventually, we reached the north gate. Looking through the gate, I could see the causeway that led to Shifara Castle. Agrélian dismounted and went to speak to the guards. He returned after a moment with another guard.

"I must return to my post," he said. "Dimas will assist you in your petition to the Court."

"Welcome to Shifara," the guard, who was evidently Dimas, spoke. He looked at Alénia. "These are from Su Lariano?"

She shrugged and looked away. "Ask them yourself. I was just showing them the way."

Dimas turned toward Mira, high on Farukan's back.

"Your pardon," he said. "You are a delegation from Su Lariano?"

"We are," Mira answered.

"You bear the armor of a White Rider," he said. "Are you also here as a representative of the Rider Council?"

"No," Mira answered. "I haven't even met them yet." She pulled a document out of her saddlebags and handed it to him.

"This is our letter of introduction from Queen Astrina Ulané Poloso."

The guard glanced at the seal.

"I am not familiar with the official seal of Su Lariano," he told us. "If you would please wait, I will send this ahead for verification. It will be returned to you unopened."

He handed the document to another guard, who saluted and dashed through the gate toward the castle. When Dimas turned back to us, Bijoux had approached him and was getting his scent. Dimas panicked at the sudden appearance of a *Jahgreet* and jumped back in a crouch, his hand going to the hilt of his sword.

"Bijoux," I called to her. "Don't scare the poor man. He's just doing his job."

Bijoux flipped an ear at me and opened her mouth in an enormous yawn. Then she flopped down and began cleaning her claws while she looked around.

Dimas straightened up, his eyes still on Bijoux.

"I am afraid you will need to use a sturdy collar and leash," he said. "We can't allow such a dangerous creature to roam the castle freely."

That might be a problem.

"We don't really have one," I told him. "I guess I could use a length of rope."

"I'll have something suitable brought," he said. He signaled to another of the guards. This one was a *Loiala Fé.*

"She likes red if you have it," I called after her.

The first guard to return was the one from Shifara Castle. The seal on the document had been verified, and we were cleared to proceed from that standpoint.

"I'm sorry," Dimas said. "But I can't allow you to continue with the animal if it is not leashed."

"You guys can go on without me and I'll catch up later," I told the others.

"Are you sure?" Mira asked me.

"I don't want to leave her," I said, "and you don't need me for this."

"They don't need me either," Kiarash said with a grin, "but I'm not passing up the chance to meet royalty."

"I will also stay," Shéna said. "I am only a maid. Not someone to be presented in Court."

That surprised me. I wouldn't have expected Shéna to volunteer to hang out with me.

"Once we have a leash for you," Dimas told us, "you will be able to proceed to the castle where your party will be quartered as diplomatic guests."

I had spotted a café close by with tables outside.

"We'll relax over here," I said. "We'll see you later."

A guard led Mira and the others out onto the causeway while Shéna and I both dismounted. Leaving our horses with the guards, we went to sit at the café with Bijoux following on our heels.

# CHAPTER TWENTY-SIX

## RISPAN

*T*he coffee served by the café was far superior to anything we'd been able to manage on the trail. I reveled in it silently as I watched people in the area go about their business. You could learn a lot by watching people. I'd always done this naturally, but the training we had received before our trip to Pokorah-Vo had taken it to a whole new level. I'd refined it even further in practice on the mission.

The street that ran through the city from one gate to the other was the main thoroughfare. There was a lot of business and foot travel. Mostly I saw *Ashae*, but there were also a number of human and *Loiala Fé*.

The guards were only semi-alert. This told me that they were competent enough but didn't expect serious trouble. Considering the only access to the gate was through the city, that wouldn't be unusual.

I heard a low whistle and glanced back at the guards. On the surface, they looked the same as before, but now their casual attitude was for show and I could tell by how they held their eyes that they were on high alert.

An *Ashae* in white armor was striding toward the gate. Dimas stepped into his path.

"Lord Tibor." Dimas nodded. "What can we do for you?"

"A party came though not long ago," the Rider said. "What was their business?"

"Your pardon, Lord, but I am not at liberty to say."

"You would deny a request from the Rider Council?" The Rider's voice was full of menace.

"It is not my place to render such a determination," Dimas told him. "If you would like to submit an official request in writing, I will pass it on immediately to the appropriate person."

"Our requests are not required to be in writing!" The Rider bristled.

"That is true, Lord Tibor." Dimas nodded. "It can be spoken during the weekly general assembly, and it can be evaluated at that time. If you would care to return for the next meeting in three days' time, we will gladly allow you to pass for that purpose."

"Your lack of cooperation and respect will be noted, Dimas."

"You pardon, Lord Tibor." No emotion showed on Dimas' face. "I have endeavored to be respectful and apologize if I have not done so. My duties are very clear and specific; I do not have the authority to do other than I have done. If I have been derelict in any way, it was not intentional, and I ask that you notify my superiors that I may be corrected."

This response left Tibor without ammunition. He glared at Dimas for a moment before turning and going back the way he had come.

Dimas watched him until he was out of sight, then he turned his eyes speculatively on me. I tipped my cup in acknowledgement before taking another sip. He huffed a single chuckle and turned away.

I shared a glance with Shéna and could tell that she had also found their exchange to be very educational. We were silently enjoying our second cups when the other *Loiala Fé* guard returned. She had something coiled in her hand and a *Loiala Fé* was following her closely.

She hesitated when she drew near, and Dimas pointed to where we waited. She saw us and headed straight over.

"I'm sorry for the delay," she said. "Finding a proper leash was more difficult than I would have imagined. And there was nothing in red."

"Good day, sir and Lady," the man with her said. "I am Karel. It was from my humble shop that we were able to supply a poor and temporary solution for you."

The guard rolled her eyes.

"We have a collar and braided leather leash," he went on. "Which might be fine for a family pet in an ordinary household, but they are not at all suited for such a glorious creature."

"Oh, really?" I looked at him.

"Use these with my compliments," Karel said. "They are far too worthless to charge a fee. But please allow me to see the animal in question and I will devise something more befitting."

I took the collar and leash from the guard. It was a simple thing of plain thick leather and a buckle, slipped through a loop at the end of the braided leash.

"Come here, Bijoux," I said to her.

Bijoux looked up at me curiously and stepped over. She sniffed at the collar. I could tell she didn't know what to think about it when I buckled the collar around her neck. She tried to push it off over her head experimentally.

"You know," I said. "The first time she gets annoyed by a tug on the leash, she'll probably bite through it like paper."

"Undoubtedly." Karel nodded. "This is one of the things an appropriate leash would counter." He looked over Bijoux. "Very good," he smiled. "I will bring you something in the morning. I'm sure you will be quite satisfied."

"I don't know where we'll be," I told him.

"No matter." He nodded with a smile as he left. "I will find you."

I grinned at the guard. "There is no power greater than that of a merchant with his eye on a sale."

She laughed, glancing briefly at Shéna. "When you are ready, I am sure Dimas will let you pass now."

"Thanks for your help," I told her.

She smiled with a nod before walking back over to join the other guards.

"You flirt very easily," Shéna commented, her eyes on her empty cup as she set it on the table.

"It doesn't hurt to be a little friendly." I scowled at her. She probably would have complained if I'd been rude, too.

"If you say so," she answered, her voice flat.

"I'm afraid to see what that guy is going to bring us," I changed the subject. "I have a feeling it's going to cost us."

Dimas allowed us to pass with Bijoux on her leash. He assigned the same guard who'd helped with the leash to guide us. Her name was Démka.

"The first thing will be to get your horses stabled with the others," she told us as we went out across the causeway that led to Shifara Castle. "Then we'll find out where you are all quartered." She glanced at me. "Have you come far?"

I nodded. "Most of us from Su Lariano, others from further, Pokorah-Vo."

"I think I've heard of Su Lariano," she said. "How far is it?"

"Seventeen hundred miles, give or take."

"Wow." She shook her head. "I think my butt would be tired after that much riding."

"Why?" Shéna asked her. "How much do you usually get ridden?"

Démka looked at her sharply, and then scowled at me.

Maybe life would be easier if I became a hermit.

Démka stopped making conversation. She spoke to the guards at the end of the causeway, then motioned for us to follow her through the gate. She took us to a small stable.

"Your party wasn't given VIP status, so you're quartered outside the keep itself," she said. "Your mounts will go in the stable here, and you will be staying in that building." She pointed to a medium-sized structure next to the stable that looked like a small mansion. "Enjoy your stay."

Shéna rode forward to the stable. As Démka turned to go, she glanced at me. "If you two were together," she whispered angrily. "You could have let me know!"

"What?" I turned to her retreating back. "We're not."

I followed Shéna into the stable. Javen was already there.

"Just grab your saddlebags," he said. "I'll take care of everything else. You won't need your blanket rolls either."

"Thanks Javen," I said to him.

"You know," I said to Shéna as we walked to the other building, "We should be trying to make friends, not enemies."

"I don't know what you mean." She shrugged. "She didn't seem to be mad at *me*."

Mooren and Kiarash were inside with Alénia.

"I thought you wanted to meet royalty," I said to Kiarash.

"We aren't officials." He frowned. "So only Mira and Tesia could go all the way."

"You must be disappointed," I laughed.

"It's not so bad," he said. "We have a kitchen. And it comes with a cook."

That ended the conversation for me, and I went in search of the cook. Not long after, I was seated at the table enjoying an omelet with cheese and onions and mushrooms.

"Isn't that a breakfast dish?" Kiarash asked me.

I looked up at him. "Do I tell you how to fly?"

He held up his hands in surrender and I went back to eating.

It was hours before Mira and Tesia joined us, and they were more than a little annoyed.

"Two days!" Mira scowled. "We waited all that time to be told to come back in two days!"

"It's not surprising," Tesia told her. "You can't just show up at the capitol and expect the king and queen to drop everything to see you when they don't know anything about you. And it's not like they see Su Lariano as an important ally."

"I know." Mira sat down heavily on the couch. "I just hate waiting."

"There's food," I said. "And a cook."

"Men." Mira scowled at me. "Give them something to eat and that's all they care about."

I started to say something about that not being *all* men cared about, but I saw Shéna looking at me, waiting for my comment, and I thought better of it.

"Food is good," was all I said.

"Eat well," Alénia spoke up, looking at Mira. "Tomorrow we can train."

Mira groaned.

"Your weapon is the staff, yes?" Alénia asked her.

"Yes." Mira looked at her. "Why?"

"It is good that you brought your strengths into the longsword," Alénia said, "but you must know the differences. When you understand them and learn how one can play into the other and how it does not, then you will be truly formidable with the blade."

Mira gave her a puzzled look. "How do you mean?"

"Tomorrow."

Mira and Alénia kept themselves occupied the next day by drilling with the longsword in the space outside between the residence and the stable. Mira had received good instruction back in Su Lariano, but no one there had been a true master with this weapon. The tips that Alénia could give her were far beyond the abilities of any of our instructors. I watched with Mooren for a bit, but eventually I went back inside.

Not long after that, we got a knock at the door from Karel the merchant. As soon as he stepped inside, he had Bijoux's attention.

Karel placed a box on the table and opened the lid.

"I had craftsmen working through the day and night to create the perfect items," he said. "Her name is Bijoux, you said?"

"That's right."

Bijoux was walking around him, smelling and sniffing.

Karel reached into the box and pulled out a collar. The leather was stained a bright red. The buckle was silver and gold. I could tell that the workmanship was of a very high quality. He removed the plain leather collar from around Bijoux's neck and attached the new one. Bijoux seemed to luxuriate in it and didn't try to remove it as she had the other one.

Karel reached into the box again and pulled out a coiled cord. One end had a clipping mechanism and he attached it to the collar. He handed the other end to me. The cord was a three-ply braid, woven of red leather and silver and gold woven chains. My end was looped back into the braid so I could put it easily around my wrist. He had really gone all out with this.

"The whole thing is magically reinforced," he said. "It will be resistant to snapping or breaking. It will even resist being cut, either from a bite or from a blade."

"It's all quite remarkable," I told him. "I'm afraid it may be too expensive for us. We're not wealthy landowners. I'm just a simple public servant."

"A public servant you may be," he smiled, "but you are also a representative of your city and your queen, yes? And official delegations are provided funds for expenses, so this would not come out of your own purse."

He'd guessed right on that. I was still afraid to ask.

"How much?"

"As I realize you may not have anticipated this need, I am willing to sell this for a much lower price that would normally befit such an item," he told me. "Normally, such an item would go for three hundred gold pieces. It pains me to say it, but I can let you have it for one hundred fifty gold, in the name of cooperation and goodwill between our cities."

"A hundred and fifty gold?" That was more than half of what we'd been given for expenses. "I'm sorry to waste your time," I told him. "I was afraid you were going to say fifty and I'd have to say it was too much. But a hundred and fifty? My queen would lock me in a cell, and I'd never again see the light of day."

"Fifty?" He acted like I'd just stabbed his mother. "That wouldn't even cover the cost of the materials alone! Let alone to pay the artisans to craft the work! There's probably the equal weight of fifty gold in the woven chain. I might be able to do one hundred ten, but even artisans have families to feed."

"They will eat better than I will in a cell," I told him. "Which is exactly where I would be if I spent a hundred and ten gold pieces of my queen's money for a collar and leash. If I was given the chance to explain the precious metals in the chain, she may forgive sixty. But I would still be taking a risk."

"Sixty? Surely your queen is more intelligent than that," he scoffed. "One glance would tell her that ninety was a bargain and she would praise you!"

"My queen is not so lax with the use of public funds." I shook my head. "I might be able to avoid life imprisonment if I didn't spend beyond seventy."

He sighed and reached for the buckle of the collar, but Bijoux growled at him, and he withdrew his hands.

"You will have to remove it from her," he told me. "She seems to like it. It is a shame you couldn't go as high as eighty to keep her happy. I will need to break the news to the artisans that their work was not adequately appreciated."

I knew full well that his workers would be paid and that the amount was unlikely to change based on what he charged me. At best, they were paid in silver, not gold. I stepped toward Bijoux, and she looked at me suspiciously.

"Perhaps if I explained Bijoux's insistence," I suggested. "My queen would not punish me too severely if I spent seventy-five for this."

His expression suggested he was experiencing extreme indigestion. "Let us not quibble over such a small difference," he said. "Let us agree on seventy-eight gold and be done with it."

"Done." I shook his hand to seal the deal. "Wait here please."

I went into the other room and dug the amount from the sack Mira had in her saddlebags. Then I went back to Karel and counted it out onto the table. He swept the coins into his own purse and nodded to me.

"It was a pleasure doing business with you," he said. "You drive a hard bargain."

"Tell me the truth," I said. "Why does Bijoux like it so much?"

"She may simply have good taste." He shrugged. There was an unmistakable glint in his eye. "Though treating the leather with catnip oil might be part of it."

I ignored Shéna's chuckle from the side of the room. Shaking my head, I showed him to the door. I unclipped the leash from the collar and set it on the table. Bijoux sat with her head held proudly. I'd have to explain it to Mira later.

We didn't know when they'd be back, and I still had time to kill. Mira always had a book or two with her, and I dug one out of her saddlebags. I sat down to read it but when I opened it up, it was poetry. I didn't mind it, but it wasn't really my thing.

Kiarash, Tabalin, and Javen had seemed to form a bond with each other and were keeping themselves occupied in the stable areas. I wasn't particularly fond of hay or the smell of manure, so I stayed in the residence with Shéna. I looked around the shelves and cabinets and found what looked like the board game that I'd seen in Gralbast's study.

"I don't suppose you know how to play this?" I asked, holding up the board.

"*Jhianki*? I am familiar with the basics," Shéna said, "but I am no master."

"Can you teach me?" I asked.

"Have you played before?"

"No." I shook my head. "I know Gralbast had one of these, but I don't know anything about it."

We set the board up on a table between us.

"What's the object of the game?"

"To capture or control more territory than your opponent," she told me. "The strategies in *Jhianki* can be very complex."

The square board consisted of a grid of lines, nineteen by nineteen, and we each had a bag of small stones, black or white.

"Stones are placed on the intersections," she told me. "Not in the squares."

We went over the rules and basic moves, but it quickly got very complicated. I set a stone on the board, and she shook her head.

"No, you don't want to do that. You will trap yourself and I'll take control of that area."

I paused to look at the board to see what she meant. By the end of the morning, I felt I was getting the hang of it, at least the general idea. It also seemed that Shéna was better at the game than she let on. It was very pleasant, and I had found that when she wasn't snapping at me for some reason, I really enjoyed her company.

"How did you learn to play?" I asked her.

She paused in placing a stone. "One of my masters enjoyed playing it," she said. "He would invite others for a challenge. He wasn't very good, but he was powerful and had a bad temper, so they let him win. I was his prize, and I would serve them while they played. But I watched and learned."

Meanwhile, Tesia was studying some books on magic she had brought along. That got me thinking.

"How hard is it to learn magic?" I asked her as we were finishing up lunch.

"It depends on what you want to learn," she answered. "A lot of it is pretty simple, but some spells can be extremely complex and mastering them can be quite a challenge. Most people stop learning once they can do all the basics. Why? Are you thinking of advancing your level?"

"I don't really have a level," I said. "I was thinking I wouldn't mind learning at some point. It could be useful."

"How far did you get in your studies when you were younger?"

"It wasn't really something they focused on at the kids' home."

"I'm sure they taught you something?" she asked.

"I learned basic numbers," I told her, "and how to read. They didn't have much of a library, but I spent a lot of time there and read just about anything I could get my hands on."

"No, I mean about magic."

I shook my head.

She looked at me like I'd slapped her.

"Fundamental magic use is required education for all children in Su Lariano," she said. "Even for the kids' home. *Ralahin* is considered a birthright for all *Ulané Jhinura*, and education of our citizens is a primary pillar of Su Lariano."

I shrugged. "I don't know what to tell you."

I'd never seen Tesia angry, and the look in her eyes told me it was something to avoid at all costs.

"I will look into this when we return to Su Lariano," she said. "In the meanwhile, I will start you on your studies."

"You don't have to do that," I told her. "I mean, of course I'd like to learn, but we have other things going on and I don't want to bother you with this."

"Nonsense!" she said. "It's simple enough to get you going. It also helps if you have some personal goals for the process. Is there anything you specifically wish to be able to do?"

I thought for a moment. "That vision thing Mira does seems like it could be really useful. And the flitting that Mira and Neelu can do."

"To see using the *Ralahin* vision is simple enough," she nodded, "and with practice you can learn to maintain it. I can also teach you how to use the *Ralahin* to move more swiftly in the common method. But as for what Neelu and Mira do, that is another matter. The only thing I know about that technique is that it is dangerous, and I wouldn't recommend it."

"Just the normal way would be good," I said. "Anything at all would be good."

"Could you teach me as well?" Shéna asked. She seemed even more embarrassed about it than I was. "Slaves are forbidden to learn magic."

"You're not a slave any longer," Tesia said firmly. She looked at us. "Both of your educations have been lacking, and through no fault of your own, either of you. We will start right away."

Any worry I'd had about how we were going to pass the time waiting for Mira's Court appointment the next afternoon was quickly dispelled. Tesia worked us mercilessly on *Ralahin* and magic basics. I'd overheard a lot of conversations between her and Mira on magic, but most of that had been far above anything I could think about or understand. By the time we broke for lunch the following day, we could connect to the *Ralahin* vision to See. I was able to light a candle, and Shéna could move small objects. She had also given us the basics for anchoring our position, which was the first step in using the *Ralahin* to move.

"Different people will have different strengths," Tesia said. "Things that are simple for one can be nearly impossible for another."

A page arrived after lunch to bring Mira and Tesia to their appointment. Mooren was allowed to go with them as a personal aide. Shéna and I kept at our lessons while they were gone. They finally returned in time for dinner.

"How was it?" I asked as Mira sat on the couch.

"Exhausting," she said. "We had an appointment, but that was just to get in line. We still had to wait for hours."

"It can be tiring," Tesia admitted, "but the good thing is that we have been officially received and granted diplomatic status."

"So, what's next?" I asked them.

"I need to go to Vaelir's estate," Mira said. "That's the center of my inheritance from killing Vaelir. Step one is to stabilize things there. Then I can send official notification to the Rider

Council of my claim, and they will tell me when to show up to present my case."

"When do we report the slavery?" I tried to keep my voice casual. I didn't need to lose control whenever this subject came up.

"As soon as we know Farukan's family is safe," Mira told me. "That's top priority."

"Then we go to the Minister of Internal Relations," Tesia put in. "We have an appointment in a week. They can escalate things very quickly through the proper channels."

"How exactly are we going to make sure Farukan's family stays safe after you talk to that Minister?"

"We'll have to send them to safety," Mira answered. "As long as they stay, they'll be in danger."

"Sounds like a plan." I nodded. "When do we start?"

"In the morning," she said. "It's at least a couple hours ride to Shianri."

# CHAPTER TWENTY-SEVEN

## MIRA

*W*e headed out after breakfast. Rispan had shown me the collar and leash for Bijoux. It was beautiful workmanship and Bijoux wore it like she was a queen, and it was her crown. I wasn't happy about the cost, but considering the materials, I couldn't deny that the price had been fair. I didn't know how much use we were going to get out of it, but it looked like Bijoux was going to be a permanent fixture with Rispan, so it would be a good idea to have something that would make a statement like that.

"I'll be sure to notate it in an expense report," I told him. "If it gets denied, I'm sure it won't take you more than twenty years or so to pay it back."

We made our way back across the causeway from Shifara astle to Shifara City. I glanced back over my shoulder at the gate to the causeway and noticed a small man watching us intently from near the gate. I couldn't make out any distinct features other than he was roughly the same height as Kiarash and had dark-red skin. It wasn't long before we had crossed the city and were out the main gates.

I'd been provided general directions from one of the minor officials we'd dealt with the previous day. I hoped I remembered

233

them well enough. If not, we could always ask someone along the way. Farukan must have heard my thoughts.

*"I know the way."*

*"Of course,"* I sent back to him. *"After all, this is your home we're talking about."*

*"Not a home,"* his disagreement rumbled. *"Our prison."*

I patted him on the neck. *"Not for much longer."*

Farukan led off once we were outside the city. The estate was southwest of Shifara, in the foothills just below a rocky range. By late morning, we were passing under an arched gate. Orchards grew on either side of the road. It was at least twenty minutes before the villa came into view ahead of us.

As we drew near, I saw a flurry of movement and more than a dozen *Loiala Fé* came to line up in the large space in front of the building. One *Ashae* stood in front of them. From her bearing, she was very much in charge of these people.

We came to a halt and her eyes were fixed on me.

"We welcome you to Shianri as our new Lord." She bowed to me. "I am Ancaera. I hope you will allow me to serve you as I served the last Master of Shianri."

Farukan kneeled to let me get to my feet. Ancaera's eyes widened with surprise at this.

"Thank you, Ancaera." I didn't know what the protocol was.

"What are you doing?" a voice demanded from the doorway. "I told you to ignore her!"

It was Niklos.

"Get back inside, all of you!" he demanded.

The *Loiala Fé* looked at each other with uncertainty.

Ancaera dipped her head, "With respect, Niklos, you are not our Master. Her claim stands unless the Council decides otherwise."

"Don't argue—"

"What are you doing here, Niklos?" I cut in.

"This is my uncle's estate." He glared at me. "I have leave to visit whenever I choose."

"Your uncle is dead, and you are standing on *my* property," I corrected him, "and you are not welcome. You do have a habit of being where you are not wanted, don't you?"

Ancaera caught her breath as soon as the words were out of my mouth. She carefully kept her eyes on the ground.

"Can you leave on your own?" I asked him. "Or do you need assistance?"

"I look forward to your slow death." He glared at me. "Groom! Saddle my horse!"

One of the *Loiala Fé* bowed and started to leave.

"Wait." I stopped him. "It may have escaped you Niklos, but everyone is currently busy. I'm afraid you're going to have to saddle your own horse. I assume you know how?"

He turned angrily and strode towards what looked like a horse barn. As I turned back to Ancaera, I noticed Rispan had also dismounted and was following behind Niklos.

"Ancaera, thank you for your welcome. I'm pretty new at all of this," I told her. "In fact, I'm new to this world. I'm going to have to rely on you, on all of you really." I turned to include the others. "I'm not here to make a bunch of changes or tell you how to do your jobs. And Ancaera, I have no idea what your role is, and I look forward to hearing about everything. There is one thing." I looked over all of them. "I don't know anything about how things were done in the past, but there is something I will insist on. Justice, fairness, and mutual respect. Anyone who can't abide by that will have no place here. I'll meet you all individually as I can. Meanwhile, please carry on with whatever you were doing. And stay clear of Niklos until he's gone."

They clearly didn't know what to make of me, but they dipped their heads and dispersed.

"Ancaera—" I was interrupted by mental shout from Farukan.

"*Akshira! No!*" Farukan suddenly bolted toward the horse barn.

I didn't wait to ask what was going on; I flitted to the inside, faster than even the big *Rorujhen* could move.

Niklos was grappling with Rispan, but Rispan only came up to his breastbone and was having a hard time of it. They were next to a dark grey *Rorujhen*, and I could see it had two deep gashes on its neck. Niklos held Rispan by the throat with one hand. Rispan had a dagger and tried a cut, but it glanced off Niklos' armor. There was a pounding against the walls from a nearby stall.

Niklos' right arm was tangled in his cloak. He shrugged it free, and I saw he held a bloody dagger.

"Time for you to die!" he snarled at Rispan.

"No!" I screamed.

Niklos' blade was moving, but I had to be faster. My daggers were out, and one slash crossed the tendons on the back of his hand, then I was between them like a whirlwind, slashing both femoral arteries and his jugular.

Rispan fell from Niklos' grasp as the Rider staggered back, confusion on his face. I stood ready in case he tried anything else. I needn't have bothered. The dagger had already fallen from his hand and any of the other wounds would kill him if not treated instantly. Even magic would be unlikely to save him from all three. His blood was forming a great puddle around him as he collapsed to the ground.

"Akshira!" Ancaera rushed past me to the wounded *Rorujhen*.

I still had my connection to the *Ralahin* and saw her start to manipulate magic. She placed her hands on the wounds and muscle and skin began to weave back together.

I turned to Rispan, "Are you alright? What happened?"

"He pulled his knife and before I knew what was happening, he'd started slashing at the mare on her neck. It's a good thing you got here when you did, though."

Ancaera was stepping back from the *Rorujhen*, her face looking tired.

"She'll be alright now," she said. "There will be scars, but she will live." She looked at Niklos' body. "This might complicate things. Are we to be allies?" she asked me.

"Allies?" I asked her. "Vaelir was your husband, right?"

"I did not choose him." Her mouth was a grim line. "I was forced to marry him so he could take control of Shianri when my father died."

"Well, you heard my conditions out front," I told her. "If that works for you, then we're good."

She nodded. "It is best to keep this quiet for now. When you go to the Council to present your claim for Vaelir, you must do so for Niklos as well. You have Vaelir's armor, yes?"

I nodded.

"You will need to bring both sets." She looked me over. "What do you know of the laws of the Riders? The strictures by which they must operate?"

"Nothing," I told her.

"Riders are not permitted to feud except through the explicit consent of the Council," she said. "They will try to censure you for this. But Niklos was attempting to kill a *Rorujhen* which was your property. Therefore, *he* must be presented as the aggressor and your act as one of defense. We need to immediately send an official notification that you are established on your estate and are prepared to present your claim."

She smiled, "You are going to be a problem for them. They don't like women to own property. And they do not like humans. Presenting your claim as both a human and a woman will upset many of their established traditions."

"You'll have to excuse me if I don't feel sorry for them," I said.

She laughed, then glanced at my armor, "The *balangur* is to be your symbol?"

"Yes." I nodded. The ravens.

She smiled, "The estate is called Shianri. In the old tongue, it means hearth or home. But in some translations, it means nest.

*Balangur* is a fitting symbol for the Master of a nest. Come, let us go inside." The groom was standing by. "Niden, you know what to do here," she said to him, nodding at Niklos.

We had all gathered in the barn at this point.

"Javen, Tabalin," I told them, "See what you can do to help here please."

We followed Ancaera to the house. Kiarash stayed to help Javen and Tabalin.

"So that is how fast you move when you fight with magic," Alénia commented with a nod. "It can make a difference."

Ancaera led us to a study where we all took a seat. She looked around the group and back to me.

"These are all sworn to you?" she asked. "They are your inner circle and privy to your plans? Your secrets?"

Alénia stood up before I could answer. "I am sworn to none," she said. "I'll be outside."

Shéna rose as well. "I am sworn only to my people. Though I see you as allies and even friends, my people will always come first." She followed Alénia out of the room.

That left Rispan, Mooren, and Tesia. Ancaera made a movement with her hand, and I could see she had raised some sort of magical barrier around us.

"No one can hear our words now," she explained. "We can speak freely. I will start, as I am the one who must earn your trust."

Rispan went to a side table and raised a decanter to pour us each drinks while she continued.

"Shianri has been in my family for generations," she said. "We bred horses. I had no siblings and when my father died, under questionable circumstances, I had to marry or lose Shianri. Vaelir arrived, pretending, though poorly, to be charming and interested in only me. I knew his true motive, but that didn't change the necessity of my choice. It wasn't long after our marriage that he went on an expedition beyond the Great Mountains. He returned with six *Rorujhen*. Two males and five females.

It was his intention to breed them. In the end, there was only one colt. He had no understanding of horses, let alone *Rorujhen* or the differences between the two."

"And you do?" I asked her.

"We are generations of horse breeders in my family," she said. "Of course, I knew they were not the same. My *husband* had been gone for some time before I learned the full extent of that difference. I assume you are aware?"

I nodded. Then I realized. "You called her Akshira! Her true name!"

Her eyes widened, "I did! That was a mistake. I hope no one noticed."

"And that brings us to another of my conditions" I told her. "I will not abide slavery."

Ancaera nodded, looking relieved. "Then we are of the same mind in this. But what do you intend to do about it?"

"Our plan was first to make sure Farukan's family was safe."

"Farukan?" Ancaera looked at me. "Akshira wouldn't tell me his name. She said it wasn't her secret to reveal. But they aren't the only ones in slavery. There are four others here, not to mention all the *Rorujhen* that other Riders have."

"We will help the ones we can," I told her, "and then we intend to report the Riders to the king and queen. Bring the slavery out into the open. We made an appointment with the Minister of Internal Relations for the Royal Court to bring forward a grievance. We have one week to take care of everything else before the appointment."

"The king and queen will gladly use this to break the Riders' power." She nodded. "The Riders have been growing in influence and this has caused much unrest and intrigue. This may even lead to civil war." She thought for a moment. "Have you thought of how you will proceed once you have made the accusation?"

"Not really." I shrugged. "I figured at that point we would turn it over to the locals and head back south."

She shook her head. "That would be seen as retracting your accusation. Once you start this rolling, you will need to see it through."

"That kind of puts a delay on getting back to Pokorah-Vo," I said, "but I can't just let it drop."

"Good," she nodded. "You have to send as many of the *Rorujhen* away as you can, as soon as you can. The Riders would kill them all to prevent the truth from coming out."

"I thought we could just keep them under guard to protect them," I said.

She shook her head. "Too risky. If they get desperate and launch an all-out attack, there's no way to keep the *Rorujhen* safe. They have to be gone."

"We can't just turn them loose to fend for themselves," I said. "They need allies. And that means someone has to go with them."

Mooren and Rispan shared a look. Rispan shook his head in disgust.

"What?" I asked him.

"It'll have to be me," he said, "but I don't like it."

I started to object, but then I saw what he meant. Mooren wouldn't leave me, no matter what I said to him. And this wasn't something Tesia could really do, even if I didn't need her to stay, and I definitely needed her knowledge and expertise dealing with officials and bureaucrats. No, I didn't like it either, but he was right.

"When?" I asked.

"We should probably send all the *Rorujhen* that are here at Shianri as soon as possible," Mooren said. "The further out of harm's way they can be, the better."

"But what about all the other *Rorujhen* enslaved by the Riders?" I didn't want to leave them behind.

"We'll just have to send them south as soon as we can and hopefully, they can meet up with Rispan's group," he said.

"I agree." Rispan nodded. "We can't put all our money on

one throw of the dice. We get out the ones we know we can get out, and then we try for the rest."

"I don't know how long it will be before I can get back to Pokorah-Vo," I told him. "You should take over as Raven while I'm gone."

He thought about that and nodded. "Just don't be gone too long."

"Don't get too attached to my hat," I told him.

"First things first," Ancaera said. She went to a small writing desk and took out a parchment, a quill, and an ink bottle. "What's your full name?" she asked me as she started writing.

"Mirabela Cervantes Ramirez."

We waited while she finished writing the document and blew gently across its surface to dry the ink.

"This says you are settled at Shianri and are prepared to submit your claim as victor to the White Rider Council," she explained, handing it to me. "Normally, it would include the name of the defeated party. When they ask you to verify the identity, you will tell them it is for Vaelir and Niklos both."

I looked at the document. "Mirabela nya Balangur?" I handed it back.

She nodded, folding the document. "You need to establish a clan name, and using your symbol lends more consistency, hence credibility." She picked up a stick of red wax. "You will need to imprint your sigil."

"My sigil?"

"Your symbol," she said. "To seal the document."

"I don't have—" Yes, I do! I removed the raven clasp from the collar of my cloak. "Will this work?"

She looked at it and nodded. "Yes. We can get something better for the future. Something set on a ring."

She pulled on ambient magic to melt the wax and then pressed the raven figure into it.

"Just a moment," she said. She made a motion and the barrier around the room dropped. "Néci?" she called.

A moment later, one of the *Loiala Fé* stepped into the room. "Lady?"

Ancaera handed her the sealed document. "Please see that this is taken to Master Dimétrian immediately."

She raised the barrier again after Néci left.

"Shéna and Kiarash should come with me," Rispan said. "We should probably bring the *Rorujhen* to Su Lariano for protection and then go on to Pokorah-Vo. Kiarash can spy out the way from above on Naga, so Tabalin can stay with you."

"And that brings us back to the question of when?" I pointed out.

"Best to get it done," Rispan said. "Give us a good night's sleep and we can leave tomorrow."

I nodded. "That will keep my promise to Farukan."

"Alright." He stood up. "I'll go break the news to Shéna and Kiarash that we're back on the road tomorrow."

"One thing." Ancaera stopped us. "I just want to say that I am proud to be a part of what you are doing for the *Rorujhen* and for the *Ashae*." With that, she dropped the barrier.

# CHAPTER TWENTY-EIGHT

## RISPAN

*T*he rest of the evening was spent preparing supplies and everything that we would need for the trip south.

I went to the barn where the *Rorujhen* were kept. They needed to know what was going on as well.

"Hi," I said to them. "I'm Rispan. I know you can all understand me. And I also know that scares some of you. It's against the Riders' rules to let anyone know you can think and talk. But all that is going to be changing. I'm sure Farukan has told you already; you are not going to be slaves anymore. Tomorrow, I'm taking you all south so that you will be safe. Mira made that promise to Farukan, and we're keeping it. Once they know you are all safe, they don't have to worry about you, and they can do what they need to do."

I had their attention all right.

"*Listen to him my brothers and sisters,*" Farukan said. "*He speaks the truth.*"

"At first, I was thinking to ride horses and lead you out," a couple of them tossed their heads derisively at that, "but that would slow us down. So, I'm looking for volunteers. I need a mount for myself and one other. And one or two to carry packs. But this is a request, not an order. Once we're out of here, you will be free. The plan is to go to Su Lariano. That's where my people are. They will recognize you as a people, not as animals or as slaves to be owned. You don't even have to come with me once we leave here, but we are stronger united."

*"You fought the Rider earlier."* The thought came to my mind. It was not as deep as Farukan's and seemed to come from the back of a dark stall. *"When he attacked Akshira."*

"Yes." I nodded. "That was me."

*"You could have been killed. You very nearly lost your life to protect her."*

"Well." I shrugged. "I don't know about that. Dying was never part of the plan."

*"You fight for those you do not know, at peril to yourself. I will be your mount."*

"Thank you," I said to him. "I would be honored. How are you called?"

*"I am Barashan,"* he said. *"Akshira is my dam. Farukan is my sire."*

*"I will carry your other,"* a female voice whispered in my mind. *"I am Akshira."*

"Thank you, Akshira."

*"You are fools,"* another voice spoke, *"but I will carry a pack. I am Bahram."*

*"And I,"* came another. *"I am Reyhana."*

"Thank you both," I said. "Sleep well tonight, all of you. We have a long day ahead of us tomorrow."

We all came together for an early breakfast. Barashan and Akshira both knelt so that Shéna and I could mount. Barashan's coat was jet black, and he stood nearly as tall as Farukan. I looked down at Mira and the others from the saddle.

"I still wish I could be there for your challenge," I said to Mira. "Not that I don't think you can handle yourself."

'I know." She nodded. "You get into too much trouble on your own. Look what happened last time I wasn't around to keep you on your toes."

A lot had happened last time we split up. To both of us.

"Kick butt, sis," I said.

Barashan saved me any embarrassment by heading out, the others fell in line behind. I could tell something was also passing between Farukan and his family. I felt like if I focused, I could understand what they were saying, but I respected their privacy and left them to their own farewells.

Unencumbered by slower horses, *Rorujhen* could practically fly across the ground. They could go for twelve hours a day and travel two hundred and fifty miles in that time. On horses, it would take us a week to travel that far. That would put us in Su Lariano in a week. Kiarash could still keep up with us on Naga, but it wouldn't be as easy for them as it had been on the trip north. Bijoux had to ride with me; fast as she was, she couldn't keep up with the *Rorujhen* for that many hours.

*"You didn't mention this creature would be riding as well,"* Barashan commented. But I could tell he was taking it in good humor.

"Yeah," I admitted. "I kinda forgot about that. Sorry."

I still tended to talk out loud to the *Rorujhen,* and it would sometimes startle me to receive their thoughts. Mira seemed to have made the transition to mental communication more easily.

I hoped Mira was doing well with her claim and challenge but worrying about it wasn't going to help anything. We were moving so quickly, I had doubts that any other *Rorujhen* would catch up when they could be sent south. Once we got to Su Lariano, we could post scouts to watch for them. The plan was that Farukan would give them a mental image of the route. My job was to get this group to safety.

Shéna looked small on Akshira's back, but she seemed much more comfortable than she had been on her horse coming north. I guessed that they'd been carrying on an internal conversation, and this had helped to reassure Shéna. She'd kept a brave face on the trip from Su Lariano to Shifara, but it seemed she was never quite comfortable. As she became more relaxed on

Akshira, her cares seemed to wash away. Her smile beamed, and the way the wind blew her hair as she rode was nothing short of breathtaking.

Ancaera had done a good job healing Akshira's wounds. Thin lines showed where the blades had cut her.

Bahram and Reyhana each carried packs that were relatively small. Other than Kiarash and Naga, the only other members of our party were three additional mares: Zaria, Triska, and Chessa.

All of the Rorujhen had been assigned pet names that had been mildly insulting and had been forbidden from using their true names. Simply the act of being able to say their own names had been empowering for them, but it was also frightening. None of them had wanted to be slaves, but they all feared the consequences of disobedience.

The story came out that they had all been captured roughly five years earlier when Vaelir had taken his trip to hunt for them. They had all been very young at the time except Akshira and Farukan. Normally, adult *Rorujhen* were too smart and fast to be caught, but Akshira had been pregnant with Barashan and Farukan wouldn't leave her.

I tried to draw them out by asking them about their story. Since the conversation was mental, they could easily talk while they ran, but only Bahram and Akshira seemed open to talking. They had been so indoctrinated against betraying their ability to speak they had a hard time accepting that the situation had changed. Even Reyhana and Bahram, who had spoken up the night before, were holding back.

Evidently, Vaelir had tried to get them to breed, but they had refused. It was one thing they could not be forced to do; they might have to submit to slavery themselves, but they would not create children for the purpose of making them slaves. There was a limit to how much Vaelir had been willing to punish them; they were too valuable. The fact that he'd had six *Rorujhen* had lent him quite a bit of status and prestige within the ranks of the White Riders. Being the only adults at the time, Akshira and

Farukan had become mother and father figures for the small herd.

As we camped on the second night, Chessa ventured a hesitant question. *"Are you to be our master now?"*

I could sense them all listening intently for my answer.

"Absolutely not," I said. "You have no owner now. No master besides yourself."

*"But where will we live? How will we know what to do? Who will give us food?"*

Her confused thoughts in my mind almost overwhelmed me.

"You can live wherever you want," I said. "You can go wherever you want."

*"But I have nowhere to go!"* Her fear was palpable. *"This was a mistake! We should go back!"*

"What about your family?" I asked her. "You can go back to them. I'm sure they would be happy to know you are safe."

*"Our families didn't want us,"* her words in my mind carried a deep pain. *"We were a disappointment. Only Vaelir was willing to take care of us, and he is gone."*

"Vaelir told you that, didn't he?" Shéna spoke up.

*"Yes,"* Chessa answered. *"He took care of us."*

"No!" Shéna told them. "Vaelir lied to you! He stole you from your families and turned you into slaves."

*"He could be cruel at times,"* Chessa argued, *"but he loved us. He was a good master!"*

I could sense mixed emotions coming from the others.

"There is no such thing as a good master," Shéna said. I could tell she was trying to be patient. "He was evil."

*"What can you know of it? You were not there. You did not know him!"*

"I have been a slave all my life!" she snapped back. "Every minute! Every breath! Every bite of rotten food and every blow and every indignity! And always being told how I deserved it! How I was lucky to get even that much!" Her face was contorted with rage.

"Look into my mind and see for yourself!" she demanded. "I know all the lies and all the manipulations. Anything to convince me that no one else could care for me or love me." I saw her gaze turn inward as her rage turned to pain. "I was worthless. Something scavenged from the refuse pile. It was all lies! Vaelir was a good man?" She shook her head. "Look in my mind and see other *good* men like *that*. But keep looking and you will see what a good man is really like, because they *do* exist!"

Shéna's outburst caught me by surprise. I suppose I never really thought much about her life in Pokorah-Vo beyond the obvious. I could sense the *Rorujhen* as their minds rushed to hers, looking through her memories as she bared them for her. Tears streamed down her face as she confronted her own memories. I got flashes of images and scenes as they bled over from the *Rorujhen*, though I couldn't look into her mind, myself. The impression I had was that they were absorbing the memories of her life. I couldn't imagine how that must have felt for Shéna. Towards the end I saw flashes that included me, bits of things I had said or done. And then they receded, drawing their minds back.

*"Thank you, little sister,"* Barashan said. *"You have honored us with your burden. Give us time to fit the pieces of our lives together in this new light. It is not easy for us."*

Shéna nodded. "I know."

"I know that there is a lot of uncertainty right now," I said to them. "You don't know what the future will hold for you, and that's scary. But have faith. And Hope. You do have a future. It will start with Su Lariano. You will have a place there and you will have the freedom to choose your own paths in your own time."

I felt their acceptance of my words, though they neither agreed nor disagreed.

"That was a very brave thing to do," I said to Shéna.

"I'm not brave." She shook her head. "I'm a coward."

"It doesn't seem that way to me at all," I told her.

"You don't understand. You *can't* understand." She looked at me. "You don't know how worthless someone has to be to be a slave. To stay a slave. You come along and you think you can understand." She took a breath. "You are a good man. And you come along and do so much, because you *are* good, and you *are* brave. And everything in me tells me I don't deserve someone to be good to me, that someone like you could never love someone like me because I am less than nothing and no matter how much I try or pretend, I will never be more than that. I can never be worthy. And so, I push you away because I could not bear it if I let you close and you pushed me away." She stood up from where she'd been sitting. "I need to sleep."

She went to where her bedroll was set up and laid down. Bijoux went over and curled up with her.

I was still reeling from what she had said, and a lot of little things clicked into place. I had to say something. She needed me to say something. What could I say that wouldn't just sound like some pathetic attempt to placate her, or like some trite and meaningless aphorism? She deserved better than that, but I didn't have the words.

Kiarash glanced at me but didn't say anything.

For a reasonably smart guy, I could be really stupid sometimes.

# CHAPTER TWENTY-NINE

## MIRA

*W*e had received an almost immediate answer to our notification to the Council, and I was given four days before I had to appear to present my claim. Meanwhile, Ancaera filled me in on what I would be facing.

"Technically," she told me. "There is a Council of eleven Riders. But the reality is that Master Dimétrian *is* the Council. He's been the Master for as long as anyone can remember, and he has too much power and too many connections for anyone to risk going against him."

"How long has he been the Master of the Council?"

"That's hard to say." She frowned. "I remember Vaelir had been trying to figure that out. He'd been checking old documents and asking around. No one could recall a time before he was Master."

"Do you think he had anything to do with Vaelir attacking me and my caravan?" I asked her.

"You can bet it didn't happen without his knowledge and at least his tacit approval."

"In other words," I said. "I'm going in there to explain how I was defending myself against Vaelir to the very guy that sent him."

"Essentially, yes."

"Shouldn't that worry me?"

"Not in terms of your claim," she said. "You would have to face a challenge either way. They will do whatever they can to keep a human from their ranks. Or a woman. And the match will be on horseback, in your case, you will be on Farukan. Dimétrian probably intended for Niklos to challenge you. He'll need to get someone else to do it now."

"He wouldn't do it himself?"

She shook her head. "Why should he risk himself when he can get any number of people to do things for him?"

"So, he's the one that's been pulling all the strings?"

"He *seems* to be." She nodded.

"You say that like there's more to it."

"Nothing provable," she said. "Vaelir had started to have suspicions that there might be someone else. But he was sent south, and he was never able to find out anything specific."

I also spent time every day, continuing to work with Alénia on the longsword, and with Tesia on magic. Tesia was still worried about how I would do with a magical battle, but Alénia was pleased with my progress with the sword.

"I have seen every Rider fight," she told me. "Blade to blade, not many of them could stand against you. The way you have incorporated other techniques and created your own style gives you a great advantage. And we have refined your competence in application."

"Thank you!" I knew that praise from her really meant something, but I also knew that the refinement she mentioned could never have happened without her. "Then I don't need to worry about the Riders except for their magical attacks."

"I didn't say that," she corrected me. "I said not many could stand against you, blade to blade. But there are definitely those it would be better for you to avoid."

That deflated my mood a little.

"Also, the fight will begin on horseback. You can't use a two-handed grip and the blade will be heavy. You must get your opponent on the ground as soon as you can." She nodded at me. "I look forward to seeing your match."

We headed out that morning. Mooren, Tesia, Alénia and Ancaera on horses, and me on Farukan.

"*Are you ready for this?*" I sent to him.

"*As ready as I can be,*" he replied. "*Challenges are not that common. This will be my first as well. But I have heard stories.*"

"*Anything you would care to share?*"

"*I would just caution you that you cannot ignore his mount,*" he said. "*Some of them can be quite brutal. Of course, I will do what I can to protect you.*"

"*Just help me get him on the ground,*" I told him. I needed to be able to use both hands with my sword.

The Hall of the White Riders was an adjunct to Master Dimétrian's estate, which was called Odaro. The ride over was only a couple of hours into the mountains to the south.

As we got closer, I started to experience a strange feeling. Not really physical, but something. I opened up my *Ralahin* vision and all the flows appeared to be moving a little faster than usual with just a little more force and urgency. It was flowing, or being pulled, to somewhere ahead of us. I turned to Tesia.

"Are you feeling this?" I asked her.

She nodded. "I can only think it is fueling an extremely powerful spell," she said, "but I've never seen anything this strong."

We continued onward and passed through the gate of the Odaro estate. Almost at once, the way forked, and we took the right-hand path. The road led to a building that reminded me of some churches back on Earth, and it was constructed almost entirely of white marble. The flows of magic were much stronger here and seemed to be focused on the building.

"Who approaches?" An *Ashae* stepped forward from the huge doors at the front of the building. He wore the white armor of a Rider.

"Mirabela nya Balangur," I answered. I was fully decked out in my own armor from Gylan. I even carried the helmet, though I had yet to put it on. Unlike the Rider who greeted us, I was not dressed all in white, and my cape was black.

He made a signal and the doors opened behind him.

"You may proceed," he said.

Evidently, we were expected to ride through the doors and they were built to accommodate riding a *Rorujhen*. Once we were inside, we could see that it was one huge room. There was a raised area on the far side, and there were several people seated at a large table that was curved so they could easily see each other. There was additional seating around the edges of the room, and to the left was an area for mounts and gear. The center of the room was a huge open space.

The flow of magic in the room was nearly a torrent at this point. It flowed through a wall to the right. The wall didn't look like it was part of the original structure.

Tesia paused and spoke just loud enough for me to hear.

"Do not try to flit," she warned me. "The flows are too strong here. It would destroy you."

That wasn't good. Flitting was one of my greatest secret weapons. If I couldn't use it, I would lose a huge advantage.

Ancaera nodded to me. Then she and the others went to the left as I rode forward on Farukan.

I looked at the Riders seated at the table on the raised stage area. Eleven *Ashae*. I assumed the older one in the center was Master Dimétrian. I wasn't wrong.

"You're Mirabela nya Balangur?" he spoke. His voice was smooth and smug, and a little whiny, like a bad salesman.

"I am." Ancaera had prepared me for how I should make my case. "I have come to announce my claim to the Council, for membership of the White Riders and for inheritance and holding, by right of victory in combat, as dictated by the laws of this Council."

"You know, I sent for you a week ago," he said. "This could have been done by now if you'd come to me."

He was departing from established decorum. He should have given me a formal reply. That gave me some leeway in answering.

"I did get that message," I said, trying to hide a smirk, "but my calendar has been a little full."

"Now, we just have to go through it," he said. "If you'd come to me sooner, I could have helped you."

"I'm here well in advance of the one-year deadline."

"You might even be a senior Rider by now, who knows?" He shrugged. "I can do things like that sometimes."

"I'm sure you can." He didn't seem to be getting to a point, other than his own importance.

He decided to move on. "You said you had victory in combat. But nobody knows who it was against. You never said anything about who it was."

"I claim victory over Rider Vaelir," I said. I reached behind me on the saddle where I had his armor tied. I united it and threw it to the ground between us.

I heard a murmur of voices and Dimétrian motioned to a guard. The man retrieved the armor and set it on the table for Dimétrian and the other members to see.

"Aside from the armor," I said. "I also provide proof through possession of his sword and his *Rorujhen*."

I didn't need to draw the sword. It was easily seen in its sheath on the saddle.

"Maybe you did, I don't know," Dimétrian said. "A lot of people say it couldn't be done. A human, not much more than a child, beating a Rider. That's what they're saying. It can't be done. Maybe they're right."

"Vaelir led a dozen humans to attack my caravan from ambush on our way to Pokorah-Vo," I said, trying to stay formal. "While my guards fought the humans, Vaelir engaged me in single combat. He lost."

I heard more murmuring from around the room.

"A lot of people are saying it couldn't happen that way," he insisted. "I mean, if it did, that would be great for you. But we have some of the best people... experts. They knew Vaelir, they say he was a great guy and a good fighter. I didn't know him very well, I can't know everyone, but they're saying he would be hard for anyone to beat."

How could someone be in charge of the Council and not be able to focus on the conversation or the process?

"I have a witness." I turned my head. "Mooren nya Su Lariano!"

Mooren stepped forward. As an *Ulané Jhinura*, he might not be physically tall, especially in a room of *Ashae*, but he strode forward as though he were a giant.

"I offer myself as witness," his voice was strong. "Mirabela nya Balangur speaks the truth. I would further say that the attack led by Vaelir on our caravan was a cowardly act, completely without justification or provocation."

Some of the mumbling voices sounded angry at that.

"Well, alright," Dimétrian said. "I think your witness is probably a friend of yours. Maybe he would say anything you wanted. I don't know. We'll have to go to the challenge—"

"Wait!" I stopped him.

He looked at me, clearly annoyed and unused to being interrupted.

"I'm not done." I retrieved the other set of armor from behind my saddle and tossed it to the ground as I had the first.

"I claim victory over Rider Niklos!"

Dimétrian's eyes shone with victory. "You killed another Rider?"

"I did." I nodded.

He motioned to the guard, who came for the armor as he had the first.

"Maybe you know," he said, "Riders, and you weren't a Rider of course, you were just a provisional Rider, you have to

255

have your claim validated first to be a Rider, so you weren't really a Rider, but even, you know, the provisional ones, there are rules about attacking other Riders. You can't have feuds or attacks without approval from the Council."

"Of course," I answered. "And I would never have harmed him if Niklos had not attacked my men and tried to kill one of my *Rorujhen*. But I am permitted within the law to defend myself and my property."

"You could," he said. "Is that what happened? I don't know that's what happened. It doesn't sound very likely. I hear Niklos was a good guy, you know. He knew the rules. It doesn't sound like something he would do."

"I have a witness." I turned again. "Ancaera nya Balangur!"

Ancaera stepped forward to join Mooren.

"That's Vaelir's widow!" Dimétrian snapped. He evidently didn't like surprises, and none of this was going the way he wanted. "You can't call her nya Balangur. You killed her husband."

"By right of victory in combat I may choose to adopt and provide for the family of the defeated. Is this not the custom?"

I could almost hear his teeth grinding from where I sat on Farukan. He pursed his lips angrily. Before he could say anything, Ancaera made her statement.

"I offer myself as witness to the attack by Niklos on the *Rorujhen* of Mirabela nya Balangur and his subsequent defeat."

This was an appropriate time for me to take it to the next level.

"Are there any who would challenge this as truth?" I demanded. "Do you challenge it, Master Dimétrian?"

He turned his head sharply to look at me, "I preside. I'm the Master of the Council. I don't challenge. We already have a challenger. Kaerélios!"

A broad shouldered *Ashae* rose from his seat at the side of the room.

"Here, Master Dimétrian."

"You registered a challenge, I have it here. You said that a human woman could never defeat Vaelir in fair combat," Dimétrian said. "That's what you said?"

"I did."

"I'm looking at it here." He held up a piece of paper. "I have it right here. You said that it could only have been murder or some trick. Is that right?"

Kaerélios looked uncertain. "That was before I had heard the evidence."

"What?" Dimétrian shifted his eyes to Kaerélios. "You put in the challenge. You can't just take it back, I have it here. If you tried to withdraw it, I know you're not trying to do that, but if you did it would imply pretty poor judgement. To put it in and then try to take it back. We have pretty high standards on who can be a Rider, you know. They have to have the best judgement. Only the best people can be in my Riders. Are you ready to go forward on this?"

Kaerélios frowned. "I am."

"Very well." Dimétrian looked back at me smugly. "Now I suppose you have to prove yourself. Maybe if you'd come to me before, we could have avoided this. But now it's all in the books. I could have helped you. It's too bad, really."

I'd had my helm hanging by the chinstrap from my saddle, and I put it on my head and drew the longsword from its sheath. I reached for the *Ralahin* and the flows in the room lit up in my sight.

Kaerélios mounted a horse he'd had ready and urged it forward.

"Stop!" Dimétrian demanded. "You can't go against a *Rorujhen* on a horse!"

"I do not use *Rorujhen*," Kaerélios told him, "and I have none."

"You will use one today," Dimétrian informed him. "Get Darkstar out here!" he ordered.

Kaerélios dismounted and waited while a *Rorujhen* was

brought forward for him to use. A large *Rorujhen* was led out. He was a good eight inches taller than Farukan. He had a startling white coat, except for a dark marking on his forehead. He also had scars on his neck and front shoulders.

*"I have heard of Darkstar,"* Farukan told me. *"He is a veteran of many challenges. This will not be easy."*

Kaerélios mounted, sword in hand, and Darkstar moved toward us. I braced myself for his attack, but when it came, I wasn't ready. As they slowly neared, Darkstar suddenly leaped forward, his shoulder plowing into Farukan and Kaerélios swung his sword. My parry was too late to do more than slow it, and his blade careened off my helmet.

Farukan staggered but stayed on his feet, snapping his teeth at Darkstar, who easily dodged back out of reach. I had focused too much on his sword and remembered almost too late that this would be a magical fight as well. I quickly formed a barrier around us that would block magical attacks. I had learned Tesia's lesson well, and quickly tied it off with a complex knot just as a lance of air came at me.

Darkstar charged again and raised onto his hind legs to pound at us with his front hooves. Farukan didn't wait for the blows but threw all of his weight against Darkstar, knocking him to the ground. Kaerélios rolled to his feet, his sword at the ready. I glanced at Farukan and saw that at least one of Darkstar's hooves had struck home and Farukan was bleeding from a gash on his head. Darkstar began to circle Farukan as Kaerélios and I began to circle each other.

Now that I could hold my sword with two hands, I was much more confident. Kaerélios came at me, hoping to use his height and reach to quickly overpower me. My recent practice with Alénia had prepared me for that and I was able to deflect his blade, though he was even larger than Alénia and his blows had a lot of strength behind them. I started my blade spinning, creating a defensive bubble.

My technique was different enough that it confused him for a

258

moment, and I took advantage and turned it into an attack. He parried with frantic movements as he backed from my advance. Then he came back with a riposte that might have worked if Alénia hadn't already drilled me on this maneuver. He tried another air attack, but it was easily turned aside by my barrier.

I heard a crash behind me and glanced to see Farukan on the ground. Darkstar had risen above him and was about to come down with his hooves. I panicked and reached for an air attack of my own. I could still only manage a blunt attack and I threw everything I could at Darkstar.

The air struck him, and he was hurled through the newer wall behind him. As the section of wall collapsed, I could see a huge swirl of magic. This swirl was what had been drawing all the flows. It was immense. Darkstar had fallen into the edge of it and was screaming in pain. He rolled and staggered away from it. When he stepped back through the wall, his white coat had turned grey. One of his eyes had the silver of a cataract. His great frame had withered, and he could barely walk. It was as if he had aged decades in only a few seconds. Farukan had regained his feet.

Kaerélios came at me again and we engaged blades. Then he jumped back and threw lightning at me. I felt him start to pull the flow and I immediately created a looped channel, and his lightning flew back at him. His eyes widened in surprise, and he tried to stop the lightning, but it struck him dead center, driving him to his knees. I resisted the urge to flit and rushed forward, touching the tip of my sword to his throat before he could recover.

"Do you yield?" I asked him loudly. "Do you concede the challenge?"

Kaerélios' eyes never left mine. He gave a nod, but then spoke loudly to the room.

"I concede the challenge. Through trial by combat I acknowledge the validity of the claim. I affirm that Mirabela nya Balangur is rightful inheritor to Vaelir and Niklos." He raised his sword between us, one hand on the hilt and the other on the blade. "Further, I offer myself as vassal and liegeman. If you will accept my service as recompense for my offense in questioning your honor."

Ancaera had prepared me for the various ways the match might play out, but she hadn't said anything about this. I knew what he was offering was no small thing. Refusing would be an insult, I was sure. He wasn't just acknowledging me, he was throwing his full support behind me. Maybe not all the Riders were bad.

"I accept your service," I said.

I shifted my own sword to my left hand and took his in my right. I was totally guessing about what I should do, and scenes from old movies went through my mind. I held his blade by the hilt and touched it to his shoulders, like I had seen when they dubbed a knight.

"You will henceforth be known as Kaerélios nya Balangur," I told him, "and our causes are united."

His expression showed that my answer was sufficient. I gave him back his sword and turned to face the council.

"If this matter is concluded," I told them. "I'm going. Unless you had anything else you wanted to talk to me about?"

Dimétrian glared at me. "Leave."

I went to Farukan. Despite his injuries, he knelt to allow me to mount. I sheathed my sword, and we rode out through the big doors as Ancaera and the others rushed to follow. Kaerélios joined us as well. None of us spoke until after we had exited the gate to the estate of Odaro.

"You did well," Alénia nodded. "He was one I would have recommended you avoid."

I looked at Kaerélios. "Does joining with me put you at risk?"

"Possibly." He shrugged. Then he looked at me. "When I registered my challenge, I didn't know that Ancaera was allied with you."

"You know her then?" I asked.

"We've been friends since children." He nodded. "I only sought to protect her."

"That's fine by me," I told him. "In fact, I'm probably not going to be around a lot. Keeping her and Shianri safe is probably the main thing I would ask of you. Is that alright with you Ancaera?" I looked over at her.

She actually blushed. There was more going on here than I was aware of.

"If you think it best," she said. "I would have no objection."

A thought occurred to me. "Tesia, what was that big swirl of magic we saw?"

"I don't know." A look of worry came over her. "It's some kind of enormous spell, that's obvious. But I've never seen anything so big or powerful. It's pulling a tremendous amount of *Ralahin*."

"No idea what it does?"

She shook her head. "But it does seem like it's getting bigger."

# CHAPTER THIRTY

## RISPAN

*I* was still struggling with what Shéna had told me. Words failed me all through breakfast. Conflicting emotions warred for supremacy and there was no clear victor. What could I possibly say that would not come across as patronizing or insincere? She had taken a huge risk, and she was coming from a fragile place. This wasn't the kind of thing I was particularly good at.

As we were packing up our bedrolls, I still hadn't spoken, and she hadn't looked at me. The longer I let this go unaddressed, the harder it was going to get. I needed to say something now.

"You're wrong," I said. That wasn't the best way to start.

She looked at me, confusion showing on her face.

"No. That's not what I mean. Let me try again." Why was this so difficult? "You were right. I can't understand what you went through. Not really. But I can understand feeling like you're a castoff. Like you don't have a place and don't deserve one. *That* I've lived. I... *almost* remember my parents. To be honest I'm not sure what's memory and what's wishful thinking. I don't know what happened to them or why they left me. Mira has given me the first family I've really known. Mira and Mouse.

But I remember the years before I had that, and it wasn't pleasant. I know, it's not the same as what you went through. There's really no comparison."

She just continued to look at me. Her face was very still, and I couldn't read her expression.

"But you were also wrong," I told her. "*You* are good and brave and strong and noble despite all that you have lived through. And you *are* deserving. Anyone or anything that says otherwise, any thought that you aren't any of these things, that's just part of the lies you were talking about before. Part of the trick to keep you down. It's just not true."

Her eyes fell to the ground. "But I was born a slave," she said. "Born into it and lived it. Nothing was my own, not even my own body. Whenever you look at me, you will always know that. You will always see the worthless slave-girl."

"That's where you're wrong again," I said. "I have *never* seen that when I looked at you. Ever. When I first saw you, all I saw was a beautiful woman. And later I learned that there was so much more to you than that." I smiled. "Sometimes I did wonder why you were being so snippy with me. True." I shrugged. "Sometimes we do things like that to protect ourselves."

She looked up at me, "Then you aren't angry at me for being... *snippy*?"

"Oh, it was pretty mild compared to some of the things I've experienced." I grinned at her. "I think I'll survive."

I hadn't realized how tensely she'd been standing until that moment when her shoulders relaxed.

"For now," I suggested. "How about we get these guys to Su Lariano where they'll be safe?"

Things felt different between all of us after that. Not just between me and Shéna, but all of us. We'd all had different experiences, but we'd all felt similar pain. And I knew that in some ways, Kiarash felt like the odd man out. But he'd been there for our sharing. A silent supporter. Just by being there, he was a part of our group. He'd accepted us, and we'd accepted him.

Chessa and the other *Rorujhen* seemed to be more focused on future possibilities. All the worry and fear hadn't gone away, but now it seemed like they felt they weren't going through it all alone. One of the scariest things to do sometimes is to let yourself hope.

Every day, the miles fell quickly behind. The pace of the *Rorujhen* was so much faster than anything I'd experienced, and it was exhilarating. I was almost sorry when we entered the forest, knowing that our journey was about to end.

We slowed to a walk coming through the outer town and approaching the gates to Su Lariano itself. Neelu was waiting for us at the gates, Arané-Li at her side.

"I thought you would be heading straight to Pokorah-Vo?" she asked me.

I shrugged. "Plans change."

"That they do." She nodded. "Mira is safe?"

"She was when I saw her last," I answered. "That was a week ago."

"I see you've brought *Rorujhen*, and I'm guessing we are extending official protection for them?"

Before I could answer, Bijoux jumped down from where she'd been dozing off across the saddle in front of me and approached Neelu.

"She's grown a lot." She smiled, reaching down to scratch Bijoux behind her ears. Then she turned her attention to the *Rorujhen*.

"Of course you are all welcome in Su Lariano," she told them.

"We weren't expecting you," Arané-Li said. "So, at the moment we don't have appropriate accommodations. For now, we only have standard horse stables. But I assure you, we will have that corrected in short order. I am Arané-Li."

"*Your courtesy is appreciated,*" Akshira spoke for them. "*I am Akshira.*"

"Your pardon," I said, remembering my manners. "Friends, this is Princess Neelu Ulané Pulakasado."

"You will discover quickly," Neelu said, "I'm not fond of formalities." She gave me a look. "At least not with most people."

I quickly bowed with as much flourish as I could manage from atop Barashan and Neelu narrowed her eyes at me.

"Shéna," she said. "It's good to see you again. And I believe I just saw Kiarash and Naga heading for the upper stables where she stayed before. Let's get you all in for some rest and refreshment. Except for you, Rispan." She turned to me. "General Dzurala and Queen Astrina are waiting to hear your report firsthand."

"The queen?" That gave me a start. I'd never met the queen and was more than a little nervous about the prospect.

"Oh, don't get yourself into a twist. It's just a report. You've done that before."

"If the rest of you would come with me," Arané-Li said, "I'll get you some refreshment and show you to your quarters, as they are for now. And if you like, I can arrange a tour of our city."

"I think I'll go to my quarters for a bath," Shéna said. She looked at me. "Have fun!"

I scowled at her and followed Neelu to the conference room to give my report, Bijoux followed at my heels. As Arané-Li led the *Rorujhen* in a different direction, Barashan's voice sounded in my head.

"*I would continue to be your mount, Rispan, and aid you in your work.*"

"*Thank you, Barashan,*" I sent the thought. "*I would be honored.*"

When we arrived, I saw two people seated at the table. Dzurala could be bad enough, but my biggest worry was the other woman sitting next to her.

"Is this the miscreant I keep hearing about?" the queen asked.

"The one and only," Neelu sighed.

Miscreant? What had she heard about me?

Don't argue. This is the queen.

Bijoux went ahead of me and jumped up on one end of the conference table. She laid down and began cleaning her claws. Despite her being nearly the size of an adult *Ulané Jhinura*, neither Dzurala nor the queen reacted to her with more than a brief glance.

"Your Majesty." I bowed as deeply as I could manage. Neelu sat down in an empty chair at the table.

"All right," the queen said. "You've had a long trip, so take a seat."

"Yes, your Majesty. Thank you."

"Agent Rispan," Dzurala's voice was hard as ever. "Your return party was missing quite a few of the people you left with. Why don't you tell us what happened on your trip?"

"It was mostly uneventful," I told her. "Well, until we got close to Shifara anyway. And Mira had to kill another Rider, but hopefully that won't be a problem. Ancaera—"

"Stop!" Dzurala cut in. "Focus. Start at the beginning."

"Right." I took a deep breath. Ignore the fact that the queen was sitting there and just give my report.

I started at the beginning and walked them through everything that had happened after we left and up to the point we left Mira and the others. I tried to focus on Dzurala, but the queen was looking at me very intently and it was distracting. I felt like a field mouse being examined by a very large and hungry owl.

"I concur," Dzurala was saying. "You should go on to Pokorah-Vo and assume the persona of Raven. I'd like to know what's going on with Mira in Shifara, but Pokorah-Vo is more pressing. How have you been doing with the telepathic communication with the *Rorujhen*?"

I shrugged. "Alright. I usually speak to them out loud, but I can manage it either way."

"Good." She nodded. "We'll want you to get started right

away. Were you aware that Mira and Tesia had been experimenting with long distance communication methods?"

"Um..." I thought back. "I may have overheard bits of conversation, but nothing specific. Why? Did it work out?"

"Not as envisioned," she said. "We just couldn't figure out how to make it loud enough to hear and soft enough that it wouldn't damage the receiver's ears. But communicating with Farukan gave us another idea that did work. It allows two people to communicate telepathically."

I was impressed. "What's the distance?"

"We assume there is no limit," she said, "but we only had time to test it to three hundred miles. We will issue you one before you go."

"Barashan, one of the *Rorujhen,* said he wants to continue as my mount for now."

"Even better." Dzurala nodded. "You can get to Pokorah-Vo that much quicker. Korashéna's business with the *Chados* in Aganaté is also of high importance. I'm thinking we should also issue one of the communication devices to her." She glanced at the queen as she said this. Astrina nodded agreement.

"How many comm-devs do you have?" I asked.

"How many what?" Dzurala asked.

"Comm-devs," I said. "It's easier to say than communication devices."

"I suppose." She arched an eyebrow at me. "The exact number is not important. We have enough for now. I'll see that both you and Korashéna are issued one and are trained in how to use them. Be ready to leave in the next few days. That will be all for now."

"I understand you are an orphan," the queen said. "Do you know anything of your parents?"

"No, your Majesty." I shook my head, wondering why she would ask. "I don't really have any memories from before I was found."

She nodded. "Thank you for your report. You have done well."

I bowed and made a fast exit, hoping I was following protocol but more concerned with getting out from underneath the magnifying glass.

# CHAPTER THIRTY-ONE

## MIRA

*M*aking our case for the Royal Court in Shifara was going to take more than just accusations. We had to show incontrovertible proof that *Rorujhen* were not simply animals. I had Discussed this with Farukan, and he had agreed. When the time came for our appointment with the Minister of Internal Relations, Farukan went with Mooren, Tesia and I to the offices. Everyone else had stayed at Shianri. Everyone but Alénia. After my challenge at the Rider Council, she had gone her own way, telling me to practice more so we could have a rematch in the future.

From what I had gathered, the Minister of Internal Relations Office was like an arbitration court. It handled issues that came up between different races in the realm, unless they were too complex or delicate and required a higher authority.

Walking Farukan through the halls of the large castle to the Minister's office drew several strange looks, but no one objected. This lasted only as far as the reception area outside Minister Rhesaeda's office.

"I'm afraid you cannot bring that animal into the Minister's office," the receptionist informed us.

"I am afraid you have that backwards," Tesia informed him. "He is not here with us; we are here with him."

The receptionist gave her a confused look. "Either way," he said, "there simply isn't room."

"In that case," Tesia said. "Please ask Minister Rhesaeda to step out here so that the matter may be presented to her."

"One moment," he said. "I will pass on your request."

He stepped into the office, and we waited while he explained the situation. After a moment, an *Ashae* woman stepped through the door. As with other *Ashae*, she had platinum hair and she towered over all of us but Farukan.

She looked around our group before speaking. "This is unusual. Even if your matter has something to do with *Rorujhen*, surely you could have spoken of it to me in my office without the animal."

"*I prefer to speak for myself,*" Farukan's deep voice rumbled in all of our heads.

"How—" Rhesaeda's pale blue eyes went from one of us to the other. "Is this some sort of a trick?"

"*There is no trick here, Minister. But a situation most despicable and heinous.*"

Rhesaeda looked at Farukan. "How is it that you can speak into my mind?"

"*It is the way of the Rorujhen,*" Farukan told her. "*This is how we speak.*"

"All of you?"

"*Yes.*"

"But… the Riders… They know?"

"*Perhaps not all Riders.*" Farukan acknowledged. "*But at the least, every Rider with a Rorujhen knows.*"

"And Master Dimétrian?"

"*Of that, there is no doubt.*"

"By bringing this to me, you have made me a target for the Riders," she said, frowning. "We have to escalate this now." She evidently made some kind of a decision. "Come with me."

She led us out of her offices and down several hallways and turnings. We eventually came through a side door in the throne room. King Kholinaer and Queen Ysiola were both in attendance, and I could see a line of people waiting to be presented. Farukan's heavy step when we came through the door got everyone's attention. Not far back in line was a group of small, redskinned figures. There was something odd about their features, or the way they were looking at us, but I didn't have time for that now.

"Wait here," Rhesaeda said to us. We watched as she quickly approached the royal couple and, after a quick bow, began speaking to them in a low voice. They looked startled and glanced our way.

"Bring them forth," King Kholinaer's voice sounded loud.

Rhesaeda motioned for us to join them. We approached the steps at the base of the thrones, and we all bowed, including Farukan.

"Now then," Kholinaer said. "What has gotten my Minister so upset?"

Farukan bowed again, tucking one leg beneath him and bending low.

"*Your Majesties,*" his voice carried to the minds of everyone in the room and they all turned with wide eyes and rapt attention. "*I am Farukan of the Rorujhen. I have come to plead against the enslavement of my people by the White Riders of the Ashae.*"

"That's quite an accusation," Ysiola said. "Slavery is illegal in Daoine. If this were true, why have we not heard of it before?"

"*The Riders emphatically forbid Rorujhen from revealing we are more than mere animals,*" Farukan answered. "*Were not my own family moved to safety beyond the reach of the Riders, I would not have risked coming forward myself.*"

"We do not disbelieve you," Kholinaer said, "but if we are to act, we will need more than just the word of a single individual. How can we know you speak the truth? That you are not some kind of an anomaly and are different from other *Rorujhen*?"

*"If any can see into my mind,"* Farukan told them. *"They can see the truth for themselves."*

Kholinaer motioned to a page, who hurried off.

"Looking into someone's mind without leave is one of the greatest violations that can be done," Ysiola said to him. "We do have someone who can do as you suggest, but you must give explicit consent."

*"I thank you for your courtesy,"* Farukan replied, dipping his head to her.

The page returned shortly with several, small airborne creatures in tow. I'd seen pixies, *Pilané Jhin*, only from a distance, but I recalled Rispan telling us about the one he met in Aganaté.

One of the *Pilané Jhin* flew to the king and queen. After a moment, it approached Farukan. The presence I felt in my mind was immense.

*"Farukan, I am Giang. Do you consent to our presence in your mind? For us to search for the information we seek?"*

*"I do consent,"* he answered. *"The truth must come out."*

*"And do you consent to this information being made public?"*

*"I do."* His answer was firm.

The *Pilané Jhin* gathered in front of Farukan. Images started forming in my mind, flying by too quickly to see. They seemed to be progressively further and further back in time. Finally, they settled on an image I recognized.

*I see Akshira. And she is very pregnant. She is being chased by several Ashae, and I see Vaelir's face among them. I am Farukan, and I am running, trying to protect her. There are ropes. On me. On Akshira. I fight them. I scream into the minds of the pale creatures, "Leave us alone!" They laugh. They strike me. They command me to silence. We are entangled and we cannot escape. My vision shifts. I see other times. Vaelir, striking at Rorujhen, demanding they breed. They refuse and he strikes them again. Vaelir, showing us to others, all of them in white armor. I see Master Dimétrian. Others in white armor. They have other Rorujhen. Always, these creatures in white speak of the rules. They laugh. They speak of the penalty of violation. They would hurt my beloved Akshira. They would maim my child. I must always obey. I must always be silent.*

The visions faded.

There was no hiding this now. Everyone in the room had seen the images.

"We have heard your plea," Kholinaer said, "and we take your cause as our own. We hereby decree that all *Rorujhen* are a free and independent people. All claims of ownership are void. This crime against the *Rorujhen* is also a betrayal of Our kingdom and Our realm. You may go to your family and be safe, knowing your cause is in Our hands."

"Your Majesties." I bowed to them. "I am Mirabela nya Balangur. I have recently come into possession of the estate of Shianri. We would be happy to receive any freed *Rorujhen* and assist them in returning home or in any way to help them to move forward in a life of freedom."

We made our bows and thanks as Minister Rhesaeda hurried us back out the side door. This was good. If I'd understood correctly, the king had taken over the matter, so we didn't need to stay in Shifara.

"This is going to have a huge impact on the political balance," Rhesaeda said. "The power of the Rider Council can't survive this. The Riders themselves may even be disbanded. This is really big."

"I don't understand why they would risk everything by doing it then." I shook my head. "Even if they didn't think anything was wrong with what they were doing, why take the risk?"

"They had their protections," Tesia said. "They thought they had everything covered."

"They just didn't count on you." Mooren grinned.

Our ride back to Shianri was lighthearted. We'd struck a giant blow against the Riders. The late afternoon was just beginning to cool with hints of the approaching autumn. I couldn't wait to get back south and tell Rispan everything that had happened. We'd won this battle! Now we could focus on Pokorah-Vo.

Something slammed into us like the stomping of a giant foot, and we were all knocked to the ground. I staggered to my feet, looking around. There was blood from Tesia's mouth, and she wasn't moving. Through blurry vision, I could see that Farukan was also back on his feet, but only barely. What happened? I could see figures coming out of the surrounding bushes. White armor. Two of them grabbed me and put something on my wrists. Mooren was on his feet, charging them. His sword was drawn. I reached for the *Ralahin*, but there was nothing. Something was blocking me. I struggled against whoever was holding me, but he was too strong. I was still trying to clear my vision. Three figures advanced on Farukan, swords in their hands.

"Farukan! Run!" I screamed at him.

He was still staggering, but he'd heard me and lurched into a run, knocking over two of them while a third struck him from behind. He was through them and gone.

I tried to reach for my daggers, but they weren't there. I tried to draw lightning, but nothing came. Something struck the side of my face, knocking me to the ground.

"We have diplomatic status!" I yelled. "You can't—"

"As a White Rider, you have broken our laws and you must pay the price," a familiar voice spoke through the haze. Was that Dimétrian? "Diplomatic status will not save you."

I heard a clash of blades and turned my head to look. Mooren had managed to force one of the Riders back, but then another slashed at him from behind, cutting his hamstring. Mooren grunted and fell to one knee. He tried to force himself back up, but another blade struck him through the body, practically pinning him to the ground.

"Mooren!"

The Rider braced his foot against Mooren's chest and pushed, pulling his sword free. Mooren fell onto his back. He turned his head and met my eyes. He managed a half smile before the Rider thrust his sword back through the middle of Mooren's chest.

"Mooren!" I couldn't see anything anymore. I didn't want to see anything or feel anything. "Mooren." I sobbed his name over and over as someone drug me to my feet, trying to hold something of him in my heart.

Something struck me again and the world went black.

# EPILOGUE

## RISPAN

*B*arashan had brought me quickly to Pokorah-Vo. We knew he wouldn't be needed in the city though, so he was out on the plains. He told me that if I needed him, to call and he would come. That was an ability they had kept secret from the Riders; if a *Rorujhen* was bonded, they would know of a call, even before it came, and they would be there. I had no idea where he was at this point, and I envied him his freedom. I had too many things I had to do. Responsibilities.

My *jahgreet* cloak was really coming in handy for my spy-work in Pokorah-Vo. As I moved down the darkened street, I knew Bijoux was close by. How something so big could move so quietly was a constant source of amazement.

At least tonight I wasn't Raven the merchant. In the three weeks I'd been here, there'd been a lot of changes in the city. Sides were being drawn; King Arugak and the slavers and everyone else. The telepathic comm-devs had worked well. I could get information to and from Su Lariano instantly. It had also allowed Shéna and I to talk a lot more while she was in hiding below in Aganaté. Kiarash had safely brought her in, and she was with Khuyen and the *Chados*.

There'd still been no news from the north about Mira. We should hear something soon, though. There was no sense in worrying; Mira could take care of herself. Besides, she had Farukan and Tesia to help. And Mooren.

### END OF BOOK TWO

# GLOSSARY

**Aganaté:** Secret underground *Ga-Né-Mo Ri* city below Pokorah-Vo.

*Ande-Dannu:* (Fae of the Summer Court) They live in the original realm of the *Ashae*.

*Ashae:* (Sidhe or Fae) *Ashae* are roughly six and a half feet tall, with pointed ears, platinum-colored hair, pale blue eyes, and light-skin.

*Balangur:* The word for raven in the common tongue used on Daoine.

**Bar:** This is an *Ulané Jhinura* rank in the Palace Guard equivalent to a private.

*Bo-ka-bo:* Martial art used and taught to the military in Su Lariano.

**Daoine:** This is the continent and realm in which the story takes place.

*Dannu Fé:* (Fae of the Winter Court) They live in the original realm of the *Ashae*.

*Darakanos:* (Dragons) This is the European type of dragon. *Darakanos* are shapeshifters and can appear in a humanoid form that is similar to *Loiala Fé*. They are extremely powerful telepaths and do not have a language as such.

*Fu-Mo Ri:* (Fomorians) Ancient race who warred with the *Uthadé* on the home world of the *Ashae*.

*Ga-Né-Mo Ri:* (Gnomes or Brownies) They are generally under two feet tall and have reddish-brown skin and green hair.

*Impané:* (Imps) They are typically well under two feet tall. They have short horns, like a goat, and cloven hooves. Their skin is rough and dark red.

*Jahgreet:* This is a six-legged, humanoid panther. They are difficult to see due to natural camouflage and are extremely fast and dangerous. They can run on two, four, or six legs. Standing upright, a fully-grown *jahgreet* can be up to six feet tall.

*Jhianki:* A board game of strategy similar to Go.

*Jhiné Boré:* (Dryad or tree nymph) They have dark, greenish-brown skin, black hair, green eyes, pointed ears, and Asian features.

*Jhiné Solé:* (Nyad or water nymph) They have pale blue skin, black hair, blue or green eyes, pointed ears, and Asian features.

*Kazan:* Musical instrument with five pairs of strings.

**Lance:** This is an *Ulané Jhinura* rank of the Palace Guard equivalent to a corporal.

**Laraksha-Vo:** This is the primary *Urgaban* city on Daoine.

*Loiala Fé:* (Fae) They are roughly the same size and appearance as humans but have pointed ears.

**Odaro:** The name for Dimétrian's estate. This is also where the White Rider Hall is located.

*Ogaré:* (Ogres) Approximately nine feet tall, with thick, hard skin that is immune to heat or fire. Found in remote mountain regions.

*Pilané Jhin:* (Pixies) Typically about three inches tall with humanoid bodies and features. Sometimes confused with *Sula Jhinara* (sylphs.) They live in flowers and primarily live on nectar and pollen. They can also be mischievous. Skin may be beige to dark chocolate, or blue or green. Blue and green pixies have butterfly wings, the others have dragon-fly wings. They are also strong telepaths. They are alternately male and female and change over a two-year period.

**Pokorah-Vo:** *Urgaban* city founded by criminal exiles from Laraksha-Vo.

*Putri firgolo:* This is an expletive or curse phrase in the common tongue.

*Rala:* A general term for magic.

*Raladolin:* A term for the specific method of used by Neelu for using magic to enhance speed or movement using magic. This method is not used by other *Ulané Jhinura.*

*Ralahin:* A specific term for magic used by the *Ulané Jhinura.*

**Raven's Nest:** Restaurant owned by Mira and Bavrana in Su Lariano. Managed by Mouse.

*Relak:* Large predatorial rodent. The body is maybe two feet long, plus a tail. They make a guttural, hissing sound when angry.

*Reshan:* Large eagle, similar to the Philippine eagle. Stands about 4.5 feet tall, 10-foot wingspan. Used as mounts for *Ga-Né-Mo Ri.*

*Rorujhen:* This race is similar in appearance to a very large horse. However, they are much faster and are fully sentient and communicate telepathically.

*Rylak:* A hard-wood tree, similar to eucalyptus.

**Sapling:** This is an *Ulané Jhinura* rank in the Foresters equivalent to corporal.

**Shianri:** The estate in the Shifara region which Mira inherited when she killed Vaelir, a White Rider. The word means hearth or home, or even nest.

**Shifara:** The *Ashae* capitol in Daoine. This includes Shifara City and Shifara Castle, each of which are walled and are connected by a causeway.

*Shyntak:* A martial arts weapon similar to nunchaku. Literally, swing-stick.

*Shyngur:* A martial arts weapon similar to tonfa. Literally, diverged-stick.

*Solénur:* (Siren) These are found in watery areas such as oceans or swamps and bogs.

**Sprig:** This is an *Ulané Jhinura* military rank equivalent to a recruit. Sprigs are not yet assigned to a specific branch of military.

**Su Lariano:** An *Ulané Jhinura* city, home to Neelu. Mira's first home on Daoine. There is an outer town, but this is primarily an underground city built into caves and tunnels under a mountain.

*Sula Jhinara:* (Sylph) Typically about three inches tall. Often confused with *Pilané Jhin* (pixies) and also known as flower fairies. They live in flowers and have wings like a butterfly, but the wings look like flower petals. They look like flowers and have blue or green skin. They are also strong telepaths. They are alternately male and female and change over a two-year period.

**Tree:** This is an *Ulané Jhinura* military rank equivalent to Staff Sergeant.

**Twig:** This is an *Ulané Jhinura* rank in the Army or City Guard equivalent to a private.

*Ulané Jhinura:* (Sprite) They are generally about four and a half feet tall, so can appear to be human children except for the pointed ears. Using magic, they are able to move very quickly. They also appear to have slightly Asian features.

*Urgaban:* (Goblins) *Urgaban* are typically around four feet tall. They are generally humanoid, but the head is noticeably larger, with a heavy jaw and wide mouth, and their arms are longer. Their pointed ears are also very long. They have pale, yellowish skin and no hair.

*Uthadé:* (*Tuatha de Danann*) Ancient race who warred with the *Fu-Mo Ri* on the home world of the *Ashae*.

**White Rider:** This is an elite group of *Ashae* warriors, all male, who are supposed to be the executors of justice in Daoine. They wear white armor of hardened leather. Higher ranking Riders use Rorujhen as mounts.

**Zerg / *Zergané* / *Zergish* / *Zergishti maloto*:** This is an expletive or curse word or phrase in the common tongue.

# ACKNOWLEDGMENTS

I would like to thank all of my online friends, writer pals (such as B.R. Stateham as well as all the members of my FB writers' group) and beta readers who have helped me to get this story into as a good a shape as it is. You are all a treasure. A special mention to my dear friend Tiffany, who read, laughed, and cried with me through the story and nagged me every step of the way.

And of course, how can I not say it? Thanks Mom!

# ABOUT THE AUTHOR

Primarily an author of fantasy and science fiction, Adam K. Watts was born in Santa Clara, California and was raised mainly in the heart of "Steinbeck Country" in Salinas, California. He has always been an artist and has made forays into writing, painting, composing, dancing, performing arts, and digital photography.

As a child, his mind was caught by the poetry of Robert Frost; the words from "Stopping by the Woods on a Snowy Evening" and "The Road Not Taken" resonated with him. The ideas of looking into the woods with longing to enter and turning away out of duty and responsibility, and the desire to travel a path few have seen, have lent his soul the aspect of the seeker. This aspect has been reflected in many of his works; images that bespeak of places that call, of paths that make you want to walk them, and corners that beg you to come look and see what is just around them, or just the wandering wind asking you to walk with her.

He was also shaped at a young age by *Man of La Mancha*, a musical play inspired by Cervantes and Don Quixote. "Tilting at windmills" is a metaphor for pushing back against the machinery of civilization advancing at the price of beauty and the human spirit. He believes that advancement can and should be achieved, but the cost should not be valor or honor or justice. An impossible dream? Perhaps.

"I've been a lover and avid reader of fantasy and science fiction since I was knee-high to a short Hobbit. I have finally escaped the confines of professional non-fiction writing to follow the purpose that has been burning in my heart since I could lift pencil to paper. Those embers, never quite cooled, have been fanned to unquenchable flame and I cannot contain the result. Enjoy!"

To learn more about Adam K. Watts and discover more Next Chapter authors, visit our website at www.nextchapter.pub.

The Merchant Prince
ISBN: 978-4-82412-687-0

Published by
Next Chapter
1-60-20 Minami-Otsuka
170-0005 Toshima-Ku, Tokyo
+818035793528

14th February 2022